T0146552

ACHALADAIR

There Is More Than Gold, in Them Thar Hills

W I L L I A M   S .   Y O U N G

authorHOUSE®

AuthorHouse™ UK
1663 Liberty Drive
Bloomington, IN 47403 USA
www.authorhouse.co.uk
Phone: 0800.197.4150

Published by AuthorHouse 11/04/2016

ISBN: 978-1-5246-6547-0 (sc)
ISBN: 978-1-5246-6548-7 (hc)
ISBN: 978-1-5246-6546-3 (e)

Print information available on the last page.

This book is printed on acid-free paper.

There is more than gold in them thar hills.

This story is purely fictional and is a follow-up to the original *Achaladair* book, which I hope you have read and enjoyed. Our main characters are still involved, but with a few newly introduced characters and a different storyline, I hope that everyone enjoys this book. The action is still centred on the Bridge of Orchy Hotel, the Orchy hills, and the mountains of Glencoe, which are as beautiful as they are dramatic.

Much obliged,
William S. Young

The Orchy Hotel

After completing their mission involving the IRA and Russian spies in the area of Achaladair and Glencoe – including saving the American president's life – the lads celebrated in the Bridge of Orchy Hotel. The night of Scottish reels and music played by the accordion players had finished. The ceilidh had gone down with a bang, so to speak, and they had all enjoyed themselves. At the end of the night, there were some tired legs. In the morning, there were probably a few sore heads.

"But it was a guid nicht," said Sergeant Murdoch as he fell into the awaiting taxi with Constable Tommy Anderson, laughing heartily at his predicament. The snow was falling quite steadily as the taxi pulled away.

"It sure was a good night," said MI6 agent Frank Mulholland to his partner, Agent Tom Sommerville. "I think I'll head off to my room; I'm feeling tired, mate."

"Is Carol too much for you?" Tom asked, chuckling to himself and smiling at his friend. Frank had been having a fling with an Irish girl named Carol McBride over the past few days. She was working behind the bar of the hotel with her friend Emma MacNamara, who had been seen slipping in and out of Agent Sommerville's room on various occasions.

Bridge of Orchy was a small hamlet on the A82 road. It boasted a hotel, railway station, and a few scattered houses around the area. It also had a church, which allowed it a village status. The Orchy Hotel was at the centre of most forms of transport and was on the route of the West Highland Way and West Highland Railway. It was a common stop-off point on many journeys. Its nearest villages were Tyndrum, five miles to the south, and Crianlarich, which was around ten miles to the south.

The head barman of the Orchy Hotel, Tam Cameron, lived in Tyndrum and was well respected by the management of the hotel. He had never missed a day's work since he started nine years ago. The bar and kitchen staffs consisted of a few locals but mainly seasonal staff who were employed for either summer or winter seasons. The hotel catered for the skiing and mountain climbers during the winter months and was an excellent base for tourists to access the Glencoe Mountains and ski centre.

Three Irish girls currently worked in the hotel. Carol McBride, her sister Lorna, and their friend Emma MacNamara all came from a little town in Ireland called Crumlin, near Belfast City. They let Tam know that they were glad to get away from the trouble over in Ireland. For the girls, the chance to move to a nice quiet area like this was pure heaven.

The following morning, Frank Mulholland awoke from a drunken sleep and noticed that Carol was gone from his side. *Geez, what time is it?* he thought, struggling out of bed. Pulling back the curtain, to his dismay, he saw a blanket of snow outside. *Christ!* he thought. *That snow looks deep, and I've got work to do today.* He dragged his six-foot-two frame to the shower room. After showering, Frank wiped the steam from the mirror with the back of his hand. Gazing at his reflection with his azure eyes, he quickly ran a comb through his blond hair. He began to get his head around his itinerary for the day ahead. Lifting his pager (or, as he preferred to call it, his bleeper), he contacted the MI6 team down at the Inveroran Inn.

"Hello, John. It's Frank here. How is Iain Macleod?"

"I'm et Fort William Belford Hospital wae him the noo," replied Big John in a broad Scottish accent. "The bullet is lodged in his shoulder, and they are operating oan it as we speak. It looks as though he is gonnae be oot o' commission fur a wee while. I've left Jim MacNeill and Brian Wilson doon at Forest Lodge keepin' an eye oan things, jist in case oanybody is snoopin' aroond."

"I've arranged for a couple of trucks to come down to Forest Lodge today to pick up all of the guns and ammunition that are down in the cellar," said Frank.

"Ah think ye hud better order a couple o' snawploughs first," said Big John with a laugh. "Come tae think o' it, how am I gonnae get back tae Inveroran if the roads are blocked?"

"If the worst happens and you can't get back, I'll get Tommy Anderson's helicopter," said Frank.

Big John B. Aitken was around six feet tall, with sandy-coloured hair and wiry, bushy eyebrows above hazel eyes. He was a tough-looking character. Many people had said that they wouldn't like to get on the wrong side of him, but he was a kind soul. His voice was generally gruff, but his bark was worse than his bite, so to speak, and Frank Mulholland trusted him explicitly.

On the previous day, the MI6 team – Big John B. Aitken, Jim MacNeill, Iain Macleod, and Brian Wilson – were involved in a takeout of IRA and Russian agents who were using the house called Forest Lodge as a gunrunning den. This was when Iain Macleod caught a bullet to his shoulder. The MI6 ground team was led by Big John Aitken (or JBA, as he preferred to be called). They had been together for a while. They fought together in North Africa and were recently deployed in Belfast, Northern Ireland, before being inducted into MI6 to make up this specialised team at Frank Mulholland's request.

"I'll give Sergeant Murdoch at Tyndrum Police Station a call and see if he can tell me what's happening about the roads over here; we're snowed in at the moment," said Mulholland.

"Get back tae me as soon as ye find oot oanythin an' let me ken whit is happenin'," Big John said.

"OK," replied Frank, ending the call.

Mulholland pressed the digits for Tyndrum Police Station. "Hello, may I speak to Sergeant Murdoch, please?"

"Yes, sir," the desk clerk, Constable George Dalgetty, replied. "Who shall I say is calling?"

"Frank Mulholland."

A few seconds later, the gruff voice of Sergeant Murdoch spoke. "Hello, Frank. Whit can ah dae fur ye?"

"I was wondering if the roads were going to be cleared sometime today, Sergeant. I was hoping to get down to Forest Lodge to check out the situation down there."

"They should be cleared in a wee while. They are stertin' et Crianlarich an' workin' alang the main roads, but ah dinnae ken when they will get oan tae the road alang tae Forest Lodge, as it is only a single-track road," Murdoch said. "Dinnae worry aboot it tho', 'cause ah kin get ye a lift oan Tommy Anderson's helicopter if yer desperate tae get doon ther."

"Great stuff, mate," said Frank. He hung up and thought about their past. Sergeant Murdoch and Constable Tommy Anderson had been working at Tyndrum Police Station for the past sixteen years, since they came through police college together. They made a good team and were well respected in the area. During the Second World War, Sergeant Murdoch was highly skilled with guns. He was an excellent shot with an automatic rifle, as he proved on the previous day, taking out Russian agents up on Beinn Achaladair, a mountain in the Orchy Hills. His fiery red hair was immaculately kept in place, typical of an ex–military man.

Tommy Anderson, a highly skilled helicopter pilot and Royal Air Force veteran, now flew his helicopter, taking tourists around the mountaintops, to boost his meagre earnings as a police constable. He and Sergeant Murdoch had been assisting MI6 agents Frank Mulholland and his fellow agent, Tom Sommerville, over the last four days. They had built up an excellent relationship with both agents. Tommy was a bit of a character who occasionally took centre stage in the Orchy Hotel by entertaining everyone with his jokes. Considering that he was a police officer, he was well liked by all.

George Dalgetty, the desk constable, was a bit of a handyman. In his spare time, he carved wooden figures and bows, arrows, and crossbows. He had a skilled pair of hands and had also been known to take his chainsaw out into the forest and turn some dead trees into exciting wildlife carvings, which were gratefully received by walkers who happened to come across them. Like many constables, he needed to get creative to supplement his pay. His wife sold the artefacts in their local shop in Tyndrum.

Just then, there was a knock at the door and Carol the barmaid walked in. "Can I be of assistance to the occupier of room number seven?" Carol offered.

Frank grabbed her into his arms and kissed her passionately as they fell onto the bed. "You sure can!" exclaimed Frank, his hands beginning to explore Carol's body.

"Wow! Slow down, Frankie boy. I'm working! I just popped in to make sure that you were coming down to breakfast," Carol said, struggling free from his grasp.

"Is Tom down at the dining room?"

"Not yet, but I was going to room eight next," replied Carol.

"I hope the occupant of room eight doesn't get the service from you that I get," said Frank, laughing heartily. "I'll pop in myself and see if Tom is OK. It's not like him to sleep in, especially when the breakfasts are ready."

"OK, darling. I'll see you both in the dining room shortly," Carol said, exiting the room.

Frank pulled on his shirt and sweater and made for Tom's room. Frank Mulholland and Tom Sommerville were both Londoners. They had been working as agents with MI6 for a number of years and had built up a good relationship.

"Hello, Tom. How are you?" Frank asked him a few moments later.

Tom was sitting at the bottom of his bed with a grimace on his face. "I've hardly slept a wink," he said, yawning and massaging his chest.

"Is Emma too much for you?" Frank jokingly asked.

Yesterday, during their confrontation with Russian agents on top of Beinn Achaladair, Tom had received two bullet wounds. One had grazed his left arm, and the other had lodged into the bulletproof vest that he had been wearing. He was quite fortunate to be alive.

"No, it's nothing like that, Frank. I've had a lot of pain in my chest where the bullet struck my bulletproof vest," said Tom.

"Christ! You are black and blue, mate," said Frank. "Maybe we should get you to hospital, just in case you have any cracked ribs."

"It'll be OK. I think it's only bruised," said Tom, dipping his eyebrows.

"How's your arm?" Mulholland asked. "Has it been bleeding again?"

"It's OK, Frank. The bullet only grazed me, and it looked clean enough when I checked it out this morning. Emma put a fresh bandage on it before she left."

"Do you think you can make it down to the dining room for some breakfast?" Frank asked.

"Of course I will. You don't think I'm missing a full Scottish breakfast, do you?" Tom grinned.

"By the way, have you seen the snow outside?" Frank said. "It's about three feet deep. I don't think we will be going very far, so maybe we can have an easy day."

As Mulholland entered his room, the phone began ringing. "Hello, Frank Mulholland speaking." It was Carol the barmaid calling him.

"Just a call to let you know, darling, that Sergeant Murdoch has informed me that it will be about three o'clock before the snowploughs will be clearing the road to Inveroran and Forest Lodge. They have been told to do the main roads first," Carol said. "Oh, and Tommy Anderson is working on his helicopter, repairing the damage from yesterday. He said you would understand."

"OK, honey. I'll see you shortly; keep my breakfast warm," said Frank.

As he hung up the phone, there was a knock at the door, and Frank opened it to be faced with his dark-haired, brown-eyed six-foot-tall friend. "Good, Tom. I'm glad that you could make it. Let's go for our breakfast," Frank said, rubbing his hands together.

As the agents made for the dining room, they observed that there were many people about.

"It looks like it will be busy in here all day, as the snow is keeping everyone inside," said Frank.

A smiling stranger approached the MI6 agents. "Greetings, gentlemen! My name is Ian Finlayson," said the man, extending his hand to Frank Mulholland. "I'm looking for donations on behalf of Nairn County Football Club. We – that is, my friends and I – are walking the length of the West Highland Way to try to boost the funds for our development fund, and we would very much appreciate anything you wish to donate."

Frank glanced over in the direction of the group as he and Tom dipped their hands into their pockets. "Will one pound and ten shillings from each of us be sufficient?" asked Frank.

"Brilliant!" replied Ian. The rest of his party waved over while giving out a cheer.

Tom asked, what they were trying to achieve in their walk along the ninety-six-mile long route?

This surprised Ian Finlayson that an Englishman would know the distance involved during their walk.

"We're walking to Fort William and then following on with a kayak paddle from Fort William up to Inverness as part of our fundraising quest," said Ian proudly.

"Wow! That's super," said Tom, enviously but admiringly.

Ian Finlayson pointed in the direction of his group and said, "The lads that are doing the sail along the three lochs are being led by David Walker, or, as we call him, 'Davy the Paddler'," said Ian, pointing the man out. "Just to his left are Bill Logan and, to his left, Alastair Nicol, who is one of the Nairn County players."

"Are you continuing with your walk even though the snow is so deep?" Mulholland asked.

"Of course we are. We are made of tough stuff up in Nairn," said Ian, laughing.

Frank gave the smiling group the thumbs up and wished Ian the best of luck on their sponsorship walk as the agents moved away.

"Look, Frank! There's Brian Greene over at the notice board. He seems to be pinning something on the board," said Tom.

Brian Greene had a cheery round weather-beaten type of face and was roughly five feet nine inches tall. He helped with the mountain rescue service, where he could be called out at any time of day or night in an emergency. Brian spent a lot of his leisure time climbing the mountains of Scotland, especially around the Orchy and Glencoe area. He knew these hills like the back of his hand.

"Brian! Can I have a minute of your time?" shouted Frank. Brian walked over, smiling at the agents. "Yes, whit can I dae fur ye?"

"There are a lot of people looking at the notice board, and I was wondering what it was all about," Mulholland said.

"There is quite a few climbers in here et the meenit, an' they are desperate tae get tae the Glencoe mountains, but there is an avalanche high alert in the area an' the notice is tae advise them that it is no' safe tae go climbing et the moment," said Brian. "But it wulnae mak' oany difference lads, as they will still go oany way, and the mountain rescue will ha'e tae go tae their aid."

"They won't be going for a while. Sergeant Murdoch has informed me that it will be around three o'clock before the roads are cleared. It looks like it's going to be a long day for us," said Frank.

An attractive dark-haired woman stepped forward, catching the attention of the men. "Hello, gents," she said, running her tongue over red painted lips. "Could, one of you help me, please? I'm looking for Brian Greene of the mountain rescue service."

"That would be me – and who am I speaking too?" Brian asked, raising his eyebrows and revealing his gray-blue eyes while taking her by the arm.

"Moira Malone … from Kilbarchan, near Paisley," she replied, smiling. "I'm here with my friends on a skiing holiday, and we would like your help and advice."

"No problem. Follow me," said Brian in a polite tone of voice, placing his arm around her shoulder and leading her away. He glanced back at the agents, grinning like a Cheshire cat.

Both agents made for the dining room. "I'm looking forward to my breakfast," said Frank.

Tom nodded in agreement. "It sounded funny to hear Brian talking posh instead of his normal Scottish lingo. That has cheered me up, mate," said Tom, laughing.

"Moira Malone! That's an Irish name. We'll have to get her checked out at headquarters," said Frank, glancing back at the clock behind the bar. "These clocks are brilliant. They give you the day, the date, the month, and the year. Look, it's nine forty-five on the twenty-eighth of March, nineteen sixty-two."

"Yes, it's a wonder it doesn't tell you your fortune as well," Tom said, laughing also as they entered the dining room. The agents found a table and looked around at some of the other guests.

"Once we have our breakfast, I'll have to give Merriday a call," said Mulholland.

Sir Jeffrey Merriday had been the head man at MI6 headquarters for many years. He had silver hair, dark eyes, and a burly figure. His relatively young fresh-faced appearance belied his age for a man in his early sixties. He was excellent at his job and had a good relationship with Frank Mulholland.

"Here's Emma coming with the food," said Tom, rubbing his hands together as she approached.

"Tom thinks you look really sexy with plates of food in your hands," Frank said, laughing.

"Oh, is that so?" said Emma, jokingly pushing Tom's back. Tom let out a shriek of pain and grabbed his chest.

"I'm sorry, Tom. I forgot about your bruising," said Emma, giving him a cuddle. "I'll leave you to enjoy your breakfast." She rushed off to the kitchen, smiling back apologetically at Tom on the way.

"I hope the snowploughs do their job well today because we have to make it down to Forest Lodge and supervise the uplift of the weapons and ammunition they have down in the cellar," said Mulholland.

"I heard on the radio this morning that this has been the coldest winter since records began," said Tom.

"Well, if it's not, then it must be close to it because it was blooming freezing last night when I stepped outside with Carol," said Frank.

"Have you noticed that there seems to be a lot more people in here this morning?" said Frank.

"Yes, mate. Emma told me that a party of climbers arrived last night but we were too busy enjoying ourselves to notice," said Tom.

"Yes … Brian Greene told me they were here and said that they are desperate to get to Glencoe for some climbing," said Frank, looking around and scrutinizing some of the faces.

After eating their breakfasts, the agents left the dining room and entered the bar. Frank noticed Brian Greene sitting with Moira Malone and gave Tom a dig in his ribs. "I wonder if there could be a romance in the air," said Frank.

"Frank, will you stop bumping into me! I'm in agony with this bruising on my chest," said Tom, grimacing with the pain.

Frank nodded to let Tom know he'd gotten the message about his bruising. "I think I'll phone Big John Aitken to find out how Iain Macleod is getting on at the hospital," he said.

He quickly made his way to room number seven. As he was about to enter, he heard a noise coming from inside the room. Turning the lock quietly, Mulholland leapt into the room, and a scream was heard as Frank threw himself at the woman, pinning her down onto the bed. "Who are you? What the hell are you doing in my room?" Frank asked angrily as the frightened woman struggled.

"I'm … the new maid, and I just started today. Carol sent me down to change the bedding in all the rooms," said the woman anxiously.

"I'm so sorry," Frank said, realising his mistake. "What's your name and where do you come from?"

"My name is Janice Irvine from Ayrshire, although it's no business of yours where I come from," replied the nervous woman.

"Well, Janice, I'm very sorry for attacking you, but I thought I was being robbed," said Frank, holding her trembling hand. Mulholland's eyes made a quick scan over the female as she made for the door and quickly stepped out into the hallway.

Mulholland instantly called Carol on the room phone and enquired as to where the new maid came from.

Frank lifted his bleeper and punched in some digits. "Hello, JBA. How is Iain Macleod getting on with his operation?"

"He's oot o' the operatin' theatre, but he is gonnae need quite a bit o' rehabilitation afore he comes back intae action, mate," said Big John.

"OK, John. Just informing you that the snowploughs should have the main roads cleared by about three this afternoon, but it may take longer to clear them all the way to Fort William, and the bad news is that Tommy Anderson is working on his helicopter. One of the bullets from yesterday has given him a problem and a repair job to do."

"Christ, Frank! I've been et this hospital since midnicht, an' i wis drivin' thro' Glencoe in the snaw tae get here. I'm bloomin' tired, mate," said JBA.

"I'm sorry, John, but there's nothing we can do until the roads are cleared. Over and out, mate."

Mulholland's thoughts drifted to visualizing driving through Glencoe in the dark and in a blizzard. His body shrugged at the thought, and he was feeling a little sorry about Big John's situation as he called Sir Jeffrey Merriday at headquarters.

"Yes, Frank. What can I do for you?" Merriday asked.

"Sir, can you check out a couple of females for me? Their names are Moira Malone, from Kilbarchan, and Janice Irvine, from Stevenson, in Ayrshire. I'm more interested in Malone, as she could be linked to the IRA. There seems to be quite a few Irish people in this area, and especially after what we found at Forest Lodge, with Sir Bernard Harkin being involved with the IRA, I think we should check out all the Irish people."

"OK, but not all Irish are involved with the IRA, my friend," said Merriday.

"Yes, I know that, sir, but I'm just being ultra-cautious. I'm stuck indoors at the minute. We have about three feet of snow up here, and we're waiting on the snowploughs clearing the roads, sir."

After hanging up, Mulholland left his room and made for the bar. Barmaid Carol called out to the guests, "Can we have volunteers help clear the snow away from the front of the hotel, please?"

Some of the men stepped forward, grabbed shovels, and made for the door as Frank shouted, "I'll do anything for you, sweetheart!" Tom laughed heartily, but he was grasping his bruised ribs, obviously in a lot of pain. "Just you sit over there and take things easy," said Frank, laughing at Tom, who was clutching his chest." The rest of the lads were heading out of the door with shovels in hand.

Carol looked sympathetically at Tom and asked, "Would you like a coffee to keep you company?" Tom nodded, and she poured him his coffee as he glanced at the clock, which showed 12.30 p.m. A few moments later, she placed his drink on the table in front of him.

"This should help your pain, Tom," said Carol, and she deposited a couple of pills on the table next to his coffee.

"Thanks, Carol. When will Tam Cameron be in today?" Tom asked.

"As soon as the roads are clear, he'll be down here like a shot."

"Carol, don't mention a shot or you'll bring on my pain again," Tom said, grinning.

Carol smiled as she made her way back to the bar, wiggling her trim figure and running her hands through her long black hair, bringing it into a ponytail.

Outside the hotel, the men were clearing away the snow. A noise in the sky brought everything to a halt. It was the reverberating sound of the rotors of a helicopter coming towards the hotel.

Good! It must be Tommy Anderson, thought Frank. The helicopter approached and landed behind the hotel, sending a flurry of snow spiralling into the air. To his surprise, a blonde woman stepped out of the helicopter. She was wearing a black Italian-style leather jacket with tight figure-hugging blue denim trousers and a pair of black knee-length stiletto-heeled boots on her feet, which seemed rather inappropriate for the present ground conditions. All eyes were focused on her as she walked towards the hotel.

Wow, she is a stunner, thought Frank Mulholland as he watched her strut through the snow and reach the entrance of the hotel. On reaching the hotel, she grasped the door handle, and with a quick double click of her heels on the paving to dispose of the excess snow from her boots, she quickly opened the door and entered. Frank made his way over to the building and peered through the window. To his surprise, he saw the blonde woman hugging Carol, Lorna, and Emma. They began laughing and dancing around in a circle.

I'll have to investigate this, thought Mulholland, making his way into the bar.

"Frank, meet Georgina Watson Burke. She's one of our friends from Crumlin, in Ireland," said Carol.

"Pleased to meet you, Georgina," said Frank.

"Oh, call me Georgie. That's what all my friends call me," she said, gliding the tip of her tongue over her painted lips. Her eyes twinkled with excitement as she gazed into Frank's eyes. Carol noticed the eye contact between them and became a little jealous at the way that they were looking at each other.

"Have you not got snow to clear away, Frankie boy?" said Carol. She was smiling but in reality trying to get him away from Georgie.

"OK, honey. I'm on my way," said Frank, smiling at Georgie as he made his way to the exit. Glancing back at the clock behind the bar, Mulholland's hand pushed the door open, allowing him to exit.

On stepping out into the snow, he told everyone that it was 1.20 p.m. and that it shouldn't be too long before the snowploughs arrived.

While he was clearing the snow away, his mind was turning over with thoughts of Georgina Watson Burke. I'll have to get her checked out by headquarters. She must have plenty of money to be able to fly around in a helicopter, Mulholland thought, noticing the motif of a phoenix on the front of the helicopter.

Meanwhile, inside the hotel, the girls were talking over old times back in Ireland. Emma was pouring some tea as they sat around one of the tables.

"Tell me, Carol, what is the script with you and Frank?" asked Georgie.

"He arrived last Saturday, and we immediately clicked, so keep your eyes off of him," said Carol.

"No problem," Georgie said, throwing a glance at Frank through the hotel window.

Carol, Lorna, Emma, and Georgina Watson Burke all went to the same school in the town of Crumlin, Ireland. Growing up together, they had been the best of friends more or less all their lives.

"You'll have to come over and visit me sometime at my house. When is your day off?" Georgina asked, raising her eyebrows.

"We only get one day off, and unfortunately we were off on Monday. It will be next week before we are off again ... unless we can speak nicely to Tam Cameron, the head barman," said Carol.

Emma nodded in agreement and gave Georgina a sympathetic look.

"I'll give you my phone number, and when you have time off, give me a buzz," said Georgina. She scribbled her number on a beer mat and handed it to Emma. "I'll have to be going now, ladies, but it's been good seeing you all again. Don't forget to phone me!" Georgina wafted her finger in their direction.

With a final gulp of her tea, she stood up, and with a slight tug on the bottom of her jacket, she prepared to leave. The girls went to the door with her to see her off.

As Georgie stepped outside, she made her way over to Frank and extended her hand. "Goodbye, Frank," she said, running her sultry blue eyes over him.

As Frank leant forward to kiss her on the cheek, a whiff of expensive perfume filled his nostrils. "It's been nice meeting you, and I hope we meet again," said Mulholland, smiling.

"I hope so," replied Georgie with a sensuous smile. She slowly slid her fingers free from his grasp and made for her helicopter. As she approached the *Phoenix*, a couple of the Nairn men whistled at her.

This brought a smile to Georgie's face, and with a quick wave of acknowledgement in their direction, she boarded the whirlybird. With a final quick glance towards Frank Mulholland, she switched on the ignition. The helicopter's rotors began spinning, whipping the riverside treetops and the soft snow into a frenzy of activity. In little time, she was up in the air and zooming away, flying in the direction of the village of Tyndrum with the beating sound of the rotors fading with each second that passed.

Suddenly, there was a shout from Bill Logan, one of the Nairn men. "Hooray! The snowploughs are coming."

Frank looked up to see a small convoy of vehicles heading towards Orchy. "Good, they're a little early," he remarked.

"We may get some climbing in at Glencoe!" exclaimed one of the men, and a loud cheer rang out.

Brian Greene of the mountain rescue service looked at Frank and shook his head. "That is whit we are up against in the rescue service," he said.

As the snowploughs reached the Orchy Hotel, the sound of laughter could be heard at the antics of the men trying to escape from the spraying snow coming towards them. Brian Greene looked at the laughing driver of the first plough and told Frank, "It's big Harry Bain who is leadin' the snawploughs. That's why they ur early! He's my gaffer, an' he lives in the village o' Killin." Brian waved.

Harry noticed Brian and stopped at the hotel. Brian Greene instantly stepped forward and apologised for not making work today. "Nae worries, mate," said a cheery-faced Harry. Ther' is mair than you dinnae mak it in today. Jist hae the day aff 'cause we hae enough men tae clear up tae Glencoe an' the Fort William team yer workin' frae the ither direction tae meet us."

Frank Mulholland overheard this information and quickly stepped forward. "Is anyone going to clear the road down to Inveroran and Forest Lodge?" he asked.

Harry Bain tilted his arm and looked at his watch. "Mibbee' aboot three o'clock, ma friend, as we hiv tae clear the main roads tae allow the traffic tae flow. I better get oan ma way, but ah'll be back tae clear the Inveroran road."

"One more question before you go, sir. Is that the road cleared all the way beyond Crianlarith?" Frank asked.

"Jings! Ye better no' let Sergeant Murdoch hear ye sayin' that, mate, 'cause it is Crianlarich wae an *ich* at the end o' the name," said Harry smiling.

Frank smiled back at him. "Yes, I know that, but being a Londoner, I can't sound the *ich* at the end of the name."

Big Harry moved off and signalled goodbye with a wave of his arm.

"Geez, Brian. Look at the depth of the snow along the sides of the road," Frank said.

"Aye, the snawploughs really push it aw tae the side. Sometimes ye kin be snawed in fur weeks if the snaw keeps comin' doon on a daily basis," said Brian.

"Don't say that – I have to get down to Inveroran and Forest Lodge. I have two army trucks arriving shortly," said Frank.

No sooner had Frank spoken those words than Brian Greene gestured. "Ah think they are here, Frankie boy," said Brian, pointing along the road.

Mulholland stepped out between the deep banks of snow, and to his amazement, there were two trucks coming towards them, with a red single-decker bus following.

Frank directed the trucks into the car park as the bus pulled up in front of the hotel.

"Anyone for Glencoe and Fort William?" the bus driver called out. A loud cheer was heard as some of the men downed shovels and made for the hotel. People were quickly boarding the bus, carrying rucksacks and skis.

"They're heading fur Scotland's first ski centre. It's caud the Glencoe White Corries Skiing Centre, which just opened in nineteen fifty-six. It has been a tremendous success ower the past six years," said Brian Greene proudly. Brian began warning everyone about the avalanche alert that he had posted, but the others didn't seem to be paying attention. The bus eased out onto the road, which had improved considerably since the snowploughs had cleared it. Brian walked into the hotel shaking his head in disbelief that they were leaving for the mountains. Meanwhile, the Nairn County men were still trying to clear the snow from the front of the hotel and around the pathways.

Frank decided to speak to the army team and inform them about the snow situation on the Inveroran road. He directed the men into the hotel to rest at the fireside tables and ordered them some tea.

When a worried-looking woman screamed that she couldn't find her five-year-old daughter, Frank Mulholland immediately leapt to her assistance by asking her the girl's name and where she was last seen. The woman's husband was searching frantically inside the hotel, but to no avail. "Gentlemen, we're looking for a little blonde girl who answers to the name of Freya Robertson. She was last seen inside the hotel about fifteen minutes ago," said Frank.

The woman's husband appeared. The look on his face told everyone that she was not inside the hotel.

Agent Mulholland began organising the men into teams of four. "You lads check the river to the left and right of the bridge. Look for footsteps in the snow leading down to the river," said Mulholland.

Agent Tom Sommerville appeared. A quick nod of his head told Frank that the girl did not appear to be anywhere inside the hotel.

"What are the names of the girl's parents?" Frank asked.

"Their names are Scott and Lorna Robertson, and they have another daughter called Chloe," said Tom.

"Let me speak to Chloe. She may know something," said Frank.

Carol the barmaid was consoling the young girl, who was crying for her sister's safe return.

"Chloe, what was Freya wearing? Did she talk about doing anything in the last fifteen minutes?" Frank asked urgently.

"She was wearing a little pink jacket and white trousers. She was playing with her little doll called Frieda," Chloe said, trying to hold back the tears. Just then, the mother of the girls came into the hotel, crying and frantic with worry.

"What did she have on her feet?" Tom asked.

"A pair of pink wellington boots," Chloe said, wiping the tears from her eyes.

"Was she thinking of going outside?" Frank asked, looking at mother and daughter.

"She didn't say anything about going outside to me," blurted Chloe.

Her mum nodded in agreement as she consoled her daughter.

Brian Greene appeared and called out to Frank. Mulholland immediately went over to meet him.

"What is it?" shouted the girl's mum hysterically. Her husband, who had just entered the room, desperately tried to console her.

"Ah've been thinkin', mate. Is ther' a possibility that she boarded the bus alang wae the crowd and is oan her wae tae Glencoe?" Brian asked.

"Good thinking, mate. I'll get my car, and we'll check out the bus as soon as I speak to the parents," said Frank. Frank called out to the worried parents. "We think she may have boarded the bus and is on her way to Glencoe. We are going to stop the bus and check it out," Frank said.

"While we are gone, would you continue looking around the hotel and the river?" Mulholland said.

Both parents nodded and said that they would continue the search outside. Frank, Tom, and Brian Greene made for the car, and the frantic chase was on to catch the bus before it stopped in Glencoe.

"If she gets aff the bus wae the crowd et Glencoe, then we wull struggle tae find her," Brian Greene anxiously said.

The agent's car slithered through the snow in the car park and made it onto the main road.

"Put the foot down and give it some gas," said Tom as the car moved along the still slightly slippery road. "Geez! I'm surprised that the bus company allowed this bus to make the journey, but at least it will not be travelling very fast," said Frank, looking at Tom with a little trepidation.

The chase was on. As the car approached the open expanse of the Rannoch Moor, the silence was broken. "There it is! Aboot a mile ahead o' us an' we'll catch it nae bother!" shouted Brian, pointing excitedly.

As the car closed in on the bus, Frank flashed the headlights for it to slow down.

To their relief, the bus pulled into a lay-by, and the team slithered to a halt.

Mulholland jumped out into the chilled air and signalled to the driver. "Can we check out the bus, sir? We are looking for a young girl called Freya Robertson," said Frank.

Both men attentively walked the aisle, checking both sides of the bus. To their delight, when they reached the back seat, there were two non-paying passengers. It was Freya Robertson and her doll Frieda. She was sitting comfortably and minding her own business. She looked up at the smiling men.

"I think you had better come with me, young lady. Your mum is searching for you," said Frank. Taking Freya's hand, he led her to the door. Everyone was cheering. Freya was smiling back at everyone as they stepped out into the snow. *I'd better have Carol let everyone know we have found her,* thought Frank, taking his pager from his inside pocket. "Hello, Carol. We've found her on the bus and are on our way back now. We shouldn't be too long, honey."

Carol called aloud, "They have found her on the bus, and she is safe." The relief on the faces of the parents was there for all to see. A loud cheer rang out as both parents hugged each other, tears of sheer relief flowing.

The cheering continued as the car pulled into the car park. Freya walked towards her mum and dad without a worry in the world.

Both parents thanked everyone for their efforts and then flopped down on some chairs, exhausted and relieved to have their daughters back together again.

Ten minutes later, Frank was looking out the window, and he signalled to Tom that the snowploughs had returned and were crossing the Orchy Bridge to clear the road to Inveroran.

"I'll let the army truck drivers know that the road is being cleared and to be prepared to move off when we give notice," Tom said, walking over to the soldiers. The soldiers were nodding in regimental order as Tom relayed the message to them. Approximately ten minutes later,

Frank stood up, and with a quick swish of his arm towards the men, he made for the exit with Tom, the soldiers following.

"Just be careful as you go over the bridge, lads. It's not very wide, and we don't want to damage it because it has stood there since ..." Frank turned to Agent Sommerville. "How long, Tom?"

"Since seventeen fifty-one, according to the book I bought," said Tom smiling.

"Well, I'm sure you are correct, mate, but it's been there a long time anyway," said Frank with a laugh.

"In fact, the village is named after the bridge," said Tom.

"The snowploughs are disappearing over the hill now, so I think we can follow," said Frank. The agents got into their car. "Well, Tom, I'll let you say it."

"Forest Lodge, here we come!" Tom said. They had a good laugh.

Frank had been saying "Here we come" every time they had been going somewhere, and it had become a bit of a joke between them.

Forest Lodge, here we come!

The agents were about to drive off when a car turned into the hotel, blocking their exit. It was a smiling agent J. B. Aitken returning from Belford Hospital in Fort William. "Thank Christ! That has been a lang nicht fur me et the hospital," said JBA gruffly. "Oanyway, they are transferring Agent Macleod tae Glasgow's Southern General Hospital the morra."

"Brilliant! Well done, John. You're a good man. If you want to make your way to the Inveroran Inn and get some shut-eye, we will tidy up at Forest Lodge. The army trucks are on their way as we speak," Frank said.

"Aye, ah seen them squeezin' ower the Brig as ah drove in, an' they hadnae much room either side," said Big John with a smile.

"I don't think the bridge was built to take trucks," said Frank.

"More like a horse and cart," Tom said, laughing.

"I'll drop the rest of your team off at Inveroran as soon as we are finished at Forest Lodge!" shouted Frank. The agents drove off, waving back at JBA. Big John waved in acknowledgement with two fingers in the air, which brought smiles to the agents' faces.

The agents were looking at the fast-flowing River Orchy as they drove down the single-track road to Inveroran.

"It's just as well that wee girl didn't fall into the river. She would have been swept downstream to the falls in no time at all," said Tom.

"All's well that ends well," said Frank. A few minutes later, they were approaching the Inveroran Inn. The proprietor of the inn, Peter MacInnes, was standing at the entrance.

Peter, along with his wife, Jessie, had been running the business for the past twelve years. Peter also supplemented their earnings as the head gamekeeper of the Inveroran Estate. He'd first met Jessie when they were climbing on Ben Nevis, and they instantly hit it off. Kilbirnie man Peter and Paisley girl Jessie Cameron were married three months later. They decided to put in an offer for the inn, which had just come on the market. They were over the moon, so to speak, when their offer was accepted, and the happy couple moved into the inn. It was a dream come true for both of them.

Frank pulled up next to Peter and grasped his hand. "The guys will be moving back into the inn tonight. Big John Aitken is following behind us, and will be here shortly," said Frank, pointing back with his thumb.

"Yes! Big John told me they were going to Fort William and staying overnight," said Peter.

"What was all that noise yesterday? It sounded like firecrackers," said Peter.

"Yes, it was firecrackers – because of the visit of American President John F. Kennedy and Vice President Johnson. They were having a little jolly on the *Flying Scotsman* along the West Highland Railway with Scottish Secretary Michael Noble. The people of Orchy were setting off crackers and cheering them as they left," Frank said cagily. "We are heading down to Forest Lodge now, but we'll see you later." Bringing the engine to life, he moved off, waving back to Peter.

"We can't tell Peter that Big John and the team were shooting up Russian and IRA agents at Forest Lodge yesterday, he told Tom. "It would probably scare them, and it would certainly harm their business if tourists heard about it. We will have to tell the lads that we told him it was firecrackers going off."

"Yes, you're probably correct there, mate," Tom said, nodding his head.

The distance from Inveroran to Forest Lodge was approximately a mile. When the agents arrived, Tom said, "It's a lovely spot down here with the river, loch, and the mountains in the background." He had his hands on his hips as he admired the view.

"Yeah, super," said Mulholland, looking at the soldiers stuffing guns and ammunition into the backs of the trucks. "I'll be glad to see this lot cleared up and away from here."

Just then, Agents Jim MacNeill and Brian Wilson appeared, asking how Agent Iain Macleod was getting on at the hospital.

Frank answered in his official tone of voice. "Fine, guys. They have taken the bullet out and are transferring him to Glasgow tomorrow morning. I've spoken to JBA, and he is heading down to the Inveroran Inn as we speak. When we finish up here, I'll run you back to the inn."

The lodge was owned by Sir Bernard Harkin, an Irish millionaire who made his wealth in the potato business over in Ireland. Upon moving to Scotland two years ago, he bought Forest Lodge but had been a bit of a recluse since arriving. He had been plying his trade in the gunrunning business, buying and selling between Russian and IRA agents. MI6 Agents Mulholland and Sommerville ended Sir Bernard's life yesterday as he tried to escape on his boat in Loch Leven. During the attack on his boat, Sir Bernard Harkin was shot and, along with his crew, was blown up as their boat crashed into the MacDonald Island graveyard called Eilean Munde.

The army trucks were now leaving with the stash of weapons. Frank looked at Tom and sighed. "Thank goodness for that. Now I can breathe more easily."

"We'll have to lock up the place before we go. As far as I know, Sir Bernard had a family, and the lodge will probably be released to them at some point," said Mulholland.

"This is a beautiful area to be living in," said Frank Mulholland, changing the subject and glancing at his watch. "Crivvens! It's half past five. C'mon, you lot! Get in the car and I'll drop you off at the inn on our way back to the Orchy Hotel."

After locking up the lodge, the MI6 men wearily climbed into the car.

"A job well done down at the lodge over the past two days," Frank said as they made the short drive back to the Inveroran Inn.

On arriving at the inn, Frank reminded the men to tell Big John about the firecrackers *yesterday* … Both agents smiled at the firecrackers comment and walked with relief towards the inn.

Frank drove away, with Tom waving and calling out, "Orchy, here we come!"

"Now we're talking," said Mulholland, grinning.

Back at the Orchy Hotel

The hotel grounds were looking strange with piles of snow and snowmen scattered around.

"Jings! The Nairn County lads have been busy building snowmen," said Agent Sommerville.

"Yes, they sure have, mate. At least the car park has been cleared and the snowmen will guard all the cars," said Frank, laughing.

As Frank locked the car, Tom said, "I hope none of the snowmen nick our car."

"If they do, they won't get very far, because that blooming heater will melt them," replied Frank.

Tom pointed at one of the snowmen with a yellow and black Nairn County scarf around its neck. The scarf was fluttering in the chilly breeze that had arisen from nowhere.

"C'mon! You can buy me a beer, Sommerville," Frank said, blowing into his hands.

When the agents entered the bar, the head barman Tam Cameron asked, "What can I do you for?" The three regular local guys were sitting in their usual seats near the fire.

"We'll have two beers – and give the three amigos whatever they would like," said Tom, nodding at the guys. The three amigos were Tam's best customers, and usually their bicycles were leaning against the hotel wall.

Tam Cameron lived in Tyndrum, in the house above Constable George Dalgetty's artifact shop. He dressed immaculately and kept his curly fair hair covered with a trilby, which had become his trademark. The local guys generally pulled his leg about it, but Tam tended to laugh it off with a grin, usually while twisting the ends of his moustache. He was well liked by all his regular customers.

Davy Blackwood was one of the local lads, and he worked with the Forestry Commission Scotland. On average, he worked a ten-hour day, although his working day was shorter in the winter due to the decreased daylight hours. Davy was about five feet ten and had wavy dark hair. His muscular body has been enhanced by moving and using the forestry equipment. He lived in a little cottage about a mile down the road from the Orchy Hotel. He had an arrangement with the hotel to get cheaper meals, and he made it a point to eat in the hotel most nights.

He usually cycled home, sometimes a little wobbly, depending on how many beers he had consumed. He regularly climbed the mountains of Glencoe and made the occasional excursion to the alps of Switzerland and Austria.

Brian Greene worked with the Stirlingshire Council Roads Department. His working day varied, depending on the distance of travel to each job. He lived in Tyndrum, quite near Tam the barman. Brian gave up his time helping with the mountain rescue service, and he could be called out at any time of the day or night. With Brian, this was a labour of love, as he spent most of his spare time walking and climbing on the mountains and would often offer advice to anyone heading to the hills.

Ian Chapman was a loveable local rogue who would do anything possible not to work. Ian, or "Chappie", as he preferred to be called, would spend most of his time poaching in the local estates, either shooting or fishing. He was a likeable lad, and because of this, the local bailiffs tended to turn a blind eye to his activities around the area. On a nice day, Chappie would sit at the edge of the River Orchy and fish for trout or salmon with a bottle of cider by his side, of which he was very fond. He lived just along the road but still travelled back and forth on his cycle.

The three amigos all smiled at Tom. "Cheers, mate!" said Chappie. "You know the order by now."

"I didn't expect to see you lads tonight because of all the snow," said Frank.

"Ye must be jokin'. It'll tak a lot mair than a wee drap o' snaw tae keep us awa!" exclaimed Chappie.

The lads all laughed heartily.

Carol appeared at the bar. "I thought I heard your voice, Frankie boy. Are you coming in for your meal?" she asked.

"Yes, honey. I think I'll check out the menu in the dining room," said Frank, glancing at Tom.

Tom nodded casually in agreement, and both agents made for the dining room, with Carol following. "I'm going to have fish tonight," said Frank.

Tom was studying the menu, with Carol standing over him and impatiently tapping on her notepad with her pencil. "Am I not ordering quickly enough for you?" Tom asked jokingly. "I'll take the haggis and neeps." He grinned at Carol and said, "Emma wouldn't rush me like that." Carol walked away giggling.

Tom had the hots for Carol's friend Emma and had spent a few nights with her in room number eight, his room since they arrived on Saturday, 24 March.

"I'm going to question Carol about her friend Georgie Watson Burke tonight, mate. I'll see if Sir Jeffrey Merriday at headquarters can check her out," said Frank.

"Is this an Irish thing with you, Frank? You are checking out every Irish person in the place at the moment," said Tom, smiling.

"It's better to be safe than sorry," replied Frank, dipping his eyebrows.

"Don't say anything to Carol," said Frank quietlyas she approached with the meals.

"Enjoy your meal, guys," said Carol. She winked at Frank and with a quick flick of her fingers tucked her dark hair under her cap and headed back to the kitchen.

"She won't be pleased if she finds out we are investigating her friend," said Tom.

"I know that, but I did the same with Carol, Lorna, and Emma. So say nothing to them, my friend. Now let us enjoy our meal."

About an hour later, Frank and Tom walked into the bar and the three amigos gave out a cheer. "We've got you a couple of beers over here, lads," Brian Greene said.

After a few hours and a few more beers, the lads were feeling a little merry.

"Where did you sleep last night?" Tom asked.

"I couldnae walk hame, as the snaw wis startin' tae come doon, an' It is a five mile journey tae get tae Tyndrum frae here," said Brian.

"Why did you not go home with Tam when he left?" Frank asked.

"Ah dinnae see the bugger goin' hame because he left sae early. Carol fixed me up with a bed in the staff quarters," said Brian, laughing.

"So that's why you were here this morning. I wondered why you had arrived here so early, with all that snow lying around." Frank said, glancing at the clock behind the bar. "Geez! It's going on midnight, and I forgot to call Merriday at headquarters."

"You'll have to leave it till the morning now," replied Tom.

Just then, a taxi arrived to take Brian back home to Tyndrum. "Will ye drap us aff oan yer wae hame?" Davy asked.

"We hivnae' got oor' bikes because o' the snaw," said Chappie, quickly finishing off his cider.

Frank and Tom said goodnight to the guys and made their way to their respective rooms.

Suddenly, a voice called out, "Would sir like a coffee delivered to room number seven?"

It was the voice of Carol, her dark eyelashes flickering at Frank from behind the bar. Frank gave her the thumbs up that it was a good idea and made for his room, with Tom walking ahead and smiling back at him.

A couple of minutes later, the door eased open. In walked Carol with a tray, which she placed on the bedside table. Frank grabbed her and pulled her down onto the bed, kissing her passionately, with Carol responding. Frank's hands slipped over her sexy body. They quickly and frantically began removing their clothes, desperate to get at each other's bodies. Frank rolled back the sheets and leaped into bed, Carol quickly joining him. They were in a high state of excitement as their bodies melded. Carol was moaning in Frank's ear as they reached fever pitch together.

"Oh my God, Frank. Please! Please! Please! Don't stop," she pleaded as both their bodies exploded in the height of passion. Carol's arms clung onto Frank, squeezing him tightly as they both collapsed with exhaustion.

"Geez, Carol. That was fantastic. Just what I needed," Frank said, snuggling into her warm body. "Pass me my coffee, honey?" he asked, his fingers running over her soft breasts, adding to her excitement.

"Get it yourself," replied Carol, knowing that he would have to lean over her to reach it.

As Frank leaned over her, Carol's hands ran down his back. He responded to her demands.

A few minutes later, Frank collapsed onto the bed at the side next to his coffee.

"You worked that one out well, Frankie boy," said Carol.

Frank grabbed his coffee and took a sip from the cup. "Geez, I must be losing my touch because it's still quite warm. Usually it's cold when I drink it," said Frank, laughing quietly. On hearing his remark, Carol smiled and then smacked his bottom.

Frank decided to question Carol about Georgie Watson Burke. She was not too happy at his timing, and she asked why he had an interest in her.

"It's my job, honey. I have to check out a lot of people and make sure they are not up to any mischief," replied Frank.

"You were pretty excited when we made love, Frank. I hope you weren't thinking of her," said Carol.

"Of course not, honey. I have to check her out professionally and inform headquarters of any information that I may find," said Frank.

"I hope you're telling me the truth, Frankie boy, or you and I will be falling out," Carol said, laying her head down on the pillow.

I should have waited until the morning, Frank thought as he lay his head down next to Carol's.

Carol pretended that she was tired and closed her eyes, but her mind was on Georgie Burke.

After a few minutes of silence, Carol's dark eyes opened and she spoke. "She comes from the same town as me, called Crumlin, near Belfast. She met a Scottish guy and moved over to a place called Penilee, in Glasgow. They married, and she became Mrs. Burke.

The company she worked for is called Rolls-Royce Aerospace Engineering. They are based in Hillington, near Glasgow. They produce aeroplane engines and then test them out," said Carol. They moved up to this area about two years ago and bought a large house in the Cononish Glen, near Dalrigh, about a mile from Tyndrum. That, I'm afraid, is all I can tell you."

"Thanks. I really appreciate what you've told me," whispered Frank, snuggling into her responsive body.

"How thankful are you, Frankie boy?" Carol asked in a sultry voice as their lips made contact. The excitement was building inside their bodies as they writhed together, breathing heavily and clinging on to each other. "Oh, yes, Frank! Hold me and don't let go," Carol said as the excitement reached fever pitch inside her trembling body. "Yes! Yes! Yes!" cried Carol as their lovemaking reached a crescendo.

Frank collapsed in a heap beside her. "Geez, honey! That was fantastic," said Frank, lifting up his cup of coffee. "Jings! My coffee is cold now," he said, chuckling.

She gave him a little smack on the bottom. "I think we'd better get some sleep because I have to be up early to feed all the walkers and skiers," she said, gazing into Frank's eyes. "According to Tam, now that the roads are cleared, they'll be leaving for the hills early." Carol closed her eyes and snuggled into Frank's muscular body.

Thursday, 29 March

When Frank awoke, as usual he noted that Carol had gone to tend to her duties in the kitchen. Frank tried to get his head around his Itinerary for the day ahead. *I'll have to give headquarters a call and check out Georgina Burke,* he thought. Pulling back the curtain, he peeked out and was faced with a clear blue sky. Suddenly, Frank's pager bleeped, and he quickly grabbed it. It was Sir Jeffrey Merriday at MI6 headquarters.

"Frank, I checked out Moira Malone and Janice Irvine. They are both as clear as a bell, so keep your mind at ease," said Merriday.

"Good, sir. But I have another request for you. Could you check out a female called Georgina Burke? She is Irish and came from Crumlin, near Belfast, in Ireland," Frank said. "I know a little history about her. See what you can find out and let me know as soon as possible, please."

"OK, Frank. I'll see what I can do. Over and out," said Merriday.

Frank made for the shower room and quickly switched on the faucet. After brushing his teeth vigorously to erase the taste of the previous night's beer, he stepped into the shower and sighed as the warm water flowed over him. *Oh my God, this is brilliant,* he thought while rubbing the soap around his body. After a few minutes of showering, he quickly turned off the shower. Grabbing a towel, he made for the bedroom. Dressing quickly, he headed for Agent Sommerville's room.

With a quick rap of his knuckles on the door, he entered. To his surprise, he found his fellow agent in a compromising situation with sexy barmaid Emma MacNamara.

"Whow. Sorry, folks," said Frank, embarrassed at what he had seen. Dark-haired Emma quickly dove beneath the covers while Tom pushed Frank out of the room, with Mulholland mumbling his apologies.

"I'm going to breakfast … *now!*" exclaimed Frank. He quickly made his way to the dining room.

A few minutes later, a slightly red-faced Emma passed him on her way to the kitchen. Frank smiled at her. Frank's pager bleeped, and he noticed that it was headquarters.

"Mulholland here, sir. What have you to tell me?" asked Frank.

"I've just had a call from Commander Peter Heuitten down at Coulport Naval Submarine Base. He would like to speak to you urgently," Merriday said. "He asked if you could come down at one o'clock today, and I told him that it would be OK. So would you try to make it, Frank?" Merriday asked.

"I hope the roads are cleared of snow, sir," said Mulholland.

"Yes, they will be. Over and out," replied Merriday.

Tom appeared, shaking his fist at Frank.

"Sorry about walking in on you and Emma. We're going for a visit down to Coulport at one o'clock today," he said, quickly changing the subject. "How's your bruised chest, mate? Although … it didn't seem to trouble you back in your room a few minutes ago." He grinned.

"It's not too bad, you sod," Tom said, laughing.

Emma and Carol appeared with the breakfasts. "Enjoy your food, gents," said Emma. Slapping the back of Frank's head, she made her way back to the kitchen.

"This looks good so get tucked in, mate," Tom said.

There was a lot of activity out in the hallway, and both agents took notice. "It looks as though the bus has arrived to take the skiers off to Glencoe Mountains," said Frank.

"I was reading my book on this area, and it seems that the Glencoe White Corries Ski Centre opened only six years ago, in nineteen fifty-six," Tom said, showing off his knowledge of the area.

"Yes, I know that; Brian Greene told me about it yesterday," said Frank. He looked at his timepiece. "It's ten twenty, mate. The bus is running a little late. It should have been here at ten on the dot. Maybe, we better allow more time when we leave for Coulport," said Frank.

Tom nodded in agreement, and they left the dining room and made their way into the lounge. Frank lifted a book from the table. Whilst tapping it on the table, his mind was deep in thought. "Could you get that book of yours and check out how far the walk is from the main road through Cononish Glen, to reach Ben Lui?" Frank asked.

"Do you not mean how far it is to reach Georgie Burke's farmhouse?" Tom said, smiling at Frank.

"You are not as daft as you look, buddy. I think we may have to put on the walking gear and head for the hills to check her out, as soon as Merriday gets back to me and confirms my doubts about her."

"I don't need to go for my book, because Davy Blackwood has just walked into the lounge," said Tom.

"Davy, can I speak to you for a minute?" enquired Frank.

Davy shuffled over and asked how he could help.

"Where do I park the car to walk through the Cononish Glen?" Frank asked.

"Are ye gonnae climb Ben Lui?" Davy asked excitedly.

"Well, we were thinking of going for a walk along the glen," said Frank.

"Ye kin stop et a wee parkin' place aboot a mile the ither side o' Tyndrum, where ye see a sign fur Dalrigh. Ah micht warn ye, though, that it is aboot a four-and-a-half-mile walk alang a country road tae get tae the hill," said Davy.

"Are there any houses along this road?" Tom asked.

"Ther' is a couple at the stert, but efter ye cross the river, yer in open country, and there is only the fermhoose, which is aboot four mile alang the road. I wid hiv tae warn ye, though, that the snaw will still be lying oan the road, as the owners o' the fermhoose hiv got a helicopter, an' because o' that, the council doesnae' treat the fermhoose road as a priority unless they phone it in."

"Thanks for the info, mate," said Tom, looking at Frank with a worried expression.

"That'll be all for now. Continue with what you were doing, and thanks for your time," said Frank.

"Ah'll mibbee see ye's the nicht for a beer," Davy said as he walked away.

"It looks as though we may have a bit of a hike ahead of us," said Frank.

"Don't be so worried, mate. The snow is only three feet deep," said Tom, laughing at the expression on Frank's face.

"I think we should leave for Coulport Naval Base around half past eleven," said Frank. "It took an hour to get there when we last visited, so we'd better allow more time for the road conditions."

"Okey-dokey, Frankie boy," said Tom, jokingly clicking his fingers.

Coulport Naval Base

om's eyes were focused on the road, and Frank stared out of the car window. "That's a cracking-looking bridge over there," said Frank.

"Yes, mate. It's called the Auch Horseshoe Viaduct, and it was built by a Glasgow company around eighteen ninety-four," said Tom.

"I take it you saw that in your book," said Frank. "What was the name of the company that built it?"

Tom hesitated. "I can't remember at this moment," said Tom with a grin, knowing that Frank had caught him out.

A devilish smile appeared on Frank's face. "Yippee! I've finally caught you out, mate. You better read your book again."

About an hour later, the agents were nearing the submarine base.

"What was that? I saw a glint coming from the snow beneath that big rock face on the hill across the water," said Tom excitedly.

"Yes, there it is again. It looks as though somebody is checking us out," said Frank, staring over at the far side of the loch.

When the agents arrived at the base, a security guard stepped forward and asked who was calling.

"Frank Mulholland and Tom Sommerville, to see Commander Heuitten, please," replied Tom.

"Yes, you are expected, gentlemen," said the guard, handing Tom two passes and pointing him in the direction.

"It's OK. We've been here before. I know the way," said Tom politely. The guard raised the barrier, allowing the car to drive through. The car pulled up at the commander's quarters, and both agents entered the building.

"Good afternoon, gentlemen!" a voice spoke out. Both agents stopped in their tracks and looked at each other in shock. The commander's secretary, Marilyn Young, was sitting at her desk.

"Good afternoon, gentlemen. What's wrong? You would think you had just seen a ghost," said Marilyn.

"Yes … I think we have," replied Mulholland.

"What do you mean by that?" she asked.

"We're here to see Commander Heuitten," said Frank, changing the subject but looking anxiously at Tom.

Marilyn leant forward and spoke into the intercom. "Your guests have arrived, sir … Shall I show them in?" she casually asked.

Frank Mulholland was thinking that she was a bit too informal with the commander, and he wondered if they had more than a working relationship going on between them.

"Yes, show them in, and could you bring in some tea and biscuits, please?" said the voice at the other end of the line.

"OK, gentlemen, just go in," Marilyn said with a smile. Her hand shot forward, and fingers with pink painted nails grasped their passes and placed them in a basket on the desk. Frank and Tom were bemused, and they were still staring at the secretary as they entered the room.

Commander Peter Heuitten had served in the navy for forty-three years, and he was highly qualified in all areas of seamanship. His six-foot body frame was fit for a man his age, and his fresh-looking face was topped up with silver hair which was smartly in place. A line around his hair indicated that he had just recently taken off his cap and hung it on a coat stand in the corner of the room. He was held in high regard by all of his men. He had confidence in all his staff and preferred to be called by his nickname, "Porky".

"Good afternoon, gentlemen! Thank you for coming down here today at my request," said Commander Heuitten, his deep blue eyes scanning the agents.

"Hello, sir! It's good to see you again," said Mulholland.

"When you were both here last Sunday, I told you that we were on a high alert but we had not found anything to concern us. Well … things have changed, my friends," said the commander.

"What's the problem, Por—," Frank began.

"Oh, it's OK. You can call me Porky. Everyone does," said Commander Heuitten.

"Yes, you told me that the last time we were here, Porky," said Frank, smiling nervously.

"One of our guards had been killed, and the other was knocked unconscious. If he hadn't been found in time, he would possibly be dead too," said Porky. "We have checked the area many times over, and have found nothing."

"Have you checked under the submarine at the dock, sir? Because we know that there are Russian agents around this area who have been trained on two-man mini subs, and they may have planted explosives under the submarine, below the surface of the water," said Frank.

"We have checked all areas, including the submarine, and found nothing," replied Porky.

"Is it possible that they came here just to be a distraction for their activities elsewhere?" Frank asked.

At this point, Tom butted in. "What about the glint of light we saw on the way here, Frank?"

"It looked as though someone was watching us as we approached, about a mile back from the entrance to the base, sir," said Tom.

"It looked like the sunlight was reflecting on someone's binoculars," said Frank.

"That could have been our men. I've positioned two men on the hillside at the far side of the loch to keep an eye on the area, although they are not as far away as you are telling me," said Porky with a little concern. "I think we'll have to check farther along the loch side, in case there is someone snooping around."

Tom tapped the table with his fingers as if to make a point. "Sir, could you check along as far as the large boulder or cliff face, because that's where we spotted a reflection of some kind. Just below the cliff face," said Tom, emphasizing the location.

"Gentlemen, we will do our best to get to the bottom of this, and yes, it will be checked out," said Porky.

"Could it be possible that a Russian submarine would come up the River Clyde and drop agents off to cause trouble in this area?" Frank asked.

"Our radar hasn't picked up anything unusual in that area," said Porky.

"They must have been after something to go to the trouble of killing a guard, sir," said Frank.

"Did they go near your ammunition depot?" Tom asked.

"No. According to our records, everything is in order. Anyway, the ammunition is not kept at the base. It is brought in from another depot when required."

"Who keeps the records of the weapons, sir?" Tom asked.

"The guards take note of what goes in and out of the base, and they pass it on to my secretary to update at all times," said Porky.

The agents looked at each other with alarm.

"Is there a problem with that?" Porky asked with a frown.

"Sir ... may we ask you some questions about your secretary?" Frank asked.

"Fire away, Frank. But she has been working here for nine years and is very reliable," said Porky.

"Last Tuesday, as you know, JFK and Vice President Johnson were visiting your base," said Frank. "They then went on to Crianlarich for a little jolly on the *Flying Scotsman* along the West Highland Railway line, where we had to eliminate some Russian agents who were perched on top of Beinn Achaladair, preparing to assassinate the president. We thought your secretary, Marilyn Young was, one of them. So we took her out, and believe me ... she was dead. Her helicopter crashed into the mountain and finished up in a ball of flames. Now, sir, you can understand why we were surprised when we saw her today, sitting at her desk and welcoming us to Coulport."

Porky pressed his intercom. "Marilyn, can you come in here for a minute, please?" As she entered the room, Porky was laughing. "Marilyn, when did you take your training for a helicopter course?" Porky asked.

"Me!" replied the surprised secretary, brushing her hand through her blonde hair. "I would never get in a helicopter, sir. I don't trust them," said Marilyn, flicking her painted fingers in the direction of Commander Heuitten.

"Have you got any sisters?" Tom asked expectantly.

"No, sir," she replied.

"Well, believe me when I say this, but you had a double, and she was a Russian agent called Alexandra Vasnetsov," said Tom. "That was why we were surprised to see you today. We thought you were a double agent that we saw being killed."

"That's all for the moment," said Porky with a smile. She walked away with a swagger.

"Gentlemen, if I find that anything is out of place, I will get in touch with you," said Porky. "But for the time being, I'll have to end the meeting. Thank you once again for taking the time to come here."

The agents smiled at Marilyn as they left the room. As they approached her desk, Porky called out, "Will you come in here, Ms Vasnetsov?" Both agents grinned at Porky's remark, and Marilyn reminded them to hand in their passes at the gate on the way out.

As the agents made their way to the car, Captain Walter Duffy appeared and asked them if they had enjoyed their visit.

"Unfortunately, we couldn't help Commander Heuitten as much as he would have hoped," said Frank.

"Captain Duffy, may I ask you a question about the submarine?" Tom asked.

"Certainly, sir. How can I help you?" the immaculately dressed captain asked, tipping his cap up and revealing deep-set blue eyes sitting beneath thick greyish eyebrows.

"Has the submarine been checked for any tracking devices that may have been planted beneath the waterline? Would it be possible for a mini sub to sail underneath the submarine undetected as it entered the base?" Tom asked.

"The answer to both questions is yes, my friend," said Captain Duffy. "But if anyone was going to enter the dock, he would most likely come across the loch, beneath the water." He pointed towards the far side of the loch. "This area is Ministry of Defence territory, and we have it well secured."

"OK, Captain. Thanks for your help. Continue with your business," said Frank.

As they made for their car, the agents discussed the meeting.

Commander Heuitten was looking out of the window, and he signalled for Captain Duffy to come to his office. "What were they asking you, Walter?" Porky asked.

"They were wondering if the submarine had been checked for any bugs that may have been planted on it. I told them it had been checked, sir. They also enquired whether it was possible for a mini sub to enter the dock undetected beneath our submarine. I said that it was possible but it was more likely to come from the opposite side of the loch."

"Maybe we would be better running another check around and under the submarine, just in case we have missed something, Walter," said Porky. "Oh, and maybe check the opposite side of the loch for any hidden mini subs." He laughed.

"OK, sir. But you won't be laughing if we find something," said Captain Duffy, replacing his cap and smiling as he exited the room.

Meanwhile, at the gate, Frank handed the passes to the guard and thanked him for the visit.

As the agents drove off, they quickly glanced across the loch.

"Bridge of Orchy, here we come!" said Frank.

"Jings! The hills look good with snow on them, especially when the sun is shining," said Tom.

"You won't be saying that when we are trudging through the snow to get to Georgie Watson Burke's house later," Frank replied with a laugh.

"Do you think headquarters could arrange for us to have training on two-man mini subs? I've always fancied trying that," Tom said.

"I had my training on them about seven years ago, at the deep water training base in Kylesku, up on the west coast of Scotland, and, it was quite scary when you dove under," said Frank. "I stayed in the Kylesku Hotel, and the views were tremendous from the hotel, looking along the loch and across to the mountains. They had a small ferry to take cars and people across the loch. I think it was called the *Maid of Kylesku*, but ideally they could do with building a bridge over the loch to speed things up for road users."

"Maybe Captain Duffy could fix me up with a quick training course down here," Tom said with a chuckle.

As they were nearing Tyndrum, Tom spoke. "Look! There's the sign for Dalrigh and the road to Georgie's house. That must be Ben Lui and the Cononish Glen over there."

"Good … At least we know where to come to tonight when it's dark," said Frank.

"Tonight," Tom mumbled to himself.

As the agents were nearing Orchy, Tom glanced over at the Auch Horseshoe Viaduct and said, "I remember now. It was built by Foreman and McColl of Glasgow," said Tom, looking at Frank and grinning.

"Keep your eyes on the road, ya sod," Frank said as the Orchy Hotel came into view.

Back at the Orchy Hotel

The agents made for the bar. "I'll buy the beers since you remembered who built the viaduct," said Frank. "Two beers, my good man," he said to head barman Tam Cameron, who was behind the bar.

"Whaur hiv you twa been tae today?" Tam asked.

"Ach, we've jist been oot an' aboot, daein' a wee bit sichtseein," said Frank, laughing at his own attempt at Scottish language.

"Crivvens! Yer stertin' tae sound like me," said Tam, tipping his trilby.

"We were thinking of going for a walk to Ben Lui tomorrow," said Frank. "Jings! The snaw wull be deep alang the road tae the mountain, as it is oany' a single-track road up tae the fermhoose."

"Dae ye's ken that its aboot a four-mile walk alang tae it?" asked Tam, twirling his moustache.

"Do you think it will be OK to undertake such a walk in those conditions tomorrow?" asked Frank.

"If ye dae go, then tak' yer gold pannin' stuff wae ye and ye kin always guddle yersel's a fortune," said Tam.

"What do you mean by gold panning?" Frank asked.

Tom quickly butted in. "According to my book, there is gold in the burns around the mountains of this area," he said with a laugh.

"Oh, ther' definitely is gold ower ther. My wife's wedding ring is made oot o' the gold fae the Dubhchraig Burn that I panned maself aboot fifteen years ago," said Tam, trying to work out in his mind how long he had been married.

"Where does the gold come from, Tam?" Mulholland asked.

"I think it aw comes frae under the ground oan the mountains aroond the Cononish Glen. It is swept doon by the watter in the burns.

40

In fact, ther' daein' some test drillin' the noo, ower oan the hill caud Easie Anie, which is jist up frae the fermhoose."

"That'll be four and tuppence, please. Will ah jist add it oan tae yer bill, Frank?" Tam asked.

Mulholland confirmed that he should do that. The agents sat down next to the fire, placing their beers on the table. Just as Frank was about to take a sip of his beer, his pager bleeped.

"Oh, I wonder if this is Merriday," said Frank. Tom looked at him inquisitively as the pager emerged from his pocket. A quick nod from Frank confirmed that it was him.

"Hello, sir. What can I do for you? What have you to tell me?" asked Frank.

"Frank, I have found out quite a lot about Georgina Burke," said Sir Jeffrey Merriday.

"OK, sir. Fire away and I'll take notes," Frank said, pulling a notebook and pen from his inside pocket.

"Mrs. Burke was born and lived in a little place called Crumlin, near Belfast, said Merriday. "When she was twenty years of age, she moved over to Penilee, near Glasgow. She attended Glasgow University and studied aviation aerodynamics, in which she passed with flying colours, if you'll excuse the pun. She then joined Rolls-Royce Aerospace Technical Development Division, where she was very much involved with a new engine for the Ministry of Defence, or MOD, which was of a high security. Unfortunately, she has gone underground – and probably taken a lot of high-security information away with her. We're not sure where she is at the moment."

"What kind of engine was she working on at Rolls-Royce?" Frank asked.

"It is of high security, my friend, so keep this information close to your chest. She was working on a silent engine made with special materials. By that, I mean materials that cannot be picked up by radar. So you can understand why it is of high security, as it would be almost undetectable. She then married, and her name changed to Georgina Burke. Her maiden name is …" Merriday paused. "Now, my friend, is this a coincidence or not? Her full name is Georgina Watson Harkin Burke," he said.

"Harkin! Do you mean that she is the daughter of Sir Bernard Harkin? The man we killed on Tuesday down at Kinlochleven?" said Frank, a little startled and surprised.

"Yes! It looks like it, but she is a clever little cookie. Keep an eye on her if she comes around to check out her father's house down at Forest Lodge," said Sir Jeffrey Merriday.

"Sir, she has already been around," said Mulholland. "I can update you now because she is living at the farmhouse down in Cononish Glen, near Tyndrum, and has been for the past two years. Her husband works in the oil business and spends most of his time out on the rigs in the North Sea."

"She may have been involved in gunrunning with her father, so keep an eye on her, Frank," said Merriday.

"It is possible, sir. Leave things to me. I'll sort this little madam out," said Mulholland, smirking.

"OK, Frank. Over and out," said Merriday.

Frank stared at Tom with a worried look on his face.

"What's wrong, mate?" Tom asked.

"We may have a problem with Mrs. Georgina Watson Harkin Burke," said Frank, emphasizing the name Harkin.

"Harkin. She's not related to Sir Bernard Harkin, is she?" Tom asked with alarm.

"I'm afraid it looks like she is. We are going to check her out tonight," said Frank sternly.

"Are we going to walk four miles along that road in the darkness?" Tom asked warily.

"Leave it with me and I'll phone Sergeant Murdoch and ask him if we can hitch a lift on Tommy Anderson's helicopter," said Frank.

"But, Frank, they are bound to hear the helicopter from the house if we go too near," said Tom.

"We'll leave that up to Tommy. I'm sure he will be able to drop us off somewhere along the glen without us being heard; then we can continue on foot," said Frank, trying to reassure Tom as he punched the digits on his bleeper.

"Hello, Sergeant. It's Frank Mulholland speaking. I wonder if you can help me out later on tonight."

"Ah'll see whit I kin dae fur ye, once ye tell me whit ye want, Frank," said Murdoch, laughing.

"Could you ask Tommy Anderson if he could take us on a flight in his helicopter down into the Cononish Glen tonight around eight o'clock, mate?" Mulholland asked.

"Whit dae ye want doon in Cononish Glen at that time o' nicht?" Murdoch asked excitedly.

"I would rather keep it to myself for the time being, Sergeant. But I can assure you that we are not breaking the law," said Frank.

"Hav' ye a job oan? If ye hiv, can ah come doon ther' wi' ye?" Murdoch asked, thinking back to Tuesday, when he helped the agents out.

"We would prefer to go down there by ourselves, just for investigation purposes. But the road has about three foot of snow on it, and it would be hard going on foot," said Frank.

"OK, Frankie boy. Ah'll ask Tommy tae pick ye up et the Orchy Hotel aroond eight o'clock. If ah dinnae phone ye's back, then ye ken bet he'll be there," said Murdoch, ending the call.

Frank gave Tom the thumbs up that they were going tonight. "We better get the walking gear and white snowsuits out of the car while it is daylight," said Frank, taking a sip of his beer. "It's a good pint of beer that you get in here."

What's the time?" Tom asked, and both agents glanced at the clock behind the bar.

"Jings! It's five fifteen. We'd better go to the car and bring the gear into my room," said Frank. They quickly made for the exit.

"It'll be cold down there tonight, so we'd better wear our boots, snowsuits, and white tammies to keep our heads warm," said Tom.

"Crivvens, you are a right softie, mate," laughed Frank as the two jogged towards the car.

A few minutes later, the agents re-entered the hotel. A voice from behind the bar asked, "Are you two going painting again? I see you've got your white suits with you." It was the lovely Carol speaking. This cheered Frank up, as he had been wondering where she had been earlier, when Tam was working behind the bar.

Can we have an early evening meal tonight, honey – around six o'clock?" Frank asked. "We are going out tonight, and we don't know when we will get back."

"OK, darling," said Carol with a little frown. As the agents made for their rooms, she wondered where they were going tonight.

A few minutes later, Frank and Tom reappeared. Lifting their beers, they told Carol that they were going into the dining room to check out the menu.

Almost immediately, Emma appeared with a notepad and pen.

"We're going for the gammon steaks and all the trimmings tonight, darling," said Tom.

"Is he speaking for you too, Frankie boy?" asked Emma, smiling.

"Of course, sweetheart," said Frank, grinning at Tom, who was pinching Emma's waist.

As Emma made for the kitchen, she stopped in her tracks and said, "Carol is worried about where you are going tonight. You better put her mind at ease."

"Tell her we are going to the Inveroran Inn to see the rest of the guys. We have a bit of business to attend to," said Frank.

Tom stared at Frank. "Do you realise that she can phone the inn later on and check if we have been there?" said Tom, tugging at Frank's arm.

"It's OK, mate. If she asks me, I'll tell her it was classified business we were attending to," said Frank, knowing that he couldn't tell her he was staking out her friend Georgie Watson Burke. Frank took a sip from his beer, but in his mind, he knew that he had just made a big mistake.

After their meal, the agents made for the bar and settled down next to the fire. Frank glanced at the clock. "It's half past seven, mate," he said. "It won't be long until Tommy arrives with the helicopter. We better go to our rooms and put on our walking boots. We'll put on the snowsuits when we are at the helicopter, as we don't want to attract any unwanted attention as we leave."

"Let's go now," Tom said, rising from his seat. He walked to his room, Frank following.

As Frank reached his room, his pager bleeped and his hand dove into his pocket. It was Sir Jeffrey Merriday on the other end of the line. "Frank," said Merriday, "I have just heard from agent John Kane, who is surveying the area down at Loch Linnhe. He has informed me that four men have come in off a boat down near Ballachulish and are heading in your direction as we speak."

"Sir, we are going to check out what is happening down in the Cononish Glen tonight. I'll let you know in the morning if we find anything untoward going on," said Frank.

"OK, but be careful, my friend. Over and out," said Merriday.

Approximately ten minutes later, there was a knock on Frank's door and in walked the dark-haired six-foot Constable Tommy Anderson, a broad smile on his face.

"Good man. It's nice to see you are early," said Frank.

"Nae problem, mate. Ah a'wis try tae be early, nae matter whaur ah'm goin'," said Tommy.

"Will it be OK for you, flying us into Cononish in the dark? I don't want us to be seen or heard by the occupants of the farmhouse," said Frank.

"The on'y problem we hiv is the noise aff the rotors and my navigation lichts tae see whaur we are landin', as they micht mak' them aware that we ar' aboot," said Tommy.

"Can we be dropped off farther away from the farmhouse?" Mulholland asked.

"If ah wis tae drap ye aff aboot twa mile frae the fermhoose, then ye widnae be seen or heard, but it wid be a bit o' a trek alang the road wi' aw the snaw," said Tommy, offering a sympathetic shrug of his shoulders.

"That will be our problem, my friend. As long as you can put us down safely and pick us up later," said Frank.

Just then, Tom entered the room with his snowsuit tucked under his arm. He smiled at Tommy.

"Would you like a cup of tea or coffee before we set off?" Frank asked.

"Naw, thanks! I'd rather get oan oor way noo," said Tommy.

Frank opened a map that he had lifted from the bookcase in the hallway and asked Tommy to show him roughly where he would put them down.

"Just aboot the bend, whaur ther' is a lot o' tree cover an' they wulnae see me frae the hoose," said Tommy.

"How far away from the farmhouse is that?" Tom asked, showing some concern.

"Ye'll still hae a guid walk ahead o' ye. Mibbee a guid mile an' a hauf, or even twa mile," said Tommy.

"OK, gents. It is now dark enough. I think's time to go," Frank said, staring out the window.

Mulholland nonchalantly flicked the curtain closed and picked up his gear.

As the three lads made for the front exit with their snow gear under their arms, the three amigos called out, "Aye! Aye! Whaur are you three goin'?"

On hearing this, Carol instantly called out to Frank and waved for him to wait. Frank's immediate thoughts were that he was in a spot of trouble, but Carol walked over and gave him a kiss. "I understand that in your position, you have to keep some things secret, darling, but make sure you come back to me safely," said Carol.

Frank was pleased to hear this. As she kissed him again, the three amigos called out and whistled at the embarrassed agent.

"See you later, honey," said Frank. Holding two fingers up in the direction of the laughing trio, he made his exit.

When the team reached the helicopter, Frank and Tom pulled on their snowsuits and white tammies. "We'll be ther' in aboot five meenits," said Tommy, firing up the rotors. In almost no time, they were up in the air and zooming away. "I'll fly richt ower Taigh an Droma."

"Where?" asked Frank.

"Tyndrum," Tom answered quickly. "That is the Gaelic name for Tyndrum, my friend."

"You and that flaming book of yours," said Frank, smiling as they flew over Tyndrum far below.

"We ar' nearly ther', guys," said Tommy as the helicopter swung around, descending and touching down onto the soft snow. Tommy switched the engine off, and silence was the only sound to be heard. "This is as far as I kin tak' ye, but if ye look in the distance, ye kin see the licht o' the fermhoose. Ye wull hiv tae mak' it oan foot frae here, an' I wull get ye's here in aboot three hours frae noo'. Say … aboot eleven o'clock-ish."

"Is that going to give us enough time to get there and return to this spot?" Frank asked with concern.

"Ah'll come back doon here aboot eleven o'clock, mate. Ah'll hang aboot fur a wee while tae gie ye's a chance tae get back tae me," said Tommy.

"Okey-dokey! We'll see you then," said Frank, itching to get going. Within a few seconds, both agents had disappeared into the night.

The sound of the helicopter lifting up and flying away was a rather intimidating experience for both MI6 agents, as they were plunged into darkness. "We better march on because the light of the farmhouse looks a long way off, and this road is not too good for walking on," whispered Frank.

"Have you noticed, Frank, that some kind of vehicle has recently travelled along this road? Feel the depth of the tread marks of the tyres."

Both agents knelt down, desperately trying to see in the dark. "Yes! You are spot on, mate," said Frank. "But at least it has flattened the snow down. If we follow the tracks, they should lead us to the farmhouse." He gazed up at the starlit sky and the bright almost-full moon, which was reflecting on the snow and river further along the glen. "Geez, it is amazing how many stars you can see up there," he said.

"Aye, it is super," said Sommerville, pointing out some of the constellations.

After what seemed to be an eternity, the agents began closing in on the farmhouse. Frank tugged at Tom's arm and whispered for him to stop. "We better be extra careful around here. It is so quiet out here that the least little noise we make may be heard," said Frank.

"How long has it taken for us to arrive here?" Tom asked with some concern.

Frank quickly shone his torch onto his wristwatch. The agents could see that it was 9.30 p.m. "Christ! It has taken us an hour and a half to get here. Can you hear the sound of water?" asked Frank, whispering.

"That'll be the River Cononish down below us," said Tom.

"Wait here, mate. I'll approach the farmhouse and check it out. If everything is OK, I'll flash my torch a couple of times and you can come over and join me," said Frank.

Agent Mulholland moved off towards the farmhouse, disappearing into the night. As he approached the grounds of the farm, he had to crawl through the snow and under the fencing. *I hope this fencing is not electrified,* he thought, trying desperately not to touch the wiring around the fence as he crawled under.

Phew! Thank God for that, he thought a few moments later.

Creeping towards the window on the side wall of the farmhouse, the outline of Georgie Burke's helicopter could be seen at the back of the house in the dim light that was coming from one of the rooms. Frank took out his torch and signalled to Tom. A few minutes later, the ghostly figure of Tom was crawling towards him.

Mulholland edged closer to the window of the dimly lit room. Peering through a small gap in the curtain, he quickly realised that it was a bedroom with a small dimly lit bedside lamp. There was another brightly lit room at the far side of the bedroom.

Suddenly, the naked figure of a woman emerged from brightness and walked into the room while wrapping a towel around her head. Frank's eyes were homing in on her. He soon realised that it was Georgie Watson Harkin Burke who had walked across the room. Frank couldn't believe his eyes.

I wish she would switch the light on, he deviously thought to himself. No sooner had that thought entered his head than both agents were thrown into a state of alarm as the security lights around the helicopter lit up. Frank's arm shot out, and he pulled Tom back against the whitewashed wall of the house. The lights coming on attracted the attention of Georgie, who walked over to the window. As she edged the curtain over to peer out into the garden, her naked breasts lightly touched the windowpane as she strained to see what had caused the lights to come on.

Mulholland pressed himself firmly against the wall. A young roe deer appeared and stopped, staring over at the agents for a few seconds before turning and running away. This was a bit of relief for Georgie, as she now realised why the security lights had come on. But it was more of a relief to both agents when she closed the curtain and turned away. Frank couldn't resist peeking into the room again, just in time to see the naked figure of Georgie lifting a negligee from the bed and heading back to the brightly lit room.

Frank was startled as he felt a hand tapping on his shoulder. "Christ, mate! You scared the life out of me there," whispered Mulholland. Tom was pointing back down the glen at two headlights in the distance, coming towards them. "We better get away from here and back towards the river," said Frank. They quickly scurried through the snow and slipped under the fence.

"It will be safe enough to dig in just below the road, and maybe we can get a look at whoever is driving the vehicle," said Frank.

"I don't think so, mate. It's far too dark," said Tom, quietly laughing.

The headlights were getting closer, and the tension began to increase. "It looks as though they are coming to the farmhouse," said Frank, lifting his head to check on its progress.

"They'll reach us in a few minutes at this rate," said Tom. Both agents were on edge as the rumbling sound of the engine echoed in the night air, getting closer by the minute. As the vehicle closed in on them, both agents snuggled into the steep banking just below the edge of the road.

The loud rumbling noise of the engine and the crunching of the snow told them that the vehicle was almost upon them. Suddenly, headlights shone overhead and the agents dove into the snow. As the vehicle drove past, the agents gazed upwards at large wheels, which were now spraying snow on top of them. "Geez! Did you see the size of the wheels on that thing?" said Tom, wiping the snow from his face.

"Hurry up, mate. We'll try to get closer to see who was driving it," said Frank, jumping up onto the roadway. I'll see if I can get a photo with my new night camera."

They watched the truck, expecting it to stop at the farmhouse. To their astonishment, the truck veered off to the right and headed uphill, away from the farmhouse.

"Christ! Where is it going?" Frank asked, watching the truck disappear over the crest of the hill. The race was on for both men as they clambered to the top of the hill. Collapsing onto the snow, exhausted by their efforts, they were just in time to see the truck disappear into a lit-up entrance leading into the mountain.

"Jings, Frank. The door is closing. It looks as though they have an underground tunnel over there. Could this be the gold mine where they are test drilling?" Tom asked, breathing heavily from his uphill scramble.

"Maybe it is, mate. But we will have to check it out in daylight."

"We'll come back here tomorrow as hill walkers," said Frank, panting heavily while shining the torch onto his watch. "It's almost ten, mate. We are going to be late getting back to the pick-up position. We'd better get cracking." They set off downhill past the farmhouse.

After about an hour of trudging through the snow, in the distance, the agents could see a light in the sky.

"That must be Tommy returning, and we've still got a fair wee bit to walk."

"My chest is getting sore," Tom said, groaning.

"I'm sorry, mate. Maybe I should have gone on this assignment by myself," said Frank. "Jump on my back and I'll carry you the rest of the way." He laughed softly.

"If I could see you, I would clip your ear, Frankie boy," Tom joked.

The agents marched onwards and listened to the snow crunching under their feet. Suddenly, a voice in the darkness spoke. "Wid you twa guys like a lift hame?" It was Tommy Anderson. "Ah could hear ye's comin' aboot five minutes ago," Tommy laughed.

"Crivvens! I'm glad to see you," said Tom. The weary agents climbed into the helicopter.

Tommy started the rotors spinning, and Frank said wearily, "Bridge of Orchy, here we come!"

"Thank heavens for that," said Tom with a sigh. A few minutes later, they were hovering behind the Orchy Hotel. Frank checked the time on his watch and realised that it was ten minutes past midnight as Tommy brought them in to land.

"I really appreciate what you have done for us tonight," said Frank, extending his hand to the police officer.

"I'm just gonnae leave the whirlyburd here fur the nicht an' tak' a taxi hame," said Tommy.

"You'll be well covered for expenses, mate," Frank said, pulling out his bleeper.

"Could you send a taxi to the Orchy Hotel, going to Tyndrum, please?" Frank asked. "Right." He turned to Tommy and slipped him a five-pound note. There will be a taxi here shortly to get you home."

When the three lads entered the hotel, they noticed that all the guests had gone to their rooms.

"We'll wait with you until the taxi arrives," said Frank as they settled near the fire, which had burned down to a little glow.

"That fire is like me. It's burned out," said Frank, poking the ashes of the burned-out logs and smiling.

"Yeah, you're spot on with that assumption, mate. I didn't want to tell you that, but now you know," said Tom, offering a hearty laugh.

Suddenly, a beam of light shone onto the window and the sound of an engine was heard.

"Oh, that looks like your taxi, Tommy," Frank said. They made for the exit.

"Geez! Is that a flicker of snow I see?" Tommy asked, jumping into the taxi and waving to the agents.

As the agents made for the hotel, they gazed skyward at the dark and angry clouds moving in from the north-west. They were hoping that the snow wouldn't come to anything.

"I think I'll leave a message for Merriday at headquarters, about what we have seen at Cononish Glen tonight. I don't know about you, mate, but I'm going to my bed. I'll see you in the morning," said Frank, yawning as he made for room number seven. When Mulholland entered his room, he was disappointed to find that Carol was not there. He was wondering if she had taken the huff with him because of his escapade tonight.

Oh, what's this? thought Frank, as he picked up a piece of folded paper from behind the door.

It was a note that read as follows: *There is more than gold in them thar hills. So watch your back.* Those last three words caused Mulholland some concern. *Well, it looks as though I'll struggle to have a good night's sleep.*

As he crawled into bed, his thoughts ran over the message, wondering who had slipped it under the door.

Roughly two hours later, Frank felt the chilly body of Carol snuggling into his back and responded immediately by turning and cuddling her. "I couldn't sleep by myself, darling. I was missing you," Carol said in her husky Irish voice. Frank's lips pressed hard against hers. They fell into a passionate embrace and made love that seemed everlasting.

"My God, Carol, that was fantastic," said Frank. They snuggled into each other and fell fast asleep.

In what seemed to be no time at all, Frank awoke to the sound of Carol running the shower. *Is it that time already?* he thought. The clock showed 6.30 a.m.

About two minutes later, Carol was dressed and rushing out of the room to make her way to the kitchen when she heard a noise in the hallway. To her surprise, it was her friend Emma leaving room number eight and rushing down to meet her. Both girls began giggling as they made their way to the kitchen.

Happy birthday to you

F rank Mulholland was awakened by the noise of his pager sounding off. "Oh, geez! What's the time?" he asked himself, reaching into his bedside cabinet.

It was Sir Jeffrey Merriday, the head of MI6, and Frank felt like throttling him for waking him up.

"Hello, Frank! I got the message you left for me," said Sir Jeffrey.

"Sir, we may have a problem down there."

"Well, Frank, in light of what you told me about Georgie Burke and the mine down at Cononish, and the impending problem at Coulport Submarine Base, I think I'll be sending you another couple of agents just to make sure we are covered for any problems that may arise."

"Who will you be sending to me?" asked Frank.

Merriday hesitated. "Well, first of all, we require a man to cover for Agent Macleod, who is now in Hospital, as you well know. And an additional man to boost the team in the result of any unforeseen problem down at the mine," said Merriday with a little trepidation.

"Sir, who are you sending over here to assist me? Because it sounds to me as if you are holding out on me," said Frank sternly, feeling a little worried.

"Frank, I'm sending you Agent Brian McDonald, the explosives expert, and ..." Merriday paused and then added quietly but abruptly, "Agent George Hardie."

Frank was a little shocked at this. "Sir, Agent McDonald will be fine, but you do know that there is a bit of history between Agents John Aitken and George Hardie," said Frank anxiously. "This may cause me problems, which I really can't afford to have at this particular time."

"I'm sorry, Frank, but you'll just have to deal with it. They will be arriving at the Orchy Hotel today around late afternoon, so the best of luck, my friend. Over and out," said Merriday, quickly ending the conversation.

Frank puffed his cheeks and called Peter MacInnes, the proprietor of the Inveroran Inn. "Hello, Peter. Can I book another room with you at the inn? It's for a Mr. George Hardie. And can I replace Mr. Iain Macleod with a Mr. McDonald? Iain Macleod is in hospital for a little while."

"No problem, Frank. I have another room available, my friend. When will they be arriving?" Peter asked.

"Sometime later today," said Mulholland.

"OK, Frankie boy."

Frank then called Agent John B. Aitken with the news of both agents arriving.

"Who are they?" JBA asked.

"Agent Brian McDonald, whom you worked with in North Africa," said Frank.

"That's aw richt. He's a guid yin tae hiv oan yer team. An' wha's the ither yin?" Big John asked.

Frank hesitated and then said quietly, "It's George Hardie." Mulholland screwed his face up in anticipation of some kind of reaction from JBA.

"Whit! That big bastard!" John shouted down the phone.

"I'm sorry, John," said Frank, anxiously. "But headquarters are sending both of them, and they will be arriving later today. Before you continue ranting, I did try to get him changed for someone else, but Merriday wouldn't oblige."

Big John cursed and slammed the phone down.

Christ! It's only quarter past eight and I'm landed with this problem already, thought Mulholland, making his way to the shower room. As the water flowed over his face, Frank was planning his visit back to Cononish Glen. He was wondering if they would be back in time to meet the new agents arriving at the hotel.

Big John B. Aitken was working with George Hardie over in North Africa at the Suez Canal Crisis. He felt as though Hardie had endangered the mission, and it almost cost him his life. He vowed that he would never work with him again. Up until this day, only they know the reason. But there was certainly bad blood between them. Hence the reason Big John was not too happy at the thought of Agent, Hardie arriving today.

Frank Mulholland turned the calendar to show Friday, 30 March 1962. *Geez! It's my birthday today, and it looks like. As Frank sings, "There may be trouble ahead."* Dressing quickly, he then made for Agent Sommerville's room.

After a quick knock on the door, Tom called out, "Come in, Frank. I know your knock by now."

As Frank entered the room, to his surprise, Tom, Emma, and Carol began singing "Happy Birthday" to him. Carol had a cake in her hands with the number thirty-two written on it. "How did you know it was my birthday?" Frank asked, slipping an arm around Carol's slim waist.

"Merriday called me yesterday and told me about it," said Tom, grasping his hand.

Frank blew out the candles to a cheer from them all and then thanked them for being so considerate. He planted a kiss on the girls. The girls then made their apologies that they had to get back to the kitchen to prepare breakfasts for the guests.

"We'll be down right away, honey. We have some business to attend to today, and, we don't have a lot of time," said Frank to Carol, at the same time letting Tom know.

As soon as the girls had left the room, Frank filled Tom in on the info about the new agents arriving and the impending problem they may have with Agents Hardie and Aitken.

"Maybe time will have mellowed their feelings. After all, it has been six years since they were at the Suez Crisis," said Tom.

"By the way JBA reacted when I told him fifteen minutes ago, I don't think so," said a worried Frank Mulholland. "Anyway, let's go for breakfast, and then we will drive down to Dalrigh and walk up the Cononish Glen to check out the gold mine."

While they were at breakfast, Frank passed the piece of notepaper over to Tom.

"Crivvens! Somebody in the hotel knows we are investigating the Cononish Gold Mine," said Tom anxiously, staring at Frank.

"It looks like it, mate. I wonder who," Frank said.

After a slightly rushed breakfast, both agents made for their rooms to change into hillwalking gear. Frank was trying to work out roughly how long it would take to get there and back again.

"The sooner we can leave here, the better. Probably a round trip of five-plus hours," said Mulholland, glancing at his watch. "That means it will be about half past two before we get back."

"So when are the agents arriving?" asked Tom.

"According to Merriday, sometime in the late afternoon, whatever the hell that means," said Frank.

They left the hotel. Arriving at the car, Frank opened the car boot and peered inside. "Take a handgun for each of us – and make sure they have bullets. You never know, but we may need them." Frank checked the cartridge of his Smith & Wesson. "Right, Tom, I'll let you say it," said Frank.

"Cononish Glen, here we come," whispered Tom.

It's a long, long road

The twenty-minute drive to Dalrigh was slightly precarious, due to the small amount of partially frozen snow that had fallen overnight, causing the road to be slippery.

"Well, we won't be walking in darkness this time. At least we'll be able to see where we are going," said Tom.

"It won't make it any easier, though, because we have to walk the full distance this time," Frank said, closing the car boot. The agents set off on what would prove to be a strenuous walk along Cononish Glen's long and winding road.

"Geez! Is that Georgie's farmhouse away in the distance?" Frank asked, shading his eyes from the sun.

"It sure is, mate. According to Davy Blackwood, it's at least four miles, and this snow is not helping one little bit," Tom said with a frown.

"Oh well! Let's get our heads down and feet moving," said Frank, sighing.

"Have you noticed the depth of the tread on those tyre tracks?" Tom said.

"Yeah! That truck we saw last night must have been carrying something pretty heavy," said Frank. They made for the hills.

An hour of silence passed as the agents trudged along the snow-covered road. Suddenly, the silence was broken when Tom spoke out. "Jings, Frank. We have to make this same return journey back to the car. We'll be shattered, mate. Have you noticed Ben Lui ahead of us? It's a cracking mountain, and it looks good with the snow on it."

"Yes, it looks nice, but I wouldn't like to be climbing it at this moment. I didn't realise that this embankment was so high and as steep when we hid here last night," said Frank, puffing his cheeks.

The agents were looking down towards the fast-flowing River Cononish.

"Crivvens! We forgot to bring our gold panning equipment," Tom said, laughing.

Frank smiled at Tom's remark and glanced at his watch. "We're keeping quite good time. We should be at the farmhouse by approximately eleven thirty if all goes well," he said.

"I wouldn't have liked to walk this road if the snow hadn't been flattened down by that truck," said Frank, looking a little anxious.

"It looks as though Georgie Burke is at home," said Tom. "I can make out the helicopter at the back of the house. Are you OK, Frank?"

"Yes, mate. It must be palpitations caused by thinking about Georgie," laughed Frank.

The time was showing 11.15 a.m. as the agents reached the farmhouse and diverted uphill towards the gold mine. On reaching the top of the hill, both men were exhausted with the combination of the deep snow and the steepness of the hill.

"Christ! I don't know about you, mate, but I need to take a rest," Frank said, gasping for breath and flopping down onto the snow.

"Yes, I can understand how you feel, buddy, now that you're a year older." Tom grinned.

"Oh, we are being watched, mate," said Tom, pointing and staring up at the sky. High above, a golden eagle was soaring, searching with beady eyes for any movement on the ground far below.

"Have you noticed that those tracks on the road appear to go into the mountain but there doesn't seem to be a door into the mountain?" Tom said, raising his eyebrows.

"We'll have to get closer to the point where the tracks disappear. It looks as though there is a concealed entrance," whispered Frank as they edged closer to their target.

Nearing the entrance, they were brought to a halt when a sudden gunshot rang out. Quick as a flash, they dove into the snow.

"Don't move a muscle," said a man's gruff voice.

The agents looked up at a giant of a man standing before them. He was a rather intimidating person, with bushy eyebrows protruding over deep-set piercing dark eyes. Around his face was a jet-black bushy beard, and on top of his head was a strange-looking hat, with bushy unkempt hair protruding from under the headgear. His left ear had an earring hanging from it, and his physique matched his six-foot, eight-inch height. On the back of his left hand was a tattoo of a hammer and sickle, which could be seen as he grasped the barrel of his rifle. All of a sudden, three men carrying rifles surrounded the MI6 agents.

"I could have shot you if I had wished," said one of the men, who spoke with an Irish accent. "What are you doing here?" He flashed uneven teeth that possibly required dental attention. The agents noticed that he had one gold tooth to the right of centre and a three-day-old stubbly growth on his chin, which matched his auburn-coloured hair. He wore round rimmed glasses encased in gold frames.

"We were going to climb Ben Lui, and we saw the tracks leading up this way. We thought it was maybe an easier route to get to the mountain," said Tom quickly.

All three men looked at each other, and the bearded giant asked in a strange accent, "Why were you lying down in the snow a few minutes ago?"

"It was quite a steep uphill climb through the snow, and it was very tiring. We were only resting," said Frank, nervously smiling at the man.

Glancing at his two partners, the bearded giant of a man pointed back downhill and said, "This is private property. Now be on your way because the next time we may not be so friendly."

The agents began walking sheepishly back downhill towards the farmhouse.

"Well done, Tom. You handled that superbly," said Frank as they were nearing the farm.

Suddenly, there was a call from the farmhouse. It was Georgie Watson Harkin Burke. "Frank! What are you doing out here? What was the gunshot I heard a minute ago?"

"We are going to climb Ben Lui, and we thought that the track uphill would be an easier route, but we didn't realise it was private property," said Frank, raising his eyebrows.

"Here was me thinking that you were coming to see me," Georgie said, frowning.

"I'll come and see you anytime, sweetheart," Frank said, giving her a seductive look.

"Yes, but not when your dad is around," said Tom, pointing to a man who was checking out the helicopter.

"Oh, that's not my dad. It's my uncle Denis," said Georgie, calling him over.

A man walked over and extended his hand towards Frank and Tom. A quick observation by Frank Mulholland revealed that he was approximately five feet ten inches tall. His hair was slightly auburn in colour, and he wore dark rimmed glasses which hung low on his nose, giving the appearance that he was looking over them.

"Denis Wadsworth is my name, gents," said Denis, observing both men. The agents took turns grasping a large hand with stumpy shaped fingers.

"Tom and Frank. Pleased to meet you, sir. That's a nice Irish accent you have there," said Frank. "You couldn't give us a lift to the top of the mountain in your helicopter?" Frank jokingly asked.

"Oh, I'm sure that you would prefer to climb it, my friends," Denis said, laughing.

"Yes, you can be sure about that, sir. There is no other way to get up there," said Tom, joining him in laughter.

"Well, folks, I think we will have to be on our way, as we have a bit of a climb ahead of us," Frank said, looking at Georgie and winking. The MI6 agents followed the track around the front of the house and waved goodbye.

Both agents stared up at Ben Lui towering above them.

"Crivvens! I'm glad that we're not climbing this hill today, mate. It looks intimidating," Tom said, nodding at Frank.

"Yes, now let's get back to the car," said Frank.

As they reversed direction, the agents were checking that they couldn't be seen from the farmhouse. On the journey back, they discussed everything that had happened.

"It doesn't look as though Denis Wadsworth recognised us," said Frank.

"It's a wonder that he didn't, considering that we thought we killed him last Tuesday," said Tom.

On Tuesday, 27 March, Frank and Tom were flying in Tommy Anderson's helicopter along with Sergeant Murdoch of the Tyndrum Police. They were hunting down Irish gunrunner Denis Wadsworth as he sped away on a cabin cruiser heading down Loch Etive. As Wadsworth reached the Connell Bridge and the Falls of Lora, Sergeant Murdoch fired a flare into the boat which had set fire to Denis Wadsworth. He was last seen diving into the turbulent waters of the falls to extinguish the flames. It seemed that there was no way he could survive the flowing rapids, considering that Frank Mulholland had believed that he had shot him a few seconds earlier.

"I wonder who the three guys were that held us up with the guns at the gold mine," Tom said.

"We'll find out when I send the photos to Merriday," Frank said.

"You managed to take their photographs?"

"Of course I did. With this fancy new camera," said Frank, pointing to the tammy he was wearing on his head. On the front of the headgear was a small badge.

"Do you mean that the badge is a camera?" said Tom, smiling at how devious Frank had been.

"Yes, mate. I tried it out on you earlier to make sure it was working. According to Merriday, it can take pictures in the dark. Now all I have to do is send the photos to Merriday by pressing this button."

"That's fantastic, mate," Tom said, wondering if Frank was pulling his leg.

"By the time we get back to the hotel, Merriday will probably have the names of those guys," said Frank, as the agents trudged onwards through the snow.

Meanwhile, back at Georgie's farmhouse

Georgie had noticed footprints outside her bedroom window and called on her uncle Denis to come over. "Last night I saw the security lights coming on, and I looked out the window, only to see a deer standing in the garden. I took it to be that it had caused the lights to come on," said Georgie.

"Yes, I saw its hoof marks in the snow as I was checking the helicopter this morning," said Denis Wadsworth.

"Well, I don't think that was the only reason the lights came on," Georgie said, pointing to the footprints below her window and the tracks going under the fence.

"It looks as if there may have been two of them, whoever they were," said Denis.

Georgie now realised that she had had intruders at some point during the night.

"Oh my God! I'll be scared to go to my bed tonight," Georgie said, frowning.

"I hope it wasn't any of those Russian perverts who are working up in the mine," said Denis with a smile, trying to comfort her.

"I'm going over to Bridge of Orchy to bring my friends over for a chat and a little refreshment," said Georgie.

Lifting the keys to the helicopter, she made for the kitchen door and left, Denis close behind.

Back with the MI6 agents

F rank and Tom were almost back at their car when they heard a high-pitched sound that only lasted for a few seconds.

"Wow! What was that noise? Did you hear it, mate?" Frank asked, alarmed.

"Yes, I heard it, and it was quite sore on my ears," said Tom, painstakingly rubbing his ears.

Both agents were looking around but were still in the dark regarding the sound that they had heard. Then Frank noticed the helicopter up in the air. Glancing at his watch, he muttered. "Christ! It's almost two o'clock, and we still have a twenty-minute drive back to the Orchy Hotel," Frank said, dipping his eyebrows in a frown.

"We'll have to put the boot down as we drive back," Tom said.

Both agents quickly ran the final four hundred yards to reach the car and jumped inside.

"Bridge of Orchy, here we come!" said Tom, huffing and puffing as the car slithered out of the car park.

When they arrived at the hotel, there was a bit of a commotion which caught the attention of the agents. Inspector M. D. Johnstone of the Glasgow Criminal Investigation Department (CID) was close by. Frank quickly approached him. "What's brought you up here, Inspector?" enquired Mulholland.

"Inspector Hugh Smith, of Crianlarich headquarters, and I were discussing last week's death of forestry worker George Nixon, when the call came in about a body being found down at the falls. He asked me to investigate this while I was in the area. I'm heading down there at this very minute."

"Do they know who the dead body is down at the falls?" Frank asked.

"Sergeant Murdoch left along with Constable Anderson to drive down there, just after they informed Inspector Smith of the situation. He's going to speak to the person who reported the dead body to us," said the inspector, pointing in the direction of the falls.

"I think we will follow you down to the falls, if that's OK with you," Frank said.

"No problem, Frank," replied the inspector.

As the agents were making their way down to the scene of the incident, they were discussing the fact that this was the third death inside the past week. "For a place of surrounding beauty, this seems a bit much to take in," said Mulholland, showing concern.

On approaching the scene, Sergeant Murdoch and Constable Anderson stepped forward to meet them. "Hello, gents," said Murdoch. "I received a call frae a Moira Malone et the Orchy Hotel. She had seen the body flowin' doon the river when she wis standin' oan the brig' behin' the hotel. By the time ah got doon, the canoeists had seen him lyin' doon on the wee beach below the falls."

"Do we know who it is?" asked Inspector Johnstone.

"No' yet. But his face has taen' a wee bit o' bashin' aff o' the rocks. Probably when he went ower the falls," said Murdoch.

Frank stepped in after hearing this. "Can I take a photo of him to check him out?" Frank asked as they looked down at the body lying on the beach some forty feet below.

"Tom, could you wait here and speak to Constable Anderson?"

"We'll make our way down onto the beach where he is lying," said Frank, nodding at the inspector and sergeant. As they cautiously made their way down to the body, Tom called Constable Anderson over.

Before Tom could question the constable, he noticed Constable Anderson shaking his head with a bemused look on his face.

"There seem tae be quite a few deaths in this area lately, an' ah canny understand why," said Constable Anderson.

"Surely this is not normal around here?" Agent Sommerville asked.

"Naw! Ahve' been here fur aboot sixteen years noo, an' we hivnae hud a death that wisnae normal in aw that time," said the perplexed constable.

"Unfortunately, my friend, we have a few bad apples in the barrel around here at the moment.

It all stems from Sir Bernard Harkin, the gunrunner from Forest Lodge," said Sommerville.

"But we killed him last Tuesday doon et Loch Leven," replied the worried constable.

"Yes, but more seems to be going on than we envisaged. Certainly there are more bad apples in the barrel, if you know what I mean," said Agent Sommerville.

Constable Anderson had a blank look on his face as he stared back at the agent.

I better explain to him, Tom thought. "What I mean, Const—"

Before he could continue, the constable interjected, "Ah ken whit ye mean. Ah'm on'y windin' ye up 'cause we country yokels ur not as daft as we look."

Agent Sommerville tried to hide his embarrassment by quickly asking the constable a question.

"How long do you think it would take for the body to travel downriver from the bridge to the falls?" he asked.

"Aboot ten meenutes maximum goin' by the speed an' the flow o' the watter," said Constable Anderson, pointing to the water gushing over the falls.

Just then, one of the canoeists came forward and asked if the man was dead. The woman was wearing a tight-fitting wetsuit which glamorised her obvious natural curves. A glimpse of auburn hair could be seen at the edge of her waterproof headgear, framing her friendly face.

"Yes, I'm afraid so," replied Agent Sommerville.

"I'm the person who saw him going over the falls," said the woman in a sexy, husky voice.

"I'll have to ask you for your name and address. We may want to speak to you later," said Agent Sommerville, quickly observing her pouting lips and facial features.

"Diane MacIntosh is my name, and I come from Kilbirnie in Ayrshire. I will be living in the Orchy Hotel for the next six months. Beginning tomorrow morning, I'm working here for the summer season."

"Oh, I'm staying at the hotel at the moment. You'll be working with Carol and Emma," Tom said flirtatiously as he looked into her gray-blue eyes.

"Tam Cameron is my boss, and he told me that I will be sharing a room and duties with a Janice Irvine," Diane said, flashing her eyelashes and smiling at the agent.

"Can you tell me if he was alive before he went over the falls?" Tom asked.

"I couldn't tell because he was almost at the falls when I saw him," said Diane apologetically.

"Thank you, madam. I'll speak to you later, when we have more time," said Tom.

She returned to her canoeist friends, glancing back at the agent on the way.

Down below on the rocky beach, Inspector M. D. Johnstone was turning the body over to allow Frank to take the picture he was required to send to Merriday at headquarters for identification.

"Ye'll notice ther' ur nae stab wounds oan his back like the ither twa bodies we found," said Sergeant Murdoch, looking at Frank. Suddenly, both men jumped back, startled.

"Christ! It looks as though he has been shot with a crossbow or a similar weapon. There's a broken arrow stuck in his neck," gasped Frank, looking at Inspector Johnstone for confirmation.

"Yes, it looks like it. We'll have to get him to the lab for forensic tests," said the inspector, staring at both men.

"Jings! Ah'll hae tae let Inspector Hugh Smith ken aboot this. How long dae ye think he has been in the watter, because he wull probably ask me tae pit it intae ma report?" Murdoch asked.

"If it happened at the riverside, then probably not long, judging by the way the river is flowing. But if it happened up in Loch Tulla, then he could have been in the loch maybe a day longer. But I would say a maximum of two days, judging on past experiences," said Inspector Johnstone.

Sergeant Murdoch made his way up to his police Land Rover to call Inspector Hugh Smith at Crianlarich headquarters and inform him of the situation. Frank Mulholland called MI6 headquarters on his bleeper.

"Hello, sir. Mulholland speaking. I'm about to send a photo through to you, and I need an identification as soon as possible because the body is about to be taken away to the forensic lab."

"OK, Frank, send it through. When I find out, I will let you know, along with the other three photos you sent to me. You sure like your money's worth, my friend. Over and out," said Sir Jeffrey Merriday, laughing.

Frank made his way up to the car and the awaiting Agent Sommerville. "I think we'll get back to the hotel and speak to Moira Malone, the woman who saw the body from the bridge.

We can also check if the new agents have arrived," said Frank, looking slightly perturbed.

As they entered the car, Tom was informing Frank as to what Constable Anderson had been saying about the time it would take for the body to reach the falls from the bridge at Orchy.

"Well, if we base it on that time, then it would probably be twenty minutes from the Loch to the bridge at Orchy, which would mean about half an hour altogether," said Frank. "Inspector M. D. Johnstone said that his approximate guess would be anything between one and two days in the water. If that was the case, then he was possibly killed around Loch Tulla and thrown into the water."

"Are you thinking the same as me, Frank – possibly around the Forest Lodge area?" Tom asked.

"You may be correct with that assumption, considering the amount of Russian agents that were based down at the lodge," said Frank.

"Bridge of Orchy, here we come!" said Frank.

"It's amazing how deep the snow is at the side of the road, and this place is really scenic," said Tom.

Upon arriving at the Orchy Hotel, Frank looked around for signs of Agents Hardie and McDonald. Suddenly, a voice called out to Frank.

It was Ian Chapman waving over to the agents as he leaned his cycle against the hotel wall. "Ah've jist come up frae Forest Lodge area, an' ah saw a helicopter landin', Chappie said excitedly. "A guid-lookin' blonde woman stepped oot o' it, and she went intae the lodge."

"Was she on her own?" Tom asked.

"Naw, ther' wis a guy alang wi' her as they went inside."

"Did they see you, Chappie?" Frank asked.

"Naw, ah dinnae think so! Ah jist hightailed it oot o' ther oan ma bike," said Chappie, pulling the door open to allow them entry to the hotel.

"Oh, you've arrived," said the voice from behind the bar. It was Carol, and she didn't look too pleased with Frank.

"Two beers – and a cider for Chappie," said Frank. He smiled and blew Carol a kiss.

Chappie sat down at his usual seat near the fire as Frank looked around the lounge.

Sitting over in the corner were Agents George Hardie and Brian McDonald.

"Come over here, lads, and, I'll introduce you to everyone," said Frank. Both men made their way over to the fireside table and sat down beside Chappie and Agent Sommerville.

"Gentlemen, meet Agent Tom Sommerville and one of our best informants, Mr. Ian Chapman," said Frank. Chappie's chest stuck out with pride at the way Frank had described him.

"George Hardie and Brian McDonald, guys," said Frank, patting both agents on the shoulder.

George Hardie was about six-one. He had dark brown hair and deep-set brown eyes with bushy eyebrows that were the colour of his hair. He was the reigning army swimming champion and had held the title for the past three years, over the distances of one hundred and two hundred yards.

Brian McDonald, the explosive expert, was around five-nine in height. He had dark jet-black hair and deep dark eyes under slim eyebrows. His initial appearance was of a handsome guy a few years younger than his actual age of twenty-five. His part in the mission they were about to undertake would be crucial.

"Two more beers over here, please, Carol," said Frank, blowing her another kiss.

Carol shook her fist, letting him know that she was not too happy with him.

"It looks as though you're in the bad books with her," Brian McDonald said, smiling at Frank.

"I've booked you guys into the Inveroran Inn, along with the rest of the team," said Frank.

"Who's in charge of the team for this mission?" Agent Hardie asked.

"Me," said Frank sternly. Mulholland went a little quiet, and he smiled over at Agent Sommerville.

Hardie stuttered, "I mean—"

Agent Sommerville quickly interrupted. "We know what you mean, and the team leader is Big John B. Aitken," said Tom, staring at George.

"Have you a problem with that?" Frank asked.

Hardie stared back at Frank. "No problem as far as I'm concerned, but I don't know if J. B. Aitken will feel the same about me." He shrugged his shoulders.

Suddenly, Frank's pager bleeped, and he took it from his inside pocket. He whispered that it was Merriday at headquarters. Frank listened and then walked over to the window, distancing himself from the agents, who were trying to listen in on his conversation.

"Frank, the three photos you sent me last night are IRA and Russian agents," said Merriday.

"Do we know their names?" Frank asked.

"Yes, the bearded giant, as you called him, is named Vladimir Bazarov, and he specialises in mechanical aerospace engineering. He trained at the aviation factory in Novaya Derevnia, in Leningrad, Russia, and then served in the Russian army at a base near Murmansk. He then moved to Rolls-Royce Aerospace in Hillington Glasgow and attended night classes at Glasgow University. The other two are Sean Macateer and Stanislav Balsunov, who are linked to the IRA and the KGB, respectively. Believe me, Frank! They are all dangerous characters and would kill anyone in the blink of an eye."

"What about the dead body in the river, sir?" Frank asked.

"Frank, we don't know his name. It could be that he is not linked to anything that was happening in the area at this present time."

"Sir, he had an arrow in his neck, and that didn't get there by itself," stated Frank. "If you find out his name, let me know, sir. Over and out."

Agent Mulholland walked back to his men and lifted his beer. They all looked up at him for a reaction to the call from Merriday. "How did you get here today?" asked Frank.

"I brought us up by car," said Agent McDonald.

"When we finish our drinks, gents, I think we will head down to the Inveroran Inn. You can follow me," said Frank, looking a little worried.

Carol appeared at the bar, and Frank moved over to speak to her. "Honey, I need your help," said Frank, appealing to her better side.

"What can I do for you?" Carol asked, grinning as she realised what she had just said to him.

"If Constable Tommy Anderson comes into the hotel, would you ask him to call me?" Frank asked, winking at her.

Frank introduced Carol to both agents and told her that he was taking them down to Inveroran. He watched as the men gulped down their drinks.

Inveroran, here we come!

"Right, lads, I think it's time we set off for the Inveroran Inn. Time is marching on," said Frank, making for the exit. As the team reached their car, Frank asked what equipment they had with them.

"The normal guns and ammo and rifles," said Agent McDonald. He was looking at Frank and wondering why he asked the question.

"I'll have to see about getting both of you snowsuits and white headgear. It's currently a requirement," Frank said, pointing at the snow around the area.

Both agents looked at the snow and nodded in agreement as they climbed into their car. "Follow me down to Inveroran!" shouted Frank as they moved off. "Drive carefully because this is a single-track road and it may be a little icy."

Tom looked at Frank and cagily whispered, "Inveroran, here we come!"

On the way down to the inn, the agents noticed how high and how fast the river was flowing.

"I think our assessment of the time for the body to travel down to the falls will not be too far off," said Tom, nodding at Frank. "Yes, mate. In fact, it may be quicker than driving along this slippery road," Frank said, laughing.

Eventually, they arrived at the inn, to be met by the team of agents who were hovering around the entrance. There were no introductions required, as they had all known each other for quite a few years. The agents were shaking hands and chatting when suddenly there was a commotion. They looked around in time to see Big John Aitken slamming his right fist into George Hardie's chin. Both men were immediately sprawling around in the snow, throwing punches, and calling each other all sorts of expletives. Hardie stuffed a handful of snow into big Aitken's face and kicked him over onto his back. Leaping on top of the Agent Hardie, who was over six feet tall in his socks, was ready to throw a punch just as Frank and Tom grabbed him, splitting them up. The other guys moved in to assist by pulling Hardie clear as Big John Aitken kicked out at him from below. Both men were kicking at each other as they separated. Frank called out that this kind of behaviour was not acceptable and if they didin't calm down, then he would have to report them to Sir Jeffrey Merriday immediately. This brought both agents to their senses, and the situation calmed down. Both men were wiping snow from their clothes while still growling at each other.

Frank decided that he had to let the men know who was in charge, and he directed them into the inn. The owners of the inn, Peter and Jessie MacInnes, were not too happy at the commotion and showed Mulholland their displeasure. Frank apologised on behalf of his agents and asked them if he could use the conference room. Upon entering the inn, Frank directed both men into the room, the other agents following.

"Gentlemen, what happened out there must never happen again," said Frank, looking angrily at the two agents involved in the fighting. "JBA! You are the team leader and should know better." He thumped his fist on the table to get the point across. Big John Aitken sheepishly acknowledged his request for calm but still threw an angry glance towards Agent Hardie.

"Now, if we can all calm down, I have some information to tell you regarding some Russian agents that are in the area. I would rather you save your energy for them, as we will have to deal with them eventually." Frank thumped his fist on the table again.

"Tom and I have been investigating a certain area around here. I will reveal this to you, possibly tomorrow, when I have decided what our procedure should be," said Frank, looking around at all the men and letting them know who was in charge. Frank stared at JBA angrily and questioned him.

"Since you took out the Russian agents down there, what was the situation at Forest Lodge?" asked Mulholland.

"It had been clear until aboot twa hours ago," said JBA.

"What has happened in the past two hours?" Frank asked, although he already knew from talking to Chappie back at the Orchy Hotel.

Agent Jim MacNeill stepped forward. "I wis keepin' an eye on the hoose an' this helicopter came in tae land, an' oot stepped this female with a man followin' oan behind, said agent MacNeill. "They wer' checkin' oot the damage tae the hoose, an' then they went inside for mibbee aboot hauf an hour. They jist left at sixteen hundred hours."

"Did you recognise the man who was with her – and did they take anything away with them?" asked Frank.

"Oh, aye! It wis Denis Wadsworth, the guy who escaped in the helicopter last Tuesday when we took them Russki agents oot at the lodge; and naw, they didnae tak' onythin' awa' wi them," said MacNeill.

"Good, Jim! And well done, mate," said Mulholland.

"Who wis the nice-lookin' blonde woman onywae?" asked Agent MacNeill.

"She's Sir Bernard Harkins's daughter," said Frank. "Her name is Georgie Watson Harkin Burke, and she lives in a farmhouse down in the Cononish Glen. Denis Wadsworth is her uncle."

"Whit aboot the Russian agent's ye telt us aboot?" Big John asked.

"I'll let you know about them tomorrow night, gents, when we discuss our approach to the situation," said Frank. "Unfortunately, we have lost the services of Agent Iain Macleod, who is now recovering in a Glasgow hospital. According to Merriday at headquarters, he is coming along nicely, but I am sure that we will manage with the help of Agent's Hardie and McDonald," said Frank, looking around for some backing from the team. All the agents responded with a resounding cheer, although Big John Aitken was a little slow with his acknowledgement as he stared at Hardie from across the table.

"I'll arrange for another two snowsuits for Agents Hardie and McDonald. Where we are going, we'll need them," said Frank.

Frank called an end to the meeting and asked Big John B. Aitken to wait behind. The rest of the team chatted happily as they made their way into the barroom.

Frank approached Big John B. Aitken. "John, I want you to put your differences from the past with Agent Hardie behind you because we have a very dangerous mission ahead of us and we can't have problems within the camp," Frank said, appealing to the big man's better side.

"OK, Frank. But ah hope ah dinnae hiv tae coont' oan him fur help when we ur oot ther' oan duty," said JBA, trying to convince Frank Mulholland of his mistrust of Agent Hardie.

All three men made their way to the bar. When they entered the bar, Frank whispered to Tom that they'd have to keep an eye on JBA and Hardie from now on.

Frank asked the proprietor, Peter MacInnes, if he could show the new agents to their rooms so they could get settled in. "Keep Mr. Hardie as far away from Mr. Aitken as possible," said Frank.

"It's OK. Big John has already asked me to do that, Frank," Peter said.

"Good! Have a round of drinks on me, lads," said Mulholland as he and Tom left the inn.

"We may have problems with them two buggers. I've tried my best to calm Aitken down," said Frank, puffing his cheeks out.

"Bridge of Orchy," Tom said as the car pulled away.

"Thank goodness for that," said Frank, muttering, "Here we come!"

The drive back to Orchy was in absolute silence. The gears were turning in Frank's head as he tried to decide which order to tackle the information he had accumulated.

The silence was broken as the car went over the old Bridge of Orchy. "We've arrived, Frank," Tom said. "It's not like you to be so quiet."

"Yes, mate. I'm sorry, but I'm wondering what way to tackle what is ahead of us in the next couple of days," said Frank.

"Would it help if we could talk it over?" Tom asked.

"Probably, but maybe tomorrow. I'm going to try to contact Constable Anderson now and see if we can get a flight on his helicopter tonight," said Frank, looking anxiously at Tom.

The agents were entering the hotel when Frank's bleeper bleeped. "Yes, sir. What have you got for me?" Mulholland asked.

Sir Jeffrey Merriday was informing Frank that the body at the river was a Russian agent by the name of Igor Volvakov. "According to Agent John Kane, he came in on a submarine that we had been tracking down to the Firth of Lorne last week," said Merriday. "He was dropped off along with some of the other agents that you eliminated earlier in the week. He did his training at Severomorsk Naval Base, near Murmansk, in Northern Russia. At least now that he's dead, it's one less thing to worry about."

"One question, sir. Who would have shot him with an arrow?" Frank asked.

"I've spoken to Inspector M. D. Johnstone," said Merriday. "He has told me that George Nixon, the forestry worker who was killed last week, was a crossbow champion. It's possible that he made contact with the Russians in some way prior to his death – and maybe he had to fight them off. Maybe he shot Volvakov! I think, unfortunately for Mr. Nixon, that he was in the wrong place at the wrong time."

"Sir, Inspector Johnstone said that he thought the body was only dead a maximum of two days," said Frank.

"The forensic lab told me that the snow, or cold weather, has possibly slowed the decomposing of the body. It is early days in their investigation, but I'll keep you up to date with everything, my friend. I think, in view of what is going on, that I will engage Agent John Kane to assist you on a stake-out of the area. I'll send him over to you in the morning, Frank. Over and out."

As the agents walked into the bar, Tam Cameron called out to Frank. "Tommy Anderson has taen some people oan a flight aroond the mountains, but he should be back oanytime, as they left aboot an hour ago."

"Thanks, Tam. Could we have two beers for us and a cider for our friend Chappie over here at the fireside?" said Frank. The agents moved over and settled down beside the fire, warming their hands.

"Well, Chappie, what have you been up to today?" Tom casually asked.

"Ach, jist the usual," said Chappie, not giving much away.

Just then, Brian Greene and Davy Blackwood walked in and smiled over at the lads as they made their way to the bar.

"Aye! Aye! Ther' in here kinnae early in the day, said Chappie. "They dinnae usually come in tae aboot seven o'clock, when Davy usually oarders a meal fur himself."

Brian and Davy shuffled over to the fireside table and placed their beers on the table.

"Yer in awfy early the nicht," said Chappie, a puzzled frown on his face. "It's oany twenty past five," he said, pointing to the clock behind the bar.

"Ach, its murder in thae wids when aw that snaw is aboot. Ye cannae move the machines aboot as easy, but we'll hiv tae mak' up fur lost time when the snaw goes awa'," said Davy with a smile.

"It's much the same wae me oan the roads," said Brian, smiling and saying cheers.

The banter was flying around, and everyone was having a good, relaxing time.

Frank glanced at the door just as Tommy Anderson walked in, and he quickly jumped up to meet him.

"Can I have a word with you, mate?" asked Mulholland.

"Nae problem, Frankie boy. Whit can ah dae fur ye?" Tommy asked.

"Would there be any chance that you could take us out in the helicopter tonight? Under cover, I might add."

"Oh, jings! This is the nicht ah play a darts match. Whit time wid ye be talkin' aboot?" Tommy asked.

"Would eleven o'clock be too late for you?"

Tommy was giving it a bit of thought as he walked around rubbing his fingers on his chin.

"Could we mak it a wee bit later, say aboot eleven forty-five. The match dinnae feenish tae aboot hauf ten, an' ah wid hiv tae mak it back frae Killin, as we ur playin' awa' frae hame. It's aboot a forty-minute drive back tae Orchy in the dark." Tommy pushed two hands forward apologetically.

"That will be fine with me, and you'll be well compensated for your trouble," said Frank, smiling at the big man. "Can I buy you a cup of tea?" Frank asked. Tommy, with a nod of his head, accepted his offer.

While Frank was standing at the bar, waiting on Tam Cameron pouring Tommy's cuppa, suddenly Tam Cameron called out to Chappie, "Ta' fur the rabbits and the salmon, wee man. Ah'll square ye up efter," said Tam, tipping his trilby in gratitude.

This aroused Frank's curiosity. "What was that all about?" he asked.

"Ach, it's the on'y wae the wee man kin afford tae get his bevvy an' a meal, by supplyin' me wae fresh game. He is guid wi' the fishin' rod and that crossbow o' his," Tam said.

On hearing about the crossbow, Frank's eyes light up like a beacon. He made his way over to the table and whispered in Chappie's ear, "Can I have a quiet word with you, Mr. Chapman?"

He moved over to another table, with Chappie following. Chappie was looking a little worried and puzzled as to what this was all about. "Whit kin a dae fur ye, Frank?" Chappie asked.

"I want to know if you still have your crossbow."

Chappie answered yes with a nod.

"Have you given it out on loan to anyone recently?" Frank asked.

"Ah've hud it fur aboot three years, an' it wis given tae me by wee Geordie Nixon, who taught me how tae use it," said Chappie.

"When was the last time you made use of it?" Mulholland asked.

"I used it earlier oan today, mate. It's hinging oan tae the haundlebars o' ma bike," said Chappie.

"What! Do you mean that you just leave a dangerous weapon lying around, hanging onto your cycle?" asked Frank with a frown.

"Ach, it's aw richt, mate. Naebody uh'll touch it aroon' here, as they aw ken it belangs tae me," said Chappie, trying to ease Frank's mind.

Frank asked him if Geordie Nixon still had a crossbow up until he met his death out in the forest.

"Oh, aye. He would still hae it. He wid regularly tak' it tae his work in case he saw some guid game that wid gie' him a meal," said Chappie.

Frank immediately stood up and ushered the man back to the fireside table.

Pulling out his pager, Mulholland dialed Sergeant Murdoch's number as he walked over to the window.

"Hello, Sergeant! It's Frank Mulholland here. Could you answer a question that is baffling me?"

"Fire awa', Frankie boy," Murdoch said.

"When you went to George Nixon's house, did you notice if there was a crossbow anywhere inside his home?" asked Frank.

"His hoose wis turned upside doon lookin' fur clues, an' ther' wisnae a crossbow tae be seen," said Murdoch.

"Well, according to Chappie, he usually took it with him to work, and that was where he met his death.

So on that assumption, it's either lying somewhere in the forest or whoever killed him took it," said Mulholland.

"Dae ye think wha'ever taen it killed the guy doon at the falls?" Murdoch asked.

"Possibly," replied Mulholland.

"Sergeant, could you ask Inspector Hugh Smith to give me a call the first available chance he has? I need to talk to him urgently," Frank said.

"Nae problem. Ye kin talk tae him the noo, as he's at ma side," said Murdoch, passing the phone over to the inspector.

"Hello, Frank. What can I do for you?" asked the inspector.

"I was wondering if maybe we could meet, as I've got one or two things to discuss with you, sir," Frank said.

"Would one o'clock tomorrow at Crianlarich headquarters do for you, Frank?" Inspector Smith asked.

"Excellent! I'll see you then," replied Mulholland. Frank put his bleeper back into his pocket. As he made for the fireside table to sit with the other guys, he heard a burst of laughter breaking out. Tommy Anderson's was standing before the guys and his joke had just reached the punch line.

"What was the joke?" Mulholland asked.

Tommy was still laughing as he repeated his joke. "Ah bought my mother-in-law a plot in the cemetery for Christmas last year. This year ah dinnae buy her oanything. She asked me why ah didnae get her oanything this year, and ah telt her it was because … she hadnae bothered tae use last year's present yet."

Mulholland laughed aloud as he settled into his chair.

Frank had no sooner sat down than his bleeper bleeped again, and he moved away from everyone once again. It was Merriday at headquarters. "Frank, I've had a call from Commander Peter Heuitten at Coulport submarine base. He said they have found a two-man mini sub hidden in the undergrowth on the far side of the loch. According to their surveillance camera, it now looks as though two Russian agents paid them a visit the night the guard was killed. On further investigation, our Russian friends are called Igor Volvakov and Dimitry Baranovsky."

"So the dead man down at the falls is definitely Igor Volvakov, sir. Then who would have killed him?" Frank asked.

Sir Jeffrey paused. "Frank! I should have told you this earlier, but there is more information. Agent Volvakov was a double agent. He was supplying MI6 with some good information, but he was about to tell us something about the gold mine down at Cononish. Unfortunately, they got to him before he passed the information on to us. Probably his fellow agent Baranovsky killed him to keep him quiet. I think you are on to something with your investigation down there at the gold mine, my friend. But be very careful, as there may be more Russians than we envisaged."

"I think there's a possible IRA problem down there with gunrunning involvement," replied Frank.

"IRA agents Denis Wadsworth and Sean Macateer, and of course Georgina Watson Burke, may be involved."

"We're visiting the area tonight at midnight," whispered Mulholland.

"All right, Frank. But be careful, my friend. Over and out," said Merriday.

Frank informed Agent Sommerville of the information that Merriday had given him and of their visit to the Cononish mine at midnight that night.

"What do you know about one of our agents called John Kane?" Frank asked.

"Do you mean 'the Iceman'?" Tom replied.

"Yes, mate. How did he come to be called by that name?" Frank asked.

"Well, about three years ago, he was on an intelligence mission up on the Arctic Circle, checking out the Russian Naval Base in Murmansk. Seemingly, he and his fellow agent, who had been injured, had to flee the area, and they were tracked over the Norwegian border as they made for the location where their mini sub had been hidden. John had carried his fellow agent part of the way, but they came under fire from his assailants. He came to a frozen river, which created a problem, and he hid behind a partly frozen waterfall. His assailants were scouring the area in search of both agents when one of them peered inside the waterfall. Apparently, Agent Kane grabbed him and a fight ensued, with Agent Kane finishing him off by plunging a large icicle through his heart. Hence the reason that he is nicknamed the Iceman."

"Wow, that's an interesting piece of information," said Mulholland.

Agent Sommerville continued. "He is apparently very good with a knife and is used to close combat, although I have heard that the incident with the icicle took its toll on his nerves. Possibly because he clamped his hand over the Russian's mouth to stop him calling out and then had to stare into the dying man's eyes while watching his life fade away. Apparently, he is used to sleeping rough in all sorts of weather, and as the saying goes, Frank, he is a hardy bugger."

"Well, Merriday has told me that he will be joining our team in the morning," Frank said.

"I think you better get your facts right because he's just walked in through the door of the hotel," said Tom, pointing.

Frank spun around to face a stocky man with rough features. He was approximately five feet nine. He was carrying a rucksack, and on his right hand were what looked like three rings, which were exposed when he removed his glove. He had a rather rounded face with rosy cheeks, and his brown eyes sank deep into his face. In his left ear was a gold earring which hung just below black woolen headgear which had been stretched over his ears.

Frank Mulholland stood up and greeted Agent John Kane. "Welcome to the team, John. But we may have a slight problem with accommodation. You were not expected to arrive until the morning," said Mulholland.

"Nae problem, Frank," said Agent Kane with a smile. "Ah oany came in here tae introduce maself tae you an' find oot whaur ye wanted me tae stake oot. Ah've heard a lot aboot you and yer excellent team. I am noo awaiting instructions frae you as tae whar ah should position maself fur surveillance purposes." He removed his headgear, revealing wiry dark hair which had been compressed by the hat. He then ran his fingers through his hair while nodding his acknowledgement of Agent Sommerville.

Almost immediately, Tommy Anderson gave Frank the thumbs up for them meeting later, and he made for the exit, with Mulholland acknowledging his signal.

Frank called over to Tam Cameron, asking him to bring over a beer for Agent Kane. As they settled down at the fireside table, Tom introduced him to the three amigos.

Frank looked at Agent Kane and said, "We're going into the dining room shortly for a meal; you're welcome to join us, mate."

"Good stuff! Ah wid look forward tae that," said Agent Kane.

"Jings, Frank, the accordian players are coming at eight o'clock, and we're going to miss the ceilidh tonight," Tom said a little despondently.

Frank quickly replied, "We can have a few dances with the girls and stay until eleven o'clock. Tommy is picking us up at quarter to twelve on the dot, and we don't want to keep him waiting."

As the agents made their way to the dining room, the two new girls, Janice Irvine and Diane MacIntosh, strolled past, smiling at both agents.

"I wonder where Carol and Emma are. I haven't seen them since we came back," said Tom, looking at Frank inquisitively.

Five minutes later, the agents settled into their seats at the table. One of the servers approached and asked them what they would like from the menu. It was one of the new girls, and Tom's eyes were scanning her from head to toe.

"I thought you were starting tomorrow morning. Not that I'm complaining," said Tom, taking out his diary to check out her name.

"Diane's my name," she said, pre-empting what he was doing. She smiled and pointed to the name badge on her lapel.

"Oh, Frank, it looks like the girls have badges with their names marked on them now," Tom said.

"Well, at least Tam has taken my advice on something," Frank said with a smile. He introduced Agent John Kane to Diane and then cast his eyes on the menu.

"Where are Carol McBride and Emma MacNamara?" Frank asked whilst browsing.

"They went away on a helicopter this afternoon with a blonde woman, at around four o'clock. They won't be back until seven o'clock. That's why I'm filling in for them." After marking their order in her notebook, she quickly made her way to the kitchen.

Frank looked at the watch on his left wrist and showed Tom that it was about a quarter to seven. "The girls won't be too long now, and the music will start about eight thirty, said Agent Sommerville, rubbing his hands together excitedly.

"You're really enjoying the Scottish dancing, mate," Frank said.

"Yes, I sure am," Tom said.

Frank informed Agent Kane about their mission tonight at midnight down in Cononish Glen.

"Aye. Merriday telt me that ah will be surveying that area fur ye, Frank," said Kane.

"Let us enjoy our meal when it arrives because we have a long night ahead of us," Frank said, smiling.

Diane brought out the meals to a resounding cheer, which brought a smile to her face.

"When we finish in the kitchen, maybe we can have a dance later on, gents?" asked Diane, looking around the men.

"I'll look forward to that," Tom answered quickly.

She returned to the kitchen, and Frank said sternly, "You better not let Emma catch you," Frank said, wafting his finger.

"It's only a dance, mate," said Tom.

"Aye, if you say so," Frank remarked, looking unconvincingly at his buddy. After finishing their meals, the agents made for their rooms to prepare the equipment for tonight's escapade into the mountains. The sound of music was ringing through the hotel as Frank left his room and entered his friends room. To his surprise, he found Tom in a compromising position with waitress Diane MacIntosh. They were oblivious to Frank's presence as they made passionate love.

The maid was clinging on to Tom like the proverbial leach. Her head was thrown back, and her misty eyes were showing the passion that had built up inside her sexy pulsating body. They were obviously enjoying every moment of their time together. As their gyrating bodies shuddered to a halt, Frank quietly closed the door and left the room, stepping out into the hallway.

What if Emma had entered the room instead of me? he thought.

He made his way to the bar, where Agent Kane was sitting chatting with the three amigos. About fifteen minutes later, Diane MacIntosh walked back to the kitchen, just as Emma and Carol appeared to take up their positions behind the bar. Tam Cameron stopped Diane in her tracks and asked her where she had been.

"I was tidying one of rooms at the request of the guest," said Diane.

"Well, could ye let me ken whaur ye are going in future?" said Tam, twisting the end of his moustache.

She walked towards the kitchen with a devious smirk on her face. Big Tam shook his head.

Frank took out his bleeper and left a message for Merriday at headquarters to check her out. He had some doubts about her.

Frank and Agent Kane were sitting with the three amigos when Tom made his appearance. Shouting above the music, Tom told him that everything was organised for tonight.

The ceilidh was well under way, with the music and entertainment now in full flow. The guys were dancing with Carol and Emma. In the background, a slightly jealous Diane MacIntosh was looking on at Tom, who was obviously enjoying Emma's company. After spending some time in Tom's room earlier, making passionate love with him, she was feeling a bit left out and not too happy that he was showing Emma such attention. When the dance had finished, she made her way over to Tom.

"What the hell is going on between you and Emma?" Diane shouted angrily, her flailing hand smacking Tom's face.

Emma and I have been enjoying each other's company for the past three nights," Tom said.

She stepped back and screamed at him, firing a few angry expletives his way as she made for the bar. Frank immediately tried to calm the situation while everyone looked on.

Emma was now enquiring as to what was going on, and Carol stepped forward to give her friend some backing. Emma had now twigged on as to what had been going on between Tom and the new girl.

Head barman Tam Cameron was not too happy about the commotion, and he came over. He angrily told the girls to go through into the back room and sort things out between them.

Frank grabbed Tom by the arm and took him to his room, away from the problem. About five minutes later, Emma was racing out to confront Tom, and she made her way to his room. Bursting in through the door and with tears in her eyes, she cursed at Tom and then slammed the door, exiting out into the hallway. Frank looked at Tom and despondently shook his head.

"You're playing a dodgy game, mate," Frank said, glancing at his watch. To his horror, he realised that it was almost time to put on the snowsuits and meet Tommy Anderson at the helicopter. "Put your gear on and come to my room when you're ready." Trying to console Tom, he patted his back as he left the room.

Frank rushed out to the barroom and called on Agent Kane to come to his room immediately. A moment later, Agent Kane knocked on the door and entered. Frank threw a white snowsuit and tammy over to him, which Agent Kane caught in mid flight.

"Take them with you, John, so that you'll blend into the surrounding area," said Frank.

"What was aw that commotion aboot oot ther'? Agent Kane asked.

Frank was angry that his time was limited. He would like to have sorted things out between Emma and Tom. With a quick wave of his hand, Mulholland showed his disgust and ignored Agent Kane's question.

About five minutes later, there was a knock on the door of room number seven.

"Come in, mate," shouted Frank, and Tommy Anderson stepped inside.

"Hi, Tommy. I thought you were Agent Sommerville," Frank said.

"Whit wis the problem wae Emma oot in the hallway?" Tommy asked excitedly.

"I'll fill you in later, mate. We have got to be on our way," said Frank.

They quickly exited the room and made for Agent Sommerville's room.

"C'mon, Sommerville, we have to go!" Frank said. Tom stepped forward with his head stooped and his snowsuit tucked under his arm.

All four men made for the exit as the music and the ceilidh continued. Frank waved over to Carol, who was behind the bar, and she instantly rushed out after him to see where they were going. Frank kissed her and said, "We won't be too long, honey. It's secret business. If I told you, I would have to kill you." Mulholland walked away blowing her a kiss.

The men quickly stepped into their snowsuits and entered the helicopter. Frank introduced Agent Kane to Tommy Anderson as they climbed into the whirlybird.

"Pleased tae meet ye, John," Tommy said, slapping Agent Kane's back as he boarded the whirlybird.

This was to be the only time that Tommy would see Agent Kane.

The rotors were spinning as Tommy asked where they were going. Frank told him about the gold mine and said he would like to land on the hill just above the entrance to the mine. "Without being seen, mate," he added. In the blink of an eye, they were zooming off in the direction of Cononish Glen.

Tommy spoke, breaking the obvious tension among the agents. "Ah'll ha'e tae stay a wee bit further back, as I dinnae want them tae hear the rotors as we come intae land," he said, looking at Frank.

"That's OK with me," muttered Frank.

"Yer no' sayin' much the nicht, Tom. Whit's up wae ye?" Tommy asked.

"I've got a lot on my mind," said Tom, looking at Frank despairingly.

You could have cut the atmosphere in the cabin with a knife as the helicopter flew towards their destination.

Suddenly, their momentum slowed and the helicopter began hovering, making its descent and lightly touching down into the deep snow. Tommy pointed the agents in the direction of the entrance to the mine, then quickly switched off the lights.

"Jings, it's pitch black out there. How are we going to find it?" Tom asked.

"I was just thinking the same thing," said Frank, looking despondently at Tommy Anderson.

"I don't think these torches are going to be much of a help in finding our way. I think that we've had a wasted journey," muttered Mulholland.

"Ah'll lead ye's doon tae tae the entrance o' the mine, but ye's wid hae been better wae Brian Greene or Davy Blackwood wae ye, as they ken these hills like the backs o' their haunds," said Tommy. He stepped down into the deep snow, with the agents doing likewise.

Trudging along the uneven ground, and even with the occasional stumble along the way, the lads were making good time.

About twenty minutes later, the silence was broken when Tommy whispered. "Keep yer torches shining doon oan the ground so that they cannae be seen. We hiv only a couple o' hundred yards tae go noo."

"What's that up ahead of us?" Agent Sommerville asked. "Is it a beam of light coming up from the ground?"

"Christ, it is," said Frank. Throwing themselves down onto the snow, the men slithered forward. All eyes were on the shaft of light when a weird-looking flying machine surfaced from the base of the beam and lifted upwards.

Frank pressed the button on his night camera and captured a photo of this strange vehicle as it hovered above the snowy hill.

"Geez, what are we looking at here, gents?" Frank whispered.

"It cannae be a helicopter, 'cause it disnae hae oany rotors," said Tommy Anderson.

Suddenly, in the blink of an eye, the flying machine was gone. A strange high-pitched hissing noise filled the air.

"Jings, that's the noise we heard yesterday, when we were walking in the glen," Agent Sommerville said, peering in the direction of Frank.

"Quickly – let's get to the shaft of light. Maybe we can see inside before they lower the roof," Frank said.

All four men quickly scurried through the snow with eyes focused on the beam. The roof was beginning to lower as the four lads reached the edge and peered inside. Inside, they saw what looked like a helicopter pad, with quite a few people standing around. Over in the corner were a couple of machines and some wooden boxes.

"Look, there's the bearded giant over at the boxes," whispered Frank as the roof door closed, plunging them into darkness once again.

"I'd like to get inside for a closer look at what's going on," Mulholland whispered.

"You may get your chance sooner than you think," said Tom, who was looking at headlights coming down the glen towards the mine.

"It must be one of the big trucks that we saw on the previous night," said Frank, scurrying through the snow to get above the entrance to the mine. The other three men followed and caught up with him as the headlights came nearer.

"It couldn't be a car going to Georgie Burke's farmhouse, could it?" Tom asked.

"No, mate ... Surely a car wouldn't be able to drive through that snow on a single-track road," said Frank.

"How are we going to get inside the mine?" Tom asked, peering into the darkness in the direction of Frank's voice.

"Just in case there's a problem, I'm going in by myself," Mulholland whispered.

"I'm going to try to jump onto the back of the truck and slip under the tarpaulin before it enters the mine."

"But how are you going to get back out?" Tom asked.

"I'll cross that bridge when I come to it. Give me an hour inside and then you can leave," Frank said as the headlights closed in on the mine. Frank turned to Agent Kane and whispered, "Find a position somewhere close by and monitor who is going in and out of the mine and the farmhouse."

"Nae problem, Frank. Ah'll keep in touch wae ye wae ma pager," said Agent Kane.

Frank decided to move to a lower part of the slope, which would allow him to jump onto the truck without being seen. "One hour, mate! And then you leave, with or without me," said Frank, before scurrying down the slope and out of sight. Agent Sommerville and Constable Anderson were trying to peer into the darkness, but to no avail, as Mulholland had disappeared.

"He'll be aw richt, Tom. But its gonnae be richt cauld fur us three," said Tommy.

On reaching the mine, the driver of the truck jumped clear of the cab and walked over to the door.

This gave Mulholland time to slip into the back of the vehicle and under the covering.

As the truck slowly eased into the mine, Frank was peering through a small hole in the tarpaulin. To his surprise, there was a weird-looking vehicle shaped like a diamond over at the far end of the passageway. He took out his camera and captured it in a picture, immediately sending it off to headquarters. He noticed that the passageway seemed to go a long way into the mountain, and he wondered how far and what else was along there. Inside a glass unit were two figures dressed in white suits and wearing what looked like helmets or masks covering their faces. Both figures were concentrating on some kind of liquid in a large tank. Fumes were hovering around them and filling the air.

Frank was wondering what kind of liquid inside the tank could possibly be throwing off these fumes.

Suddenly, there was a noise of a hooter blowing. A few bodies were moving around excitedly and looking upwards. A few minutes later, to Frank's amazement, a diamond-shaped vehicle was lowering onto the helipad that he had glimpsed from high above in the snow. Frank was absolutely astonished, as there was hardly any noise from the engine of this aeroplane as it settled down onto the floor. The door of the flying machine swung upwards, and the pilot stepped out.

Christ! It can't be, Frank thought, his eyes focused on the pilot. Georgie Watson Harkin Burke had been flying the machine. She strolled over to ask the doorman to allow her to leave, while waving over to one of the men standing near what looked like boxes of weapons.

According to MI6 headquarters, it was Irish gunrunner Sean Macateer, standing with a machine gun hanging over his left shoulder. *Macateer's positioned like a gunslinger in a gangster movie,* thought Mulholland. He waved back at Georgie Burke, who had just stepped out into the darkness. Macateer then called on the doorman to come over and give him a hand with one of the boxes. He appeared to be in control of what was happening inside the mine, and he was quite aggressive in his actions. He stood about five feet eight inches, and he was still wearing his round framed glasses, which he continually pushed up onto his nose out of habit. As the doorman moved to assist Macateer, Frank saw his chance to escape through the closing door by the skin of his teeth.

Once outside and into the darkness, Mulholland clambered uphill to meet up with the other men, who were feeling a little on the cold side. Frank called quietly and was given a scare, as the men were closer than he anticipated. "Jesus! Why are you down here?" Frank asked as they quickly clambered uphill.

"Ye dinnae think we wer' gonnae leave ye doon here by yerself, dae ye?" said Tommy. They continued scrambling up the hill.

"Crivvens, ah'll be glad when we reach the tap o' this hill," said Tommy, who was panting heavily with each word that he spoke.

"Aye! Yer no the only wan," Frank said in a Scottish accent that made them all laugh.

Eventually, they reached the crest of the hill, ending their torturous scramble.

"Thank God for that. Now all we have to do is find the helicopter in this darkness," said Tom, knowing that it would be easier said than done.

"Where is Agent Kane?" Frank asked.

"He left at the same time as you," said Tom.

"Aye! An' the bugger dinnae even tell us he wis goin'. Wan meenit he wis ther' an' the next he wis offski," said Tommy.

As they were moving along the hilltop, Tom banged his knee on something and let out a small yell. Frank shone his torch at the object. They soon realised that it was a ventilation shaft which probably went down into the mine below.

"There must be quite a few of these about, as the tunnel seemed to go a long way back into the mountain," Frank said. They continued their trek across the snow.

With great relief, Tommy spotted the outline of his helicopter and tapped Frank on the shoulder.

"Christ, mate! You nearly frightened the life out of me. My mind was a million miles away," said Frank.

As they reached the helicopter and struggled aboard, Frank shone the torch on his watch, telling the lads that it was half past one.

With great difficulty, Tommy's cold fingers engaged the key, and to their relief, the rotors began spinning.

Tommy's face showed a cheesy grin as he said, "Orchy Hotel, here we come!"

They all laughed aloud as the whirlybird climbed upwards into the night sky and zoomed towards Bridge of Orchy. About five minutes later, the snow and treetops were whipped into a frenzy of activity as the descending whirlybird touched down.

Thanking Tommy, the agents quickly made for the hotel as Constable Anderson jumped into his Land Rover for the drive back to Tyndrum. Once the agents had entered the hotel, Frank filled Tom in on their impending visit to Crianlarich police headquarters at one o'clock.

They walked to their rooms with Frank saying, "It looks like a good night's sleep for us tonight, mate."

He smiled at Agent Sommerville, who was walking rather sheepishly to his own room. When Frank entered his room, to his surprise, Carol was looking up at him from his bed.

"Where have you been tonight, Frank?" Carol asked.

"I'm sorry, honey, but I can't tell you. I was attending to some business," said Frank.

Carol instantly sat up and leaned her arms on her knees. "I hope the business wasn't Georgie Watson Burke — or you and I are finished, Frankie boy." She was looking at Frank rather sternly.

Frank climbed into bed beside her and placed his cold lips on her lips. He was thinking to himself that the kiss might help to keep her quiet. His ploy failed abysmally when Carol spoke. "What the hell was Tom up to with the new girl when he has been seeing my friend Emma?"

Frank looked at her but simply shrugged his shoulders. He then replied, "Tom has hardly spoken a word all night since the rumpus with Emma. It doesn't make sense, because he really liked Emma." He tried to ease her mind as he snuggled against her warm body.

"I hope that you two are not taking advantage of me and Emma just for a little fun."

Frank convinced her that he had feelings for her as his hand slipped over her warm breasts. She responded instantly to his touch. Before long, they were making passionate love, with all thoughts of the earlier trouble gone.

As Frank rolled over, he switched on the bedside lamp and looked at the clock. "Christ! It's quarter to three, and I've got an early rise in the morning."

"You've got an early rise! I've got to be up by six o'clock," remarked Carol, cuddling with him. Before long, the alarm was ringing, and Carol made for the shower room.

Frank looked at her naked body as she switched the light on and entered the washroom. "Do you need a hand, honey?" Frank asked, lefting the alarm to reset it for eight o'clock.

Carol was peeking around the door. "Don't think that you are out of the woods yet, boy. I'm still angry about what was going on yesterday."

Frank pretended that he was sleeping as Carol dressed. She then left the room to head to the kitchen to prepare the breakfasts for the guests.

In what seemed to be no time at all, a rather groggy Frank Mulholland awakened with the alarm ringing in his ear. *Oh, jings! Is that the time already?* he thought, making for the shower room. His mind was already running through his itinerary for the day ahead.

Saturday, 31 March

After dressing, Frank heard a noise out in the hallway. Grabbing the door handle, he eased the door open and peered out, only to see road worker Brian Greene leaving room number twelve with a smiling Moira Malone waving goodbye to him. Frank stopped him as he passed his room and invited him to come inside for a minute.

"Yes, Frank. Whit kin ah dae fur ye?" Brian asked.

"Last week, up on Beinn Achaladair, we had a problem when Tom slipped through the snow and almost fell down a ravine. It was just pure luck that I managed to grab his hand before he plunged all the way down," Frank said.

"Ye'll be needin' a couple o' ice pickaxes. Ah'll bring them ower fur ye efter, mate," Brian said, pre-empting Frank's request.

"Good stuff, mate. I'll not say that I saw you coming out of that room," Frank said, winking at Brian as he closed the room door behind him.

Frank was thinking aloud. "Crivvens, is anyone sleeping in their own room here?"

He lifted his room phone and dialed the operator. "Hello, this is a Mr. Mulholland speaking. I wonder if you can put me through to a Diane MacIntosh who lived in Kilbirnie, Ayrshire." Giving the operator the address that Carol had given to him earlier, he listened as the phone rang at the other end.

"Hello, Diane MacIntosh speaking. Who is calling?" the voice at the other end of the line asked.

"Frank Mulholland speaking, madam … Did you say your name was Diane MacIntosh and that you're from Kilbirnie?"

"Yes, sir. How can I help you?" she asked.

Frank explained that he was given this number. But obviously not wanting to alarm the woman, he informed her that it must be a wrong number. "I'm sorry, but it was a different person I was looking for," said Frank, apologising profusely.

Mulholland was now wondering how Diane MacIntosh was back in Kilbirnie and at Bridge of Orchy at the same time. *This doesn't ring true. Is the woman in the hotel using a name and address taken from the phone book?* thought Frank. Mulholland's eyes dipped. He was in deep thought as he walked around pinching his lips and rubbing his chin. The gears were turning frantically around inside his head. Suddenly, there was a knock at the door, and in walked Agent Sommerville. Frank informed him about the phone call he had made to Diane MacIntosh at Kilbirnie and said that he had spoken to her.

"Now, the question is, mate, who is the woman who was working in the hotel?" asked Frank, raising his eyebrows.

"Ask Sir Jeffrey Merriday to check her out," Tom said. Agent Sommerville was now wondering who he had been with in his room yesterday.

"I'm way ahead of you, mate. I called him yesterday, when I saw both of you together," said Frank. "Anyway, let's go for breakfast and we'll speak to Moira Malone about what she saw over at the bridge yesterday."

After a good hearty Scottish breakfast, the agents noticed Moira Malone coming into the dining room, and they called her over.

"Good morning, gents," she said with a little curtsy.

"Mrs. Malone, may we enquire as to what you saw yesterday down by the river?" Frank asked.

"It's *Miss* Malone. And I was standing on the bridge when I saw the body floating underneath at a fair old rate. The current carried it along, and I ran up to the hotel and told the barman, who immediately phoned the police." Moira said this a little nervously, crossing her legs and revealing the top of her stocking and suspender.

This drew the attention of both agents, and their eyes focused on her exposed thigh.

"Was there anyone else around at the time you saw the body?" Frank asked, looking into her eyes.

"As a matter of fact, I was looking in the direction of Loch Tulla and was watching one of the canoeists heading down towards the bridge. I caught a glimpse of something in the water before it went beneath the bridge. It was only when it reappeared on the other side that I realised it was a body," Moira said, smiling timidly at the agents while tugging the bottom of her skirt down.

"You didn't happen to see who the canoeist was?" Frank asked expectantly.

"Oh, yes, sir," Moira confidently said. "She's working in the hotel. Her name is Diane. I saw her name on her lapel badge last night."

Frank's blue eyes widened, and he looked at his fellow agent alarmingly. He quickly thanked her for this information. "Please don't mention this discussion to anyone," Frank said.

She pulled an imaginary zip across her red-painted lips, gesturing to the agents that she wouldn't. A smile lit up her hazel eyes.

As the agents left the room, there was a bleeping sound, and Frank's hand dove into his pocket. Pulling out his pager, he whispered, "It's Merriday."

"Hello, sir. You must have been reading my mind. I was about to call you," Frank said, winking at Tom.

"I have some information about Diane MacIntosh for you, and I'm afraid that she is not who she said she is, my friend," Merriday said.

Frank informed him that he had discovered that the real Diane MacIntosh was still at home in Kilbirnie.

"Can you tell me who it is we have up here at Orchy?" Frank asked.

"I sure can, my friend, and it's not good news. She is a Russian agent called Alyona Aslanov, and she is involved with the KGB. She will have to be taken care of. By that, I mean eliminated, my friend. She was highly involved in the creation of chemical and nuclear weapons. Be very careful because she is a dangerous character."

Frank began to inform Merriday about the previous night's activity up at the Cononish mine. "Sir, when we were up above the mine, a false roof opened up from the top of the hill and a type of aeroplane that was shaped like a diamond came up out of the mine. It rose vertically, and then it hovered before disappearing right in front of our eyes. The strange thing about it was that it was completely silent. The only sound that could be heard was a high-pitched hissing noise that lasted for a few seconds as it disappeared."

Merriday was quiet for a few seconds and then asked Frank if he had anything else to report.

"Yes, sir. They definitely have a stash of weapons in there, similar to the boxes they had down at Forest Lodge. I'm assuming that it is Russian weapons being supplied to the IRA, with Sean Macateer and Denis Wadsworth being involved on behalf of the IRA. While I was hiding inside the mine, the diamond-shaped plane returned. It lowered down onto what looked like a helipad. Out of the plane stepped Georgina Watson Harkin Burke, strutting across the platform and smiling at the other agents who were scattered around."

"I got the photo you sent to me, Frank, but it's a bit blurred. I don't think it will tell us much. By the way, yesterday I received word from Agent Kane that a Russian pilot called Alexei Vispedov may have arrived in the Glencoe area."

"Sir, Agent Kane arrived at the Orchy Hotel last night and is now staked out in Cononish Glen, monitoring the situation for us, said Frank. While I was inside the mine, I took a photo of the other plane they have. I sent it on to you immediately after taking it last night."

"That's strange; I didn't receive it. I hope there's not a fault with the new night cameras," Merriday said.

"I am about to resend it to you for observation again," Mulholland said. He quickly added, "Both aircraft were similar in appearance, and they seemed to be coated with a strange substance. It's some kind of toxic liquid that they are producing in a large tank inside the mine."

"Brilliant work, Frank. Send the photo on to me ASAP," Merriday said.

"Sir, before you go, it may be worthwhile checking out Georgie Watson Burke's involvement at the Rolls-Royce Technical Development Department in Hillington, Glasgow. I know she was involved in secretive work on aircraft engines for the MOD. This may give us a clue as to what's going on inside the mine regarding these two weird-looking aircraft that she's flying around in."

"Will do, Frank. Keep up the good work. Over and out," said Merriday.

As the agents stepped outside for a breath of fresh air, Frank gave Tom a rundown on what he had just told Merriday. "Where is the Iceman going to be staying?" Tom asked.

"He's going to stake out the gold mine at Cononish, and he will be sleeping rough, probably in a snow house that he will dig out by himself," Mulholland said.

The agents were looking around and up at the mountains as Frank decided to give the team at Inveroran a call. "Hello, John. How did the team settle in last night?" Frank asked.

"Aye! We wer' awrich t,an' ther wis nae bother at aw," said JBA.

"What about you and Agent Hardie, my friend?" Frank asked.

Big John went a bit quiet and then blurted out, "Ach! Ah sent him doon tae keep an eye oan Forest Lodge. Jist in case oany o' they Russkis or IRA mob wer' hingin' aboot."

"C'mon, you were only wanting him out of the way, mate. Don't be taking him to the cleaners, if you know what I mean," Frank said, laughing.

"Aw richt, Frank. That's his turn ower,' said Big John, smirking.

"What about Brian McDonald? Has he settled in with the rest of the team?"

"Nae problem wi' the wee man. He'll mak' a guid team member, especially with his expertise in explosives," said Big John.

"OK, John, but don't be too hard on Hardie. We are going to need every man we have available. On that basis, Merriday has sent us Agent John Kane to bolster the squad," said Frank.

"Whit! The Iceman is helpin' us oot?" said JBA.

"Yes, John. I've positioned him down in the Cononish Glen to keep an eye on things," said Mulholland.

"I'll talk to you later, mate. Over and out," Frank said, breathing a sigh of relief that everything was OK down there.

"That's a nice view looking up to Beinn Dorain," Tom said, looking for some sort of response from Frank. But Frank's mind seemed to be on other things.

Frank began walking towards the hotel with Agent Sommerville tagging along. As they entered the lounge bar, they saw the maid Janice Irvine walking down the hallway towards them. "We'll have to ask her about the girl she's sharing a room with – the so-called Diane MacIntosh, or I should say Russian agent Alyona Aslanov," Frank said sarcastically.

Frank called her over, and they sat down near the glowing fire.

"How can I help you?" she asked.

Frank asked if she had noticed anything out of place with her new roommate.

"Only one thing I have noticed, and that is her accent. It is definitely not an Ayrshire accent. It would be similar to mine because that is the area where I come from," said the maid.

"Well, Janice," said Frank, looking at her name badge, "don't mention to her that we've had this discussion." He put his finger to his lips and thanked her for her time.

As she left to carry on with her duties, she suddenly stopped. "Oh, there is one other thing you may like to know about. Last night she said something while she was sleeping. It was only a couple of words, but they sounded like a foreign language." She continued on her way.

Frank and Tom exchanged worried looks. "Maybe she's been planted in here to keep an eye on us, mate," Frank said, pointing his finger to his eye.

"Yes, I think that bugger will have to be watched," Tom said. "If that's the case, then maybe that's why she came on to me," he added with a worried look.

"Only time will tell, but we will have to be on our guard from now on," Frank said, shaking his finger and looking sternly at Tom. "You better check your room for bugs or a camera."

The Robertson family was sitting over in the corner of the bar, and they called the agents over to thank them for finding little Freya when she was lost the other day.

"No problem, folks," said Frank, smiling at Freya, who was sitting with her doll on her knee. Frank knelt down and began talking to her doll as if it were a person.

"Her name is Frieda, and she is not allowed to talk to strangers," Freya said pensively.

Frank patted her head. "That's good, Freya. Always remember that," Mulholland said, grinning at her parents as he stood up.

Just then, Brian Greene walked into the hotel carrying a parcel, which he gave to Frank.

"That's the ice axes ah promised ye, Frankie boy," Brian said. "Ah thocht' a wid jist bring them doon the noo' in case ah dinnae see ye efter. He looked towards the dining room.

Frank thanked him and then said, "Are you sure that was the only reason you came down?" Mulholland laughed as Brian continued walking. Frank knew that he was going over to see Moira Malone, who was sitting in the dining room.

Frank's pager bleeped. Thinking it was headquarters with some information for him, his hand dove into his pocket. The voice at the other end of the line asked to speak to Agent Sommerville. "Don't be too long, mate," Mulholland said, passing his bleeper to Tom.

Tom listened intently and smiled. "I will be absolutely delighted, Captain Duffy. Wednesday should be fine," Tom said.

Frank stared at Tom and asked quietly, "Is it Coulport Submarine Base?"

Tom was like a kid with a new toy as he returned the bleeper to Frank. "Yes!" he exclaimed. "I'm to go for a one-day crash course on two-man mini subs on Wednesday morning with Captain Walter Duffy down at Coulport Submarine Base." He looked excitedly at Frank, hoping that it would be OK. Unknown to Agent Sommerville, Frank had asked Commander Heuitten if he could set up a short training course for Tom.

"Maybe I'll consider letting you go if you're not required up here," Frank said, smirking. He was jokingly trying to put some doubt in Tom's mind as to whether he would be allowed to go.

However, Tom was not sure if his buddy was joking or not. He clasped his hands in simulated prayer, pleading with Frank's conscience.

Chappie walked into the hotel, looking a little worried. He called out to both agents, "Did oany' of you guys see a UFO last nicht, aroon' aboot midnicht?"

Frank approached him quickly and with some concern asked, "Where did you see it, Chappie?"

"It wis jist above the trees, ower ther," Chappie said, pointing across the river.

At hearing this, Tam Cameron the barman walked over and asked Chappie if he was sure it was last night.

"Of course ah'm sure. Ah'm no gaun' roon the bend yet, ye ken, mate," said Chappie.

"Ah've got somethin' tae tell ye's. Ah saw a UFO the nicht afore, an' it wis hoverin' above Beinn Dorain. It jist disappeared in a flash, but ah wis scared tae tell onywan' in case they thocht a wis goin' doolaly," Tam said, tipping his trilby.

Frank looked at both men sternly. "Did it make any noise or sounds at any time when you saw it?" Frank asked, a serious look in his deep blue eyes.

"Naw, ah dinnae hear onythin', but it wis quite far awa'," Tam said. Chappie nodded in agreement.

Frank asked Tam to give Chappie a pint of cider, and the agents settled down next to the warm fire. Chappie nestled into his usual seat. Frank asked Chappie to keep his eyes peeled for anything unusual going on in the area and to let him know as soon as possible.

Stake-out at Forest Lodge

George Hardie was staking out the house at Forest Lodge. He glanced at his watch, wondering when his stint would be over and he could get back to the warmth of the Inveroran Inn. Suddenly, a strong hand came around his neck and pulled him down onto the ground from his kneeling position. It was the fresh-faced army middleweight boxing champion Agent Brian Wilson. He said, "If Ah wis a Russki agent, ye micht be deid the noo."

"I'm bloody freezin," George said. "It is guid tae see ye. Ah hope ye are here tae relieve me." He was thankful that it was one of his mates.

"Ah'm' here tae gie ye a wee break, mate," Brian said, brushing his hand through his dark crew cut and replacing his bonnet. There was the sound of a helicopter overhead, and both agents dove beneath the undergrowth at the base of the trees. The helicopter lowered to the ground, and three figures jumped clear and made their way towards the lodge. On entering the forest, they lifted a hidden hatch cover and disappeared underground, entering the house from a secret passage. It was Georgie Watson Harkin Burke, her uncle Denis Wadsworth, and Irish gunrunner Sean Macateer slipping into the underground passage.

"There's a secret passage intae the hoose," whispered George, looking surprised.

"Aye! We ken aboot it frae the mission doon here last Tuesday," Brian said.

Hardie's blood began to boil, and anger showed in his eyes. "Why wis ah not telt aboot this by Big John Aitken when ah wis assigned tae come doon here?" He continued ranting … "That big bastard Aitken should hiv telt me aboot this secret passage. Wis' he hopin' ah wid ha'e slipped up?"

Agent Wilson simply shrugged his shoulders and said, "It has now't tae dae wae me, mate."

There was a sudden noise from the opening hatch. The blonde head of Georgie Watson Burke appeared. Her eyes scoured the area, making sure all was clear. She motioned with her hand to the men below, and a large box slithered up from the underground passage, with Denis Wadsworth and Sean Macateer just behind.

"Whit do we dae noo, mate?" Agent Hardie whispered.

"We were only told to survey the area and report who goes in and out of the lodge," said Brian Wilson, placing his finger to his lips to signal George to be quiet.

"Ah wonder whit is inside the box," whispered Hardie.

"It looks as tho' they hiv mair boxes o' Russian machine guns than we thocht' doon ther'," said Agent Wilson. They watched as the Irish threesome loaded the box into the helicopter.

Agent Wilson explained to George Hardie that the box was similar to the boxes they took from the lodge when they overpowered the IRA and Russian agents last Tuesday.

The beat of the spinning rotors and the helicopter lifting drew the attention of both agents. They saw that Georgie Watson Burke was at the controls as it zoomed off in the direction of Tyndrum and the Cononish Glen. Hardie instantly rose and told Brian that he would pass on this information to J. B. Aitken when he reached the inn at Inveroran. He walked through the forest, waving his hand nonchalantly in the air as he left. As Agent Hardie was nearing the inn, his eyes focused on something lying in the ditch at the roadside.

Crivvens! Whit wid a crossbow be daein' lyin' aboot here? George thought, lowering himself into the ditch. The agent observed the impressive workmanship and the initials GN neatly etched on the bow. Throwing the bow quickly up to the roadside, he climbed back out of the ditch and retrieved the item. *Twa hundred yards tae go tae the warmth o' the inn,* George thought, twirling the crossbow with his fingers.

On entering the inn, J. B. Aitken walked over and asked Agent Hardie how it went down at the Forest Lodge. He informed him about the visitors that had arrived in the helicopter and what they had taken away. "When wis this aw happenin'?" asked JBA.

"They oany' left aboot twenty meenutes ago, heading ower in the direction o' Tyndrum," said George Hardie, pushing his hand forward and handing Aitken the crossbow. "Ah found it in a ditch aboot twa hundred yards frae the inn," Hardie said.

"Wow! Ah better tell Mulholland aboot this richt awa'. He wis talkin' tae me aboot a crossbow earlier oan this mornin', an' this micht be the wan."

"Well done, mate!" John said, quickly punching the digits on his bleeper.

Frank's pager bleeped. "Oh, I wonder who this can be?" said Mulholland. To his surprise, it was Big John Aitken informing him about the visitors at the lodge and the crossbow that Agent Hardie had found in a ditch between Inveroran and Forest Lodge.

"Great stuff, JBA. I'll get it from you, tonight," Frank said. "We'll have our briefing, probably around twenty hundred hours. Meanwhile, keep everyone happy. That includes you and Agent Hardie. We want harmony when we go into this mission, mate. Over and out."

Frank Mulholland informed Agent Sommerville about the discovery of the crossbow and of the visit of the Irish trio down at Forest Lodge that morning. He glanced at the time on the clock behind the bar.

"It's nearly time for us to go to Crianlarich, my friend. We'll leave in about five minutes," Frank said, noticing Diane MacIntosh strolling down the hallway with some bed sheets tucked under her arms.

Tom stared at her and whispered, "There's that Russki agent, the bitch – whatever you call her."

"You mean Alyona Aslanov, my friend." Frank grinned.

The men exited the hotel and walked into the car park. Frank threw the car keys to Tom and asked him to drive to Crianlarich.

Settling into his seat, Tom turned the key. The engine purred into action. "Crianlarich, here we come!" Tom said. A cold shiver ran through his body, causing him to shake. He glanced over at Frank, who had taken the hint and was turning the heater up a notch.

Frank called Agent John Kane. "Hi, John. How are things down at Cononish, mate?"

"A helicopter has jist landed and twa men hiv ta'en a large box intae the mine. A blonde female has jist gone intae the hoose, an' erlier oan a truck went intae the mine," Agent Kane said.

"Did you feel cold during the night? You must have been freezing out there," Frank said.

"Nae problem, Frank. I'm used tae being oot in the cauld," Kane said.

"Keep up the good work… and keep your eyes peeled. Let me know of any problems which may arise," said Mulholland.

Frank was enjoying the views of the mountains covered in snow. Tom broke the silence. "Do you know that Tyndrum is built on a battlefield?"

"No, my friend, but I think you are about to tell me," Frank said.

"Yes, I am, Frank. It was back in the year 1306, and the battle was fought between the Clan MacDougall and Robert the Bruce. The battle was won by the Clan MacDougall."

"I take it that you read that in this fabulous book of yours," said Frank, laughing at his mate's expense.

The agents were pulling into the headquarters at Crianlarich, and they saw Sergeant Murdoch approaching their car.

"Whit ar' ye's daein' doon here et this time o' day?" Murdoch asked.

"We are here to speak to Inspector Hugh Smith," Frank said.

"Is ther' somethin' goin' down that ah micht be able tae help ye wae?" Murdoch asked excitedly.

He was remembering the action he was involved in last Tuesday, up on Beinn Achaladair.

"Ye'll hiv tae wait an' see whit Inspector Smith has tae say," said Frank in a Scottish accent.

"Jings, yer gettin' as guid as me at talkin' oor lingo," Murdoch laughed.

The agents entered the building and informed the smartly dressed girl at the desk that they were expected and had to see Inspector Hugh Smith. Directing them to his office, she gave both agents an admiring glance.

"Wow, she can arrest me anytime," Frank said, smiling.

A quick tap on the office door and the inspector called them in. "Good afternoon, gents," the fresh-faced silver-haired inspector said. "What can I do to help you?"

"Sir, we were wondering if you know anything about what is going on at the gold mine down in the Cononish Glen," Frank said.

"As far as I know, the mine is being test drilled to see if there is enough gold and silver to make it worthwhile investing time and money into the project," said the inspector, looking at Frank curiously.

"Well, sir, we have every reason to believe that there is criminal involvement in what is happening at the mine at the minute," said Mulholland. Agent Sommerville nodded in agreement.

"What kind of criminal involvement are we talking about?" Inspector Smith asked.

"It looks like there is more involvement with the IRA and Russian agents. A bit similar to what went on down at Forest Lodge last week," Frank said, looking at the inspector sternly.

Inspector Smith stood up and walked around, rubbing both of his eyes while he was thinking. "What do you require from me?" he asked.

Before Frank Mulholland could answer, Agent Sommerville butted in. "Is it possible that the lead mines just above Tyndrum would extend underground all the way along the mountain and up to the gold mine at Cononish?"

The hill is about two miles long," Inspector Smith said, looking a little perplexed. "You're talking about an underground passage traveling the full length of the hill? Surely that would have taken a lot of excavation and possible blasting."

Tom explained that he was reading in his book that the lead mines had been there for hundreds of years and had been worked on and off, as lately as this century. "Could it be possible that some of the excavation was done during recent times, when the mine was being worked on up at the Clifton lead mines?" Tom asked.

"I don't think so, unless the work was undertaken from the Cononish mine, where there is nobody to hear any noise that may be made by drilling or blasting … other than the owners of the farmhouse," Inspector Smith said, wafting his finger accusingly as if he may have hit on the answer. "But we have never had any complaints from the occupants of the farmhouse." He shrugged his shoulders.

Tom still had his doubts that both mines were not joined as one.

Changing the subject, Frank asked the inspector if it was possible that he could have the services of Sergeant Murdoch and Constable Anderson if they were required. "The mission is of high security, sir, and obviously we cannot reveal it to them just yet," Mulholland said.

The inspector walked around to face Agent Mulholland and extended his hand to the agents. "After what they told me about the last mission, I wouldn't like to deprive them of some excitement. Of course you can have them, if it will help the British government."

"Brilliant! And thanks for your assistance, sir. Of course, I will inform you when I require both men," said Frank Mulholland. The agents made for the exit door, with Inspector Smith jokingly saluting them as they left. When the agents were leaving the building, they called out to Sergeant Murdoch that Inspector Smith had something to tell him. Settling into the car, they grinned as they watched Murdoch rush into headquarters.

Mulholland was showing some concern at the cold wind that had arisen and the impending dark, stormy looking clouds that were homing in on them from the north-west. "Christ, I hope there isn't snow behind that wind," Frank said, shivering and pointing to the sky.

Frank's bleeper bleeped, and quick as a flash, his hand delved into his pocket. "This will be Merriday," he said Mulholland. There was silence for almost a full minute as Frank listened. "Thank you, sir. When will we receive the equipment I've asked for?" Frank asked. Mulholland listened intently and then replied, "Over and out."

Tom glanced at Frank, who seemed to be in deep thought. "Well, what was that all about?" Tom asked inquisitively.

Frank's fingers were pinching his lips as his thoughts computed the information he had just received. "That was Merriday, and, he was telling me that Georgie Watson Harkin Burke was involved with a Russian student when she attended Glasgow University. They were both studying chemistry," Frank said, looking at Tom with some concern. "He also told me that he is now involved with the Russian Military of Intelligence and the KGB. He is one of the Russians I photographed at the gold mine, and his name is Stanislav Bulsanov. They were friendly with another Russian student called Veronika Bogrov and an Irish girl called Sharon Gallacher, but they have not been seen since they left university."

"Do you think that they were inside the glass room that was inside the gold mine?" Tom asked.

"I don't know, mate, because they were inside white suits and helmets, just like spacemen.

I couldn't see their faces," Frank said, dipping his eyebrows.

Tom smiled at Frank's reference to spacemen. "Well, if they were the spacemen. Can we take it that it is some form of chemicals inside the large tank?" Sommerville said.

"Your guess is as good as mine," said Frank, smiling back at Tom.

While the agents were driving through the village of Tyndrum, Tom pointed his finger at the lead mine of Clifton up on the hill.

"That's the mine that I was talking about when we were speaking to Inspector Hugh Smith. Do you think it's possible that there could be an underground passage all the way through to the Cononish gold mine?" Tom asked.

"It could be possible because they must have blasted out the lead mines at some point, and the noise would have been an acceptable occurrence at that time," said Frank, thinking that Tom's idea was not as far-fetched as it first sounded.

As they approached the Orchy Hotel, Frank noticed a helicopter settling down just behind the hotel.

"That looks like Georgie Watson Harkin Burke arriving," Frank said, giving Tom a little dig in the ribs.

"I wonder what she wants over here at this time of the day," Tom said as they pulled into the car park.

Frank walked over and grasped Georgie's hand, then kissed her on the cheek.

"Hello, Frank. You're just the man I want to speak to," said Georgie Burke, giving him a sensual smile.

"What can I do for you, Georgina darling?" Frank asked in a suggestive tone of voice.

"Would you like to come for a flight in my helicopter? I'll take you back to my farmhouse for a coffee," Georgie said, nudging against Mulholland and allowing him to sniff her perfume once again.

"Superb! Let's go now, honey," said Frank. Mulholland turned to Agent Sommerville, informing him of her invitation. Frank whispered to Tom that this would give him a chance to check out the air vents that were positioned on the hill above the mine.

"How do I explain your whereabouts to Carol?" Tom whispered. "She won't be too happy that you're away with Georgie Watson Burke."

"Tell her I'm on government business that's highly secretive, mate," Frank said, trying to sound convincing. He walked over to the helicopter and climbed in to be greeted.

The blonde greeted him. "Welcome aboard the *Phoenix*, Frankie boy," Georgie said, giving him the eye.

"Yes, I noticed the name and motif on the front of your helicopter. But do you know what the name means?" Frank asked.

"Of course I do. And it represents me explicitly," said Georgie in a dulcet tone while smiling seductively.

"You may be correct, honey. Because the *Phoenix* is the bird of fire, with a golden tail," said Frank, looking down at Georgie's rear end. "I hope you live up to these attributes today, madam." Frank smiled suggestively. The helicopter lifted quickly, sending the treetops whipping into a frenzy of activity as the whirlybird zoomed off in the direction of Tyndrum.

Frank called out. "What's the hurry, madam?" Georgie gave him a look that told him she was in control of the situation. As they climbed over the Clifton lead mine, Frank noticed that there seemed to be quite a lot of air vents scattered around. He thought that maybe Tom's idea about both mines being linked by a tunnel was not too far off."

Frank's thoughts were disturbed by Georgie saying, "We're almost there, Frankie boy."

The helicopter slowed down and began its descent. The swirling trees and snow on the ground were whipped into a frenzy, and a flurry of loose snowflakes showered the farmhouse just below.

"That was a super view of the countryside covered in snow," Frank said. The helicopter came to rest in Georgie's backyard.

Georgie led the way as they trudged through her garden towards the back door of the farmhouse. On entering the house, she immediately turned around and threw her arms around Frank's neck, kissing him passionately on the lips. Frank was taken by surprise at her actions but responded immediately. Making for the bedroom, they were tearing at and removing each other's clothes on the way.

"Christ, I didn't expect this," he whispered in her ear as they frolicked around on top of the bed.

Frank's hands were manipulating her firm breasts, sending her into a height of extreme passion.

Moaning in his ear excitedly, she whispered, "Take me, Frank … Please! Please!" She pulled the agent on top of her pulsating body. Both of them were losing control of their emotions as their bodies ground passionately together.

"Oh my God, Frank! This is fantastic. Please … don't stop!" Georgie screamed as they clung on to each other's gyrating bodies. Breathing heavily, they collapsed into each other's arms and began kissing and caressing each other.

Frank soon realised that this was the room that he had looked into in the darkness two nights ago. Georgie was snuggling into his muscular body and running her fingers through his chest hair. As they stared into each other's eyes, Frank kissed her lips once again. Squirming free from his grasp, she wriggled beneath the sheets, Frank joining her. This time he kissed her with a greater passion, to which she responded once again. Frank's lips ran over her neck and then worked their way down onto her breasts as his hand slipped over her sensual body. Her face began perspiring as Frank's hand explored her body beneath the sheets. Once again, she exploded into a height of passion, with Frank taking full advantage of the situation. A quiet moaning sound came from her lips as she clung to him. A few minutes later, breathing heavily, they collapsed into each other's arms. As they gazed into each other's eyes, Frank asked her what she wanted to speak to him about and why she had wanted him out here at the farmhouse.

Georgie smiled seductively and said, "Mission accomplished, Frankie boy." She laughed and wriggled free from his grasp. Jumping out of bed, she then scooped up her clothes from the floor and made for the washroom while giggling back at Frank on the way. Frank excitedly followed her and confirmed to himself that it was a shower room that was lit up when he had gazed at her through the window two nights ago. Approximately five minutes later, Frank came back into the bedroom and walked over to the window. To his horror, when he drew back the curtain, he noticed footprints in the snow beside the house.

Suddenly, two hands were manipulating his body. Georgie's fingers were massaging his chest, and her breasts were pressed firmly against his back as she kissed the back of his neck. Frank immediately responded, and they kissed passionately once again. During the passionate kiss, Frank, noticed a large truck heading uphill to the mine.

Georgie, having realised that he had seen the truck, was determined that he respond to her advances, and she held him tight, kissing him even more passionately. Minutes later, as they lay exhausted on the bed, Frank mentioned the footprints in the snow outside of her room window, his devious ploy to detract from any doubts she may have had towards the MI6 agents.

"Yes, I know about them. It must be one of those pesky workers from the mine, probably a Peeping Tom." She dipped her eyebrows.

"Don't you have any security lights around the house?" Frank asked, although he obviously knew that she had.

"Yes, I have lights, but they mainly cover the helicopter and the back of the house. Unfortunately, what I need is a man about the house," said Georgie, hinting that he would be ideal.

Frank smiled and quickly changed the subject. "When am I getting my cup of coffee, madam?"

They quickly dressed and made for the kitchen, clinging to each other on the way. While Georgie was making the coffee, Frank's hands reached around her body and began massaging her breasts. Her legs turned to jelly when she felt him pressing against her in a provocative manner.

"Oh, my God, Frank, what are you trying to do to me?" She was panting heavily.

His hands were manipulating her wriggling body, bringing her to a high pitch of excitement.

Then the back door swung open. To Georgie's embarrassment, it was her blonde-haired friend Sharon Gallacher standing before them. A rather nervous but excitable Georgie introduced her friend to Frank.

Sharon apologised for interrupting them. She looked through azure blue eyes at Georgie, who was frantically adjusting her clothing. Georgie asked her friend if she would like a coffee. Unknown to both of them, Frank had just taken a photo of Sharon Gallacher and was about to send it off to Sir Jeffrey Merriday at headquarters for verification.

"I'll not bother about the coffee. I have some work to attend to," Sharon said in her broad Irish accent. She opened the door to leave, taking her trim figure outside and ending her friend's embarrassment.

Frank watched her walking away and asked what kind of work she did. "Oh, she is doing a bit of work up at the gold mine with liquid chemicals to help preserve the mining equipment," replied Georgie nervously, trying to sound convincing. Suddenly, she burst into tears. Frank asked her what was wrong. He slipped his arms around her, desperately trying to console her.

"I'm in a terrible predicament, Frank. I'm involved with some shady Russian characters, and they are now controlling the gold mine," said a trembling Georgie.

Frank slid a chair over and sat her down. "Tell me all about it and I'll see if I can help you in some way," Mulholland said. They settled at the table with their coffee.

Georgie began by explaining about her work in the Technical Development Department for the British government when she was at Rolls-Royce Aerospace in Glasgow. "I was highly involved on a new type of engine that would have been undetectable to radar," Georgie said, looking sadly into Frank's eyes.

"What kind of engine were you working on?" Frank asked.

"It was to be a solar-powered engine. It would have been solely reliant on the sun for its power. The body of the plane would have solar panels which would capture the sun's rays and convert it into power to drive the engines," said Georgie, crying again.

Frank pulled Georgie against his body to console her and asked her why she had left her job when she was on the verge of something good.

"The British government felt that they would lose a lot of revenue and jobs in the oil Industry if they were to continue with the programme, especially because this could be made available to passenger airlines," she said. "They told Rolls-Royce Aerospace to suspend the work on this type of engine."

"Well ... I can understand that. But why did you leave when this type of plane would have been of great value to the Ministry of Defence?" Frank asked.

"The MOD has all the design work available to them. They are unwilling to use it because of the costs involved. Because of its complexity, it is more costly than it would be to build normal engines."

"But surely they would gain in the long run by not burning fuel," said Frank, smiling and massaging her shoulders, trying to make her feel at ease.

"Of course it would save on fuel to run the planes on solar, but I do understand that the oil industry would be hit hard. Jobs would be lost," Georgie said.

"Why all the tears – and what is the problem you have with these shady Russian characters?" Frank asked, showing concern. In reality, the devious Mulholland was looking for some information while she was under stress.

Georgie continued. "When I was studying chemistry at university, I was friendly with a couple of Russians who showed a lot of interest in my work, and they told me that they could get me a sponsorship from the Russian Development Authority to further my work on this type of aircraft. I was stupid enough to accept their invitation. Now I am under their control and don't know what to do." She broke into tears once again. Frank placed his arms around her, showing her compassion as he pulled her tightly against his body.

"Have you built any of these planes for the Russians?" asked a concerned Mulholland, although he already knew the answer to the question.

"Yes, the original design that I was working on for the government and MOD would have carried lots of passengers. But we have built two smaller planes similar to the original design, which have a two-man capability. They are sitting up in the gold mine, out of sight. They will kill me if they find out that I have told you, Frank."

"What are the names of these Russian friends of yours?" Frank quickly asked.

"The three chemical experts are Veronika Bogrov, Stanislav Bulsanov, and Sharon Gallacher, the Irish girl you met fifteen minutes ago. They have made a chemical substance. When it's sprayed onto the aircraft, it not only protects the surface but also makes it almost invisible when manouvering the plane."

"Christ, that would be invaluable to the Russians. They could fly anywhere and not be seen," said a worried-looking Mulholland. "What is this chemical?"

Georgie explained that when they were enlarging the mine, they discovered beryllium, which had chemical qualities. After tests, they found out that a chemical substance which had similar properties to the beryllium could be made. When it was sprayed onto the planes, and in conjunction with the solar panels and the diamond shape of the plane, it would make it almost invisible to radar and the naked eye when it was flying.

Frank told Georgie that if she wanted his help, then she would have to say nothing about him and what they had discussed to anyone. "That included your friends. So trust no one," said a determined Mulholland.

Georgie Burke agreed to this, and Frank asked her to take him back to Bridge of Orchy as soon as possible. Frank now realised that what Georgie had told him was correct, for it tied in with what he had seen inside the mine on the previous night. It immediately changed his opinion of her.

On the flight back to Orchy, Frank hardly spoke a word, but he squeezed Georgie's hand to confirm his belief in her. She looked back at him nervously through sad, watery eyes.

As the helicopter landed behind the hotel, Georgie asked Frank if she would see him again. "Of course, honey." He thanked her for the coffee and told her not to worry. Georgie smiled and waved at Mulholland as the helicopter rose upwards and zoomed off in the direction of Tyndrum.

Inside the hotel, Carol McBride had seen Frank leaving the helicopter. She was worried and a little jealous that Frank has been with her friend Georgie. She had noticed that they were making eye contact and that Frank was interested in her when they had met a few days earlier.

Mulholland walked into the hotel to be met by an angry Carol, who dragged him aside to question him about his time spent with her.

"Where the hell have you been?" Carol demanded.

"I was out on business, honey. I was checking the area around here, and Georgie offered to fly me around the hilltops," Frank said, desperately trying to convince her that nothing was going on between them.

"Don't honey me, Frankie boy. If you have been up to something with her, then we are finished!" Carol shouted. She turned around and marched back to her position behind the bar, throwing Mulholland an angry glance.

Frank nervously looked around the lounge, only to see Tom and local lad Chappie staring at him because of his predicament. To ease the tension in the air, Frank asked them if they would like a beer. He sheepishly turned to Carol and asked for two beers and a cider. While Carol was pouring the beers, she was mumbling something under her breath in her Irish accent. Frank was sure that what she was mumbling was not too complimentary. He tried not to make eye contact with her as she pushed the beers towards him. "I'll bring Chappie's cider over to him," she said grudgingly.

Frank lifted the beers and walked over to the fireside table to join his friends. He puffed his cheeks out at the scolding that he had received from Carol.

"I told you that you would be in trouble going for a jolly with Georgie Watson Burke," said Tom, feeling sorry for his buddy.

"Oh, listen to him. Is that not the pot calling the kettle black?" Frank asked, thinking back to Tom's problem with barmaid Emma on the previous day.

Carol appeared at the table and placed Chappie's pint of cider down. She marched away after giving Frank a dig in the ribs with her hips.

"It looks as though you're sleeping by yourself tonight, mate," said Tom.

Frank's pager bleeped. Frank whispered, informing Tom that it was the Iceman. "Hello, John. What have you to tell me?" Frank asked.

"Ah've jist seen a richt shifty character come oot o' a helicopter and go intae the fermhoose wae Georgie Watson Burke. They wer' in the hoose fur quite a wee while, an' ah widnae mind knowin' whit they wer' up tae," Agent Kane said, laughing heartily.

"Very funny, mate," Mulholland guffawed. "I forgot that you were down there. Jings! I'll have to watch what I'm doing now that you are around. But at least I now know that you were being observant. Over and out."

Frank informed Tom that Agent Kane was pulling his leg about being down at the farmhouse with Georgie.

Back at Georgie's farmhouse

G eorgie arrived back at the farm and entered through the kitchen door. She put the kettle, on preparing to make a coffee. Suddenly, the kitchen door flew open, and in walked her Irish friends – IRA chemical expert Sharon Gallacher and gunrunner Sean Macateer. Sharon walked over, and with the back of her flailing hand, she smacked Georgie across her jaw, sending her spinning across the room and crashing into the table leg. Before she could recover her senses, Gallacher had pinned her down onto the floor and smacked her twice across the face. Sharon was screaming at her for bringing a strange man into the area.

Gunrunner Macateer pushed Gallacher aside. Jumping on top of Georgie, he grabbed her blonde hair and forced her head down onto the floor. He was holding a bread knife at her throat whilst screaming at her that she had broken the rules of their agreement.

Georgie was in a state of panic as Macateer pressed on her throat with the point of the knife. He re-emphasized the point he had just made about breaking the rules.

Georgie's blue eyes revealed complete terror as she strained to apologise to him. She blurted out slurred words to let them know that it wouldn't happen again.

Macateer eased the pressure on her throat but slapped her across the top of her head. Standing over her, he was dominantly letting her know directly that it better not happen again.

The kitchen door swung open, and in walked Georgie's uncle Denis Wadsworth. "What the hell is going on here?" Wadsworth screamed. He pushed Macateer aside and helped his niece up from the floor.

Macateer stepped forward and told him that she had brought an MI6 agent down to the farmhouse. He was pointing a finger at Georgie in a provocative manner.

Georgie was looking at them through tear-filled eyes. "I didn't know he was a British agent," she said, wiping the tears which were streaming down her cheeks with the back of her hand.

Denis Wadsworth's mind was racing now that their work at the mine might be in mortal danger of being discovered. "We'll have to step up our delivery of the weapons," Wadsworth said. We will have to bring everything forward twenty-four hours now." He looked angrily at Georgie. "Midnight tomorrow may not be enough time. The aeroplanes will have to be prepared for the flight to Moscow."

At hearing this, Georgie screamed, "You are not taking both my babies to Russia. After all, it was me who created them!" She continued wiping the tears from her eyes.

Macateer instantly replied that she was no longer in control of the planes or the situation. He pushed her aside to leave by the kitchen door. On grabbing the door handle, he turned and emphasized that the new time for evacuating was now, midnight tomorrow. Slamming the door shut, Macateer made his way up to the mine with Sharon Gallacher by his side.

Denis asked Georgie what she was thinking of by bringing an MI6 agent down to the farmhouse.

Georgie said that it was done on an impulse when she saw him at the Orchy Hotel. "I guess it was just a fatal attraction to him."

"Come here, sweetheart, and I'll wipe the blood from your face," Denis said as his favourite niece staggered over to the sink. After consoling her, Denis informed Georgie that he was going up to the mine to try to calm things down with Sean Macateer and Sharon Gallacher, in the hope that they would change their mind about the evacuation date.

"I feel that it won't give us enough time to clear all of the weapons from the mine," Denis said.

A few minutes later, Wadsworth was on his way.

Georgie quickly lifted the phone and dialled the Orchy Hotel's number as she watched Denis trudging through the snow. "Hello, may

I speak to Frank Mulholland, please? Georgie asked. Tam Cameron had answered the phone.

"Yes, give me a minute please. Who shall I say is calling?" Tam politely asked. Tam listened and then called out to Agent Mulholland, "Frank it's a Georgie Watson Harkin Burke oan the phone wantin' tae speak tae ye."

On hearing this, it was like a red rag to a bull as Carol shook her fist at Frank as he made for the phone.

"Hello, Georgie. What can I do for you?" Frank asked.

She nervously let Frank know that the aeroplanes were being flown to Russia at midnight tomorrow night and that the Irish agents were clearing the weapons out of the mine too. "The reason for them bringing the date forward is because of you visiting me today. My so-called friend Sharon Gallacher reported me to the team up at the mine. I have to go now, Frank. It may not be safe for me after making this call," said Georgie, ending the call and staring out of the window to make sure that she was not being spied upon by the gruesome twosome.

Back at the Orchy Hotel

Frank received a call from MI6 headquarters. "Hello, sir. What have you to tell me?"

"I have some information on the photo of the female you have sent me," said Sir Jeffrey Merriday. "She is a Russian spy called Alexei Smirnoff, but she is using the alias name of Sharon Gallacher. She spent a lot of her life growing up in Belfast, in Northern Ireland. Her parents are involved with the communist party."

"Thank you for that information, sir. What's the latest on the equipment that I have asked for?" Mulholland asked.

"Your requirements will be arriving tomorrow around midday, by army truck delivery from the Coulport ammunition depot, courtesy of Commander Peter Heuitten. They will be delivered to Agent John B. Aitken at Inveroran," Merriday said in an official tone of voice.

"Good stuff, sir," said Mulholland. "I will inform JBA of their arrival, but before you go, I'd like to inform you that D-Day may have to be brought forward twenty-four hours according to information that I received earlier. We are now talking about midnight on Sunday, the first of April. Over and out."

Frank looked at the clock behind the bar and said, "Christ, it's six fifteen!" He sheepishly turned to Carol and asked if they could have a meal served immediately. "We have an important meeting that we must attend later."

After seeing him with her friend Georgie, she was a bit suspicious of Frank on hearing this. But she acknowledged that it was OK by sternly pointing to the dining room. Frank called on Agent Sommerville to come into the dining room, where he filled him in on the information Merriday had just given him.

Frank Mulholland called Big John B. Aitken, informing him that they would be down at the Inveroran Inn at twenty hundred hours for a briefing. He asked him to arrange with the proprietor, Peter MacInnes, to use the conference room.

"Aw richt, Frank. But Brian Wilson is doon et Forest Lodge keepin' an' eye oan things," said John.

"Send someone down for him. I want everyone available for this briefing," Frank said in a determined tone of voice.

"Aw richt, mate. Ah'll send Brian McDonald doon tae get him richt awa'. Ower an oot," said JBA.

Mulholland stuffed his bleeper into his jacket pocket.

"What have you ordered from the ammunitions depot?" Tom asked.

"Half a dozen snow suits and caps, bulletproof vests, and ammunition for machine guns," said Frank. "Some explosives and timers for Brian McDonald and a wee surprise for Big John and the team."

"What kind of surprise are we talking about?"

"Carol is coming with our meals," Frank said, smiling at her as she approached the table. "You'll find out at the briefing."

"Don't smile at me, Frankie boy. You are still in the bad books with me," Carol said. "Enjoy your meal, gents," Carol said rather grudgingly as she made her way back to the kitchen.

"Crivvens, mate. You're not going to get into her good books too quickly," Tom said with a cackle.

"Eat your meal, Sommerville. I'll wangle it somehow," said Frank.

Meanwhile, down at Forest Lodge

Agent Brian Wilson was positioned in the pine forest, surveying the area around Forest Lodge, when he heard a slight rustle in the forest floor over to his right. To his relief, it was Agent Brian McDonald creeping towards him. "Christ! Ye hud me worried ther', mate," Brian whispered.

Agent McDonald informed him about the meeting at the inn. "We hiv tae head back there richt away," McDonald said.

"Then we micht ha'e a problem. Twa Russian agents went intae the hoose aboot ten meenutes, ago an' they ar' still in ther'," said Agent Wilson.

"How did they arrive et the hoose?" McDonald asked.

"They've got a van et the back o' the hoose, an' they slipped doon intae the underground passage tae enter intae the hoose," said Wilson quietly.

"Hiv ye telt JBA aboot this?" McDonald asked.

"Aye, and we hiv tae tak' them oot quietly. So we wull hiv tae put silencers oantae' oor guns. JBA telt me tae wait until they hud loaded whitever thae wer' takin intae the van, as it micht be handy tae hiv extra ammo' fur oor mission."

"How dae ye ken they ar' Russians?" McDonald inquired.

"Ah heard them talkin'," Wilson replied in a whisper.

The agents' discussion was brought to a halt as the door of the underground passage lifted upwards. Moments later, two boxes were sliding out onto the floor of the forest. Two bearded men came up out of the passage and dragged the boxes over to the awaiting van.

As the MI6 agents slithered across the forest floor to achieve a better angle to their targets, a noise off to their right alerted the Russian agents that there might be a problem. Both Russkis grasped their guns and immediately dove for cover. To their relief, a young deer ran out of the forest in a panic and made for the hills.

Suddenly, two bullets from each MI6 agent tore into their bodies, and they fell to the ground. Agents Wilson and McDonald emerged from their hiding place and dragged the dead bodies over to the underground passage, dumping them below ground and out of sight. As they were walking back to the van, a smile lit up Brian Wilson's eyes as he spoke.

"Ah hope the keys ar' still in the van or you ar' gonnae hiv tae go back doon an' search ther' pockets, mate."

The keys were in the van, and they headed to the Inveroran Inn to meet JBA.

"We'll hiv tae hide this gear in the forest across frae the inn, as we dinnae want tae upset Peter MacInnes and Jessie, the proprietors," JBA said. He opened the first box. "They'll come in haundy fur you, Mr McDonald."

Brian peered into the box and smiled at the cache of hand grenades. "Aye, they will dae fine, mate. Ah'm sure ah ken whit tae dae wi' them," McDonald said.

Meanwhile, Agent Wilson had opened the other box and was faced with Russian Kalashnikov machine guns and ammunition. "Yes! These will come in haundy as weel if we require them," Agent Wilson said, smiling at his find.

"We drapped the Russki bodies doon intae the underground passage fur the time being," said Brian.

JBA informed them about the meeting with Frank Mulholland and told them to get inside and grab a bite to eat. They didn't have to be told twice, and they emerged from the forest and made their way towards the inn. JBA moved the van to a new location, out of the sight of prying eyes.

Cononish Gold Mine

Meanwhile, back at the gold mine, Sean Macateer was calling the tune and reacting to what had happened down at Georgie's farmhouse. This problem had enraged him, and his voice was ranting instructions to his fellow agents. His arms were flailing around in a provocative manner, which was causing some of his people concern. He seemed to have the backing of the giant Russian Vladimir Bazarov, who was standing by his side. Both men were intimidating individuals with their rifles hanging around their shoulders, giving out instructions in an aggressive manner.

The big Russki was firing out instructions to all of his Russian comrades. Everyone was reacting to both men by buzzing around like bees in a hive. The two flying machines were receiving a lot of care and attention by the Russian agents, in preparation for their flight to Moscow.

Sean Macateer made a phone call to Diane MacIntosh at the Orchy Hotel, informing her that circumstances had changed. "We need to have Alexie Vispedov down here to fly the plane out a day earlier. Make sure that she is available or else you will be hearing from me," Macateer snarled.

Back at the Orchy Hotel

Frank and Tom emerged from the dining room and made for Frank's room. Alyona Aslanov, alias Diane MacIntosh, walked past, staring at both agents as she made her way towards the bar. "She is checking us out, mate. We'd better keep an eye on her."

"Yep, you are spot on with that assumption. It may be time for her to take a swim down the river," Frank said as they entered his room.

"Agent Sommerville! Now is the time to collate the information we have at our disposal," Frank said, taking a pen and notebook from his bedside cabinet.

"Oh, someone has been snooping around in here," Frank said. "I stuck a hair from my head across the joint of the drawer, and it's no longer there. That means someone has looked inside this cabinet." He walked over to check the wardrobe. Frank confirmed his suspicion when he noticed that the hair was gone from there too. Both agents checked the room for possible bugging. They were relieved not to find anything, but they decided to go to the shower room to collate the information. Turning the water on to drown out the sound of their voices, Mulholland then gave the pen and notebook to Tom and asked him to take notes.

"Put these names under a heading of Cononish Gold Mine and the Orchy Hotel respectively," Frank said. Mulholland began firing information at Tom, his tongue going ten to the dozen as Tom frantically scribbled.

"Slow down, Frank. I'm not writing in shorthand, mate," said Agent Sommerville, wiping the sweat from his forehead.

Cononish Gold Mine

Denis Wadsworth – Irish gunrunner
Sean Macateer – Irish gunrunner
Stanislav Balsunov – chemical expert
Veronika Bogrov – chemical expert
Alexei Smirnoff (alias Sharon Gallacher) – chemical expert
Vladimir Bazarov – mechanical engineer
Georgie Watson Harkin Burke – aerodynamic technical development engineer.

Orchy Hotel
Alyona Aslanov (alias Diane MacIntosh) – nuclear and chemical weapons expert – unknown location
Dmitry Baranovsky–– explosive expert, mini sub man, and pilot. (Came in undercover from a submarine but had not been seen since. It was highly probable that he was somewhere inside the mine.)

These are the known people that we have to deal with tomorrow night, mate," Frank said, looking at his watch. "OK, Tom. Bring the list with you, and we'll head down to Inveroran." He turned the shower off.

The agents exited the room and made their way to the car. As they stepped out into the car park, Frank gave Inspector Hugh Smith of the Crianlarich police a call, asking for Constable Anderson and Sergeant Murdoch to be made available to him tomorrow night. "Could you please ask Constable Anderson to arrive at the Orchy Hotel by six o'clock prompt with the helicopter?" Frank asked.

"OK, Frank. But it's just as well you didn't require them today. They have gone to see the Scottish Cup semi-final between St. Mirren and Glasgow Celtic, which is being played at Ibrox Park in Glasgow. Anyway, mum's the word about tomorrow night – and the best of luck," said Inspector Smith.

Agent Sommerville brought the car engine to life, saying, "Inveroran Inn, here we come!"

The briefing at Inveroran

On the way down to the inn, the agents noticed a few flakes of snow falling onto the car windscreen. "Christ! I hope it doesn't snow during the night, tonight of all nights. We are going to have a busy day ahead of us tomorrow," Frank said, prewarning Tom.

As they pulled into the Inveroran Inn, Big John Aitken was coming to meet them, and he was looking a little worried.

"What's up, big man?" Frank asked.

"We hud a couple o' Russki visitors doon at Forest Lodge, and the twa Brians took them oot. They dumped the bodies doon intae the secret passage. We hiv a couple o' boxes of ammo and machine guns, an' some explosives, that we hiv hidden in the wids across frae the hotel," said JBA. "Whit a cannae understand is that we searched the hoose oan the day we took the Russki agents oot, and we transferred aw the weapons intae the army trucks tae be ta'en awa' the next day, an' ah kin assure ye that the hoose wis emptied. We hiv been monitorin' it aw the time since."

"Maybe they have a secret panel or a hidden stash down in the basement somewhere," Frank said as they entered the inn. Frank asked Agent Aitken if he had checked the conference room for bugs.

"Aye! It's aw as clear as a bell, mate," replied JBA.

Behind the bar, Peter MacInnes was rubbing his hands together and grinning. He called out to Frank, "Will I bring *all* of your lads a drink to the room, Frankie boy?" Frank nodded his head in agreement at the request.

Almost immediately after Frank entered the room, he walked to the drawing board and began to scribble the names on the list he and Tom had prepared back at the Orchy Hotel. A little later, there was a knock at the door and Big John Aitken eased it open.

As he took the tray of drinks from Peter, Frank Mulholland joked, "Are these drinks on the house, Mr. MacInnes?"

Peter walked away mumbling to himself as Big John dished out the beers to the agents. Frank completed the list of names on the board and then took a sip of his beer.

"Gentlemen, I want you to look at these names closely. They are all dangerous characters, and we are going to take them all out tomorrow night," Frank said.

He pointed to the top two names on the list: Denis Wadsworth and Sean Macateer. He informed the agents that they were gunrunners for the IRA and that they must be taken out at all cost.

He then pointed to the next three names on the list: Stanislav Balsunov, Veronica Bogrov, and Alexei Smirnoff – alias Sharon Gallacher. "These three are chemical experts and shall be treated as dangerous people. So do not hesitate to take them out if the occasion occurs."

Frank then pointed to the big giant's name, Vladimir Bazarov, and told them that he was a mechanical engineer. "He is fully trained in warfare, as he served for years in the Russian army. He's a dab hand with explosives." He emphasized this by tapping the board.

"The last name on the list is Dimitry Baranovsky, and we have to eliminate him. He is a great danger to our mission and to our nuclear submarines down at Coulport and Faslane bases. He is fully trained on the use of explosives and mini subs and is an experienced pilot who has flown MIG fighter planes. Frank placed a photo of each person on the board next to his or her name and asked those gathered to familiarise themselves with the identity of each person before leaving the room that night.

Agent McDonald's eyebrows dipped. He was studying the photo of the last name on the list closely. He said, "You wul nae hae tae worry aboot Baranovsky. He wis wan o' the men that we took oot an hour ago at Forest Lodge. He is noo resting doon in the underground passage that leads intae the lodge."

"Well spotted, mate. And well done to the two Brians down at the lodge earlier," said Mulholland, acknowledging their efforts.

Frank drew a rough sketch of the hill called Sron Nan Colan, with the entrance to the gold mine highlighted at the Cononish end of the hill and the entrance to the lead mine highlighted at the opposite end, near Tyndrum. He informed the agents that the distance between both entrances was approximately two miles. "There is a possibility that both entrances are linked by an underground passage or tunnel. Although we are not sure of this, it may give anyone inside the mine an escape route in the opposite direction when we strike at Eas Anie, which is the Cononish end." The other agents were nodding in agreement with what he had just said.

Agent MacNeill asked, "Is it possible tae hiv the Tyndrum end covered by a couple of agents, to pick aff oanyone who may emerge frae that end o' the tunnel?"

Frank informed them that he had plans for that end of the possible escape route. "We will discuss this tomorrow night, prior to the mission." Frank pointed to the hill with his pen and stressed that these points were ventilation shafts to let out any gases or fumes that were created by the chemical processes they were working on inside the mine.

"Chemicals! Are we gonnae hiv tae wear oxygen masks oan this mission?" George Hardie asked.

"I don't think so, mate. But we will have them with us, just in case," said Frank.

Frank Mulholland sensed that the men were worried about this and changed the subject quickly by pointing to the entrance of the gold mine. "As you will notice, I have marked two circles just up from the entrance to the mine. These are approximately fifty and eighty yards, respectively, from the entrance. This is where two special aeroplanes are positioned inside the mine. Across from the second plane is a glass room which holds the chemical tank." He again pointed with his pen to confirm the location to the men.

"What kind of special aeroplanes are we talking about, Frank?" Brian McDonald inquired.

Frank informed them that the planes could lift off vertically, and that is why there was a roof above each plane. These swung open to allow the planes to lift upwards and exit from the top of the hill. "That is where you come in, mate," said Mulholland, looking at Agent McDonald. "I will come to that when we talk about the procedure in a little while," Frank said, looking around the men to make sure they were taking in every piece of information available to them.

"Inside the mine will probably be the agents that I discussed at the start of the briefing and possibly quite a few more because they are evacuating the mine. They will be taking with them as much ammunition and weapons as they can carry – and of course the two vertical lifting planes.

I have received information, by a guaranteed source, that they plan to take the planes out by midnight. Gentlemen, we can't allow this to happen," Frank said in a determined voice.

Big John Aitken stood up and pointed to the name of Georgie Watson Harkin Burke and Alyona Aslanov.

"Ye havnae' mentioned them twa, Frank," said JBA.

"Aslanov was working at the Orchy Hotel and was probably keeping an eye on Agent Sommerville and me. Due to the evacuation, she may well be inside the mine tomorrow night," Frank said.

"Aye! But whit aboot her," said JBA pointing to the name of Georgie Watson Harkin Burke. He was looking at Mulholland sternly and waiting on some kind of answer.

Frank swallowed hard, then looked over at Agent Sommerville and said, "She is the person who informed me about the planes inside the mine. She told me that the Russians were funding the manufacture of the planes. They were assembling them inside the mine and testing them around this area. According to her, she was being forced to do this under protest," Frank said.

"Why has she given you this information now, Frank?" Agent Sommerville asked.

Frank told them that her relationship with the Russians had mellowed ever since they told her both planes were going to be flown to Russia by Russian pilots. "We can't allow this to happen, my friends," Frank said, thumping his fist on the table and looking sternly at the agents. Frank asked them not to take her out, for she had a lot of technical knowledge which would allow her to build more of these planes, if and when required, should anything happen to the planes inside the mine at this moment in time.

"Whit is sae special aboot these planes, onywae? Surely if she has been involved wae the Russkis, then we hiv tae treat her nae differently, as we will never ken when she wid defect tae Russia in the future," Aitken said, pushing the point.

Frank explained the features of the planes with their solar power. "The fact that they would be almost undetectable could be a threat to our future security," Mulholland said.

The agents were all looking at each other a little confused at what they had heard. "Whit is this solar power ye ar' talkin' aboot, Frank?" asked Agent MacNeill

"Gentlemen, solar power means that the engines are powered by the sun's rays, which energise the solar panels that are around the plane's fuselage and give the plane the power to drive its engines, or something like that," Frank said, a little embarrassed that he was not up to the terminology required to explain it properly.

"Dae ye mean that these planes dinnae need oany fuel tae be able tae fly?" Aitken asked.

"Exactly," replied Frank, looking around at the surprise on the faces of all the men.

"Well, at least we dinnae hiv tae worry aboot a fuel depot blawin' up when we go in," Agent Wilson said, smiling at everyone.

"You are correct there, mate. But we have a chemical tank that we would have to contend with," said Frank, reminding the guys that it could be a possible problem that they didn't really want.

Suddenly, Frank's pager bleeped and he dipped his hand into his pocket. "It's Merriday," he told everyone. The room became silent as Frank listened in. "Yes, sir! Over and out," Frank said, a worried look on his face. "That was Merriday informing me that six Russian agents have come in off a submarine down at Corran in Loch Linnhe. According to Agents Kerr and Balmer, they are on a truck which is heading in this direction. It looks as though they are strengthening their forces for the evacuation tomorrow night.'

Frank asked Agent McDonald how much time he would require to set explosives down inside at least six of the ventilation shafts when they were roughly thirty yards apart and approximately thirty feet deep. "I want you to blow the roof of the mine so that it closes a possible escape route through the mountain and towards the Tyndrum lead mine."

"Ah dinnae think ther' wid be a problem, but ah wid be able tae tell ye better if ah could check it oot before we went in," Agent McDonald said, swallowing hard.

"Can you give me a rough time of how long it would take?" Frank Mulholland asked.

"Possibly twenty meenutes fur each vent," McDonald said, a little worried that he may be wrong.

"Don't worry too much about it. I only need an estimate because you will be in the first drop-off.

You will have to be there roughly an hour ahead of the final drop-off in order to position your explosives. They may have extra bodies on guard now that there are more arriving in a truck." He was worried.

"It disnae' matter how many o' them ther' ar 'cause, we ar' the A-Team aroond here," JBA said with a smile, trying to build up confidence in the men.

The lads all cheered at Big John's comment, letting him know that they were behind him. Frank smiled at the reaction of the agents, and then he said, "Gentlemen, this is the procedure for tomorrow, the first of April. At around midday, a delivery will arrive from Coulport Ammunition Depot for the attention of Agent Aitken and his team. Inside the delivery will be snowsuits and white hats for each of you, which must be worn to blend in with the snow on the ground. The delivery will also have oxygen masks, ammunition, and automatic rifles. Explosives and timers, for Brian McDonald, and a couple of new toys for the attention of Agent Aitken to try to bring down the aeroplanes, should they try to vacate the mine."

Frank continued. "At eighteen hundred hours, we will all meet here at the inn and have a quick run over of the procedure while we await darkness, which should be around nineteen forty-five hours. Thereafter, the first drop-off will take place. That will be me, Agent McDonald, and Agent Sommerville.

The second delivery will be Agent Wilson, Agent MacNeill, Agent Aitken, and Agent Hardie. "Gentlemen, I must remind you to have your communication bleepers and your night goggles with you. It will be pitch dark when we are up on the mountain, and this will be our only means of communication." Mulholland walked to the drawing board and wrote the following:

1. Agent McDonald wires the ventilation shafts and the entrance door to the mine. Mulholland assists.
2. Agent Sommerville gives cover to McDonald and Mulholland.
3. Agents Wilson and MacNeill cover the entrance, ready to enter the mine after the door is blown.
4. Agents Aitken and Hardie to cover escape hatches of the aeroplanes and to bring down the planes.
5. Murdoch and Anderson to cover entrance to Clayton lead mine at Tyndrum.

Frank informed the team that Agent McDonald would be setting the explosives with a timer and they would be set to go off one minute apart. "Obviously, when the first shaft blows, this will alert everyone inside the mine, so be prepared for some action. When the first explosion occurs, they will probably try to evacuate the aeroplanes to safeguard them. If that happens, then Big John will bring them down," said Frank, smiling at the big man.

"And whit hiv ah tae bring them doon wae? A pea shooter?" Big John jokingly asked.

All the agents joined him in laughter. Frank told Big John that he would be receiving delivery of some rocket launchers tomorrow. "Just in case the pea shooters are not capable of doing the job," Mulholland said with a grin.

There was a huge burst of laughter at Big John's expense. The big man had a look around at the agents and noticed that George Hardie was laughing louder than the other guys.

This clearly annoyed Aitken, and he fired off some expletives at Hardie. "You better mak' sure ye back me up weel the morra, or a micht forget whit wae tae point ma gun," Aitken said, looking rather sternly at Agent Hardie.

Frank stepped in quickly to calm the situation before it got out of hand. "We are an excellent team, one of the best, so try to make sure we keep it that way," Frank said, giving Aitken a look that could have turned him to stone.

"Aw richt, mate. Ah'm sorry fur this disruption," said Aitken, nodding his apology to Frank and Hardie. Frank accepted the apology but was concerned that there was still a bit of agro between the two agents, especially since they would be working together the following night.

Trying to get the men to concentrate on the mission, he pointed at the board. "As the first vent blows, Agent McDonald will have set the timers for the explosives at the entrance to go off almost instantaneously. This should cause our Russki and Irish friends inside some confusion.

Is that not correct, Mr. McDonald?" said Frank, looking at the agent for some kind of acknowledgement.

Brian McDonald nodded his head in agreement with what Frank Mulholland had said.

Frank continued by saying, "At this point, Agents Wilson, MacNeill, and myself will enter the mine and take out as many of the enemy as we possibly can, without damaging the aeroplanes and the chemical tank, I must stress."

"Wull, the planes no' be damaged wae the roof explodin' and cavin' in?" Agent Wilson asked.

"I hope not, mate, because we will not be blowing the four ventilation shafts that are close to the planes," replied Frank, trying to ease the doubts of the agents. He pointed out to the men that the main objective of blowing the air shafts was to cut off an escape route through the mountain. "Just in case any of those buggers do escape, I am positioning Sergeant Murdoch and Constable Anderson at the other entrance to the mine at Tyndrum."

"Will twa civilians be able tae handle whit they may be faced wae doon ther'?" Hardie asked.

Frank answered quickly to quash any doubts. "If you had seen what those two men did during our mission last Tuesday up on Beinn Achaladair, then believe me, you wouldn't question their ability to function under pressure," Frank said. To further ease the team's minds, he informed the men that he would be in touch with both policemen during the mission.

"Agent Sommerville will cover the front entrance after we go in – mainly to make sure that no one escaped through there during the action," said Mulholland, looking at Tom.

"Just remember not to shoot up the aeroplanes or the chemical tank, especially as we will be inside the mine at this point," said Frank.

"No problem, mate. You don't have to worry about that," Agent Sommerville said, nodding at his buddy.

With his eyes focused on Agents Aitken and Hardie, Frank said, "If the roof of the mine opened up, then you would have to take out the planes with a rocket launcher before it finished its vertical climb. Because if it takes off, gents, then you won't be able to see it, never mind hit it, as its design and speed of movement renders it invisible to the naked eye. If you are sidetracked by any kind of trouble, then be aware of the possibility of the planes leaving the mine. He emphasized to both agents the importance of stopping the planes from leaving. Both agents convinced him that they got the message.

Gentlemen, I want you to study and memorise these procedures because they will have to be strictly adhered to," Mulholland said. He looked at his watch and was surprised to see that it was 10.15 p.m. He pointed to his watch, letting Agent Sommerville know that they should have left by now. He reminded the team that they would meet here at 18:00 hours tomorrow before wiping the board clean.

"Jist wan mair question afore we go, Frank. Where is the Iceman – and how is he not in on the briefing alang wae us?" Big JBA asked.

Frank's bleeper bleeped, and he raised his hand, asking the men to be quiet as he listened. "OK, John. Over and out," Frank said. "The Iceman has just answered your question, mate. That was him informing me that the truck that Merriday mentioned earlier just arrived at the mine with six agents on board. Agent Kane is going to be an effective part of the team tomorrow in the lead-up to our mission – and probably even more so when the action begins. I have already briefed the Iceman on his procedure for tomorrow night," added Frank Mulholland, easing the men out of the room.

Frank and Tom made for the exit as the team gathered around the bar to order drinks. As he and Tom stepped out into the cold night air, with JBA following closely behind, Frank reminded the men to keep a clear head for tomorrow.

"Here, Frank, dinnae forget this," said JBA, handing Frank the crossbow that was found earlier.

"I'll pass this on to Inspector Hugh Smith at Crianlarich," Frank said.

"Geez! It's bloody freezing, mate," Frank said. Making their way to the car for the drive back to Orchy Hotel, both agents blew into their hands to help keep them warm, watching their hot breath disperse into the night air.

"Well, the clocks went forward an hour last Sunday, but it doesn't feel like summertime. Maybe things will heat up tomorrow night," Tom said, laughing as they stepped into the car.

"Orchy Hotel, here we come!" said both agents, smiling as the car pulled away into the darkness for the short drive back to Orchy.

On the drive back, Tom was discussing the giant Russian. "I hope they are not all that size. They must feed them well over in Russia, because the jolly giant looks like a cross between a sumo wrestler and an American footballer," Sommerville said with a hearty laugh.

"You must be joking, mate. When I was over there on some surveillance work, I noticed that the peasant field workers were skin and bone. In fact, they fed their animals better," said Mulholland.

Back at the Orchy Hotel

A muffled sound of music greeted the agents as they approached the hotel. Both men smiled as they stepped into the barroom. The three amigos were sitting in their usual places, and they signalled to the agents to come over. Chappie called on Tam Cameron to bring over two beers fur the agents. Frank's eyes scanned the bar area, and he noticed that all the girls were working, with the exception of Diane MacIntosh. He informed Tom that she was the only girl who was missing.

As the agents settled down beside the three amigos, Frank was tapping his fingers on the table to the beat of the music. "What's the name of the band playing?" Mulholland asked.

"They ar' a new band called The Crusaders, an' they ar' no bad at aw," Davy Blackwood said.

Brian Greene reiterated what Davy had just said. "They hiv been playin' some guid stuff the nicht," Brian said, his thumb in the air.

Tam arrived with the agents' beers, and asked, "Whit dae ye think o' the band, lads?" The three amigos all gave him the thumbs up. This brought a smile to Tam's face. He made his way back to the bar, picking up some empty glasses on the way.

"What kind of dance are the people on the floor doing?" Mulholland asked.

"It's the latest dance, an' its jist come oot. It's caud the Mashed Potato," answered Chappie.

A few beers and a few Mashed Potatoes later, the band finished playing. Frank Mulholland had stepped outside, checking out Tommy's helicopter and making sure it had not been tampered with. On close inspection, everything seemed to be OK, and Frank breathed a sigh of relief. *I'll have to check it out again in the morning,* thought Mulholland, walking back to the hotel.

On entering the hotel, Frank noticed that barmaid Janice Irvine was clearing up the glasses from some of the tables. He walked over to speak to her. "Excuse me, Janice. Can I have a quiet word with you when you're free from your duties?" Frank asked.

"No problem! Give me five minutes and I'm all yours," replied Janice, slightly blushing at what she had just said. But secretly she was also a little excited at the prospect of being alone with the agent. She had had a crush on him since the first day they met, when he pinned her down on the bed in his room.

Frank asked her if she could come down to his room and he would be waiting for her. He quickly made his way to the room. About five minutes later, there was a knock on the door of his room and in walked Janice.

"Yes, Frank. What can I do for you?" she asked, sitting beside the agent on the edge of the bed.

Frank looked straight into her pale blue eyes. "What I'm about to ask you must be kept strictly between me and you," Frank said, smiling at her but emphasizing that what they discussed should go no further.

Janice nodded her head in agreement and cleared a small lump in her throat as she anticipated what he was about to ask her. "Are you going to ask me something about my roommate?" Janice asked.

Frank looked into her eyes again. He was surprised that she was aware that that was exactly what he was about to question her about. "Yes, Diane MacIntosh," Frank said. He asked her why she was thinking that way about her friend.

Janice's blue eyes widened, and she stared at Frank. Her lips twitched and then she spoke, adamantly stating, "She's no friend of mine. I wouldn't trust her as far as I could throw her. And I can assure you, Frank, that that wouldn't be very far." Janice's voice was agitated and determined.

"What gives you that impression of her?" Frank asked, gently touching her hand.

"Did you get the note that I slipped under your door, informing you of a problem down in the Cononish Glen?" Janice asked.

"It was you who wrote the note informing me to watch my back?" Frank asked, dipping his eyebrows in surprise.

"Yes. I overheard her talking to someone just the other night, and I knew they were up to no good. I didn't want to get involved in any shenanigans that were going on, but I knew something wasn't right." Janice paused and looked into Frank's eyes before continuing. "Just last night, about three o'clock in the morning, she slipped out of the bunkhouse and made her way into the hallway of the hotel. My curiosity got the better of me, so I sneaked over to the hotel and overheard her talking to someone in a foreign language. Unfortunately, I couldn't understand what she was saying, but I heard the Cononish Glen Gold Mine being mentioned."

"Was she talking to someone who was staying in the hotel?" Frank asked.

"Yes, Frank," Janice said nervously. "She was talking to the woman who is in room number twelve, but I'm not sure of her name. If you check the register, you will soon find that out."

Frank leaned over and softly kissed her lips, thanking her for the warning and this information. In almost no time at all, they were kissing passionately, and they lay back onto the bed. Frank's hands were manipulating every part of her curvaceous body, and the excitement was building between them. The extreme passion Janice was feeling inside her body was reaching a crescendo as Frank's hand slipped onto her thigh.

Suddenly, there was a knock at the door and they both sat upright, just in time to see the door opening and Carol McBride looking a bit bemused at the sight of them sitting on the bed.

"What the hell is going on here?" Carol asked, raising her voice and staring at both of them.

Frank put his finger to his lips, asking her to be quiet. He decided to put his trust in both girls and offer an explanation.

"If you give me a minute, then I will explain why I have brought Janice to my room," Frank said, desperately trying to calm Carol down.

Carol sat down on the bed beside Janice as Frank walked around to face them. He was trying to think how to explain his way out of trouble.

He spoke quietly and placed his finger to his lips, then opened the door to check that there was nobody outside listening in on them.

"Ladies, I am going to have to put my trust in both of you. What I am about to tell you should go no further. If it does, then I will have to kill both of you," Frank said sternly.

The girls were staring at each other in confusion. Frank repeated what he had just said to confirm to both girls that he meant it, telling them that it was a matter of national security. Both girls agreed that they would not mention anything about this discussion again. Frank began by saying, "I have found out that Diane is a Russian agent. She is involved with the KGB. Her real name is Alyona Aslanov, and she is a very dangerous character. Believe me, she would have you killed off without a second thought." He looked into each girl's eyes and reassured them of what he had just said.

"Oh my God! And I've been sharing a room with her," said a rather worried-looking Janice Irvine.

"You may not have to worry about her for much longer, for I have a feeling that she won't be seen again in the hotel," Frank said, trying to ease the girls' minds. "If she does spend another night here, then you'll have to pretend that nothing happened. The same may be said of the woman in room number twelve until I can investigate her."

Frank looked at his watch and told both girls that it was ten minutes past midnight. Just then, there was a knock on the door. As the door opened, Agent Sommerville's face came into view. "Geez! Is one woman not enough for you, Frank? Do you have to have two on your bed at the same time?" Tom grinned at the girls.

Both girls laughed at the funny side of the situation as they stood up.

Making for the exit, they told Frank that he would have to improve his performance or they wouldn't be back again. They walked down the hallway, giggling at his expense.

Tom closed the door behind them and asked Frank what was going on that he had both girls in his room.

"We have a problem, mate. I've just been told that Alyona Aslanov was talking to Moira Malone in her room at three o'clock this morning," Frank said.

Agent Sommerville's eyes lifted, and he stared at Frank. "That can't be possible. I just left Brian Greene five minutes ago, and he told me that Moira Malone stayed at his house in Tyndrum last night," Tom said, a confused look in his brown eyes.

Frank rang the bar phone and asked Carol McBride to come back to his room immediately. Two minutes later, the room door opened and Carol entered. She was surprised that Agent Sommerville was still there.

"Yes, Frank. What can I do for you?" asked Carol, a suggestive tone in her voice.

Frank smiled at her. "Wait until Tom leaves, honey. For the time being, it is purely business that I want to discuss," Frank said, showing concern. Frank asked Carol if room number twelve had had an occupier the previous night. At that point, Carol's face paled and she asked him why.

"We have found out that Moira Malone was not in her room last night. We were wondering if it had been let out to someone else."

A slightly nervous Carol became hesitant and spluttered out, "I was only helping one of the girls out for two nights. Her friend could not afford to pay for bed and breakfast," Carol said.

"Who is this friend of yours?" Frank asked, a little annoyed that she had done this.

Carol placed her hands to her face and began crying. She asked Frank not to let Tam Cameron know about this or she would be sacked on the spot.

"Who is this friend of yours?" Frank asked sternly, emphasizing how serious this situation could be.

"It's not my friend, Frank. She's Diane MacIntosh's friend," Carol said. "Yesterday Diane overheard Moira Malone telling me that she wouldn't be down for breakfast this morning, as she was staying in Tyndrum overnight. That was when she asked me if her friend Alexei could use the room. Obviously, we are not allowed to do that kind of thing, so please don't tell the management."

"What is this Alexei's surname?" Mulholland asked.

"I don't know," replied Carol, brushing away tears with the back of her hand. Frank stepped forward and put his arms around Carol's waist. As she looked up at him through tear-filled eyes, Frank kissed her forehead and then wiped the tears from her cheeks.

"Don't mention this to anyone, honey, and we won't say a thing. But we will have to try to repair the damage that may have been done because of this situation." Frank walked Carol to the door. On her way out, Carol asked if she could come back to his room when she had finished her chores. Frank winked and nodded yes to her request. He blew her a kiss as she made her way down the hall.

No sooner had the door closed than Frank mentioned to Agent Sommerville, "Could this Alexei be the Alexei Vispedov that Merriday spoke to me about on Friday?" he asked with great concern.

"What's so special about this girl that it concerns you?" Tom asked.

"Sir Jeffrey Merriday told me that she was a pilot – and a very capable one at that. She flew with the Russian Air Force on many sorties. She would be more than capable of flying one of these special planes that are down at the mine," Frank said.

There was a sudden knock on the door, and Frank opened it to be faced with Carol and Emma, who were each holding a cup of coffee and wearing a smile. Carol entered Frank's room and told Tom that Emma was going to his room. Emma wiggled her finger, inviting Tom to follow her to room number eight. He followed quickly. "I better hurry in case my coffee gets cold," Tom said with a grin at his buddy.

Frank sat down beside Carol and stared into her eyes. They fell into each other's arms and kissed passionately, removing each other's clothing and slipping beneath the sheets. Their naked bodies were grinding together in the heat of the moment as both of them reached fever pitch. Carol purred with delight as Frank collapsed by her side and reached out for his coffee.

She smiled, realising that he had grabbed his cup to drink the coffee before it got cold. "You are a fox, ya beggar," Carol said, cuddling against his muscular body.

After making love again, they both fell into a deep sleep. Five hours later, the alarm clock began ringing, and Carol leaned over Frank to switch it off.

"Is that six o'clock already?" Frank groggily asked.

"I'm afraid so, darling," replied Carol. Her naked body leapt from the bed and made for the shower room. Frank immediately reset the alarm for eight o'clock and closed his eyes, falling into a deep sleep.

Sunday, 1 April

All Fools' Day

The alarm began ringing again, and a shattered Frank Mulholland leaned over to switch it off. Through bleary and slightly bloodshot eyes, he was checking that the time was 8 a.m. Frank lay in deep thought and considered his itinerary for the day ahead. He was trying to get everything into some sort of perspective while he had some time to himself to think. Fifteen minutes later, he jumped out of bed and made for the shower room, his mind a little clearer as to his procedure for the day ahead.

After his shower, the agent was dressing when he heard a noise out in the hallway, and he eased the door open slightly. Peeking out, he was faced with Brian Greene and Moira Malone leaving room number twelve. He quickly closed the door. With some relief, he thought, *At least Alexei Vispedov wasn't in that room; she's probably down at the Cononish Gold Mine.*

Mulholland lifted his room phone and asked the receptionist to put him through to Sergeant Murdoch at Tyndrum Police Station. "Let him know that it is Frank Mulholland," Frank said. Frank was tapping his fingers on the bedside table rather impatiently, waiting on a reply.

"Hello, Frank. How kin ah help ye?" Murdoch enquired.

Frank reminded him about the meeting at 6 p.m. down at the Inveroran Inn.

"Whit meetin' is this?" Murdoch asked. Frank instantly began reminding him, but Murdoch laughed aloud and said, "Ah'm ony windin' ye up, Frankie boy. Ah ken aw aboot the meetin the nicht," he said.

"Thank goodness for that, Sergeant. I thought I'd remind you in case, at your age, you may have forgotten all about it," Frank said with a grin.

Sergeant Murdoch also laughed and then said, "Frank, dae ye ken this. Ah've noticed that the aulder ah get, the mair proficient ahv'e become at forgettin' things."

Frank Mulholland laughed heartily at the comment and then changed the subject quickly by asking how the football match had turned out yesterday.

"Brilliant! The Saints beat the Celtic three to one, an' it wis a super game. We ar' noo in the final, alang wi' the Glasgow Rangers, et Hampden Park," Murdoch said, shouting, "C'mon, Saints!" Then a moment later, he said, "Ah'll hae tae go Frank because something has jist cropped up." He then ended the call. Frank lifted his bleeper and called Big John Aitken down at Inveroran, reminding him of his delivery, which would arrive at midday.

"Nae problem, Frank. Everythin' is in haund, an' ah'll see ye the nicht et eighteen hundred hours," Big John said. Suddenly, there was a knock on his door, and in walked Carol.

"I'm just making sure that you are up and about and coming down for breakfast, darling."

When Carol left the room, Frank walked over and thumped his fist on the adjoining wall to Agent Sommerville's room. A minute later, Tom appeared, asking, "What's the problem, mate?"

"Are you ready to go down for breakfast? We have a busy day ahead of us," Frank said, easing him out of the room. As they made for the dining room, Frank discussed the plan for the day ahead.

Cononish Glen farmhouse

Georgie Watson Burke was making her way into the kitchen when she noticed two people coming towards her house. It was her uncle Denis Wadsworth and IRA leader Sean Macateer struggling through the deep snow in her garden. As she lifted the kettle to make some tea for her impending guests, she was wondering what was about to happen. She was thinking back to the beating Macateer handed out to her yesterday. The men entered the house, Denis leading the way. He walked over to Georgie. As he kissed her cheek, she peeked over his shoulder at the figure of Sean Macateer, who was pointing his hand towards her, replicating a gun. He pulled his finger as if pulling the trigger. Georgie knew that Macateer was not the kind of person to fall out with, as he would kill her without a second thought. This scared her immensely, and she swallowed hard.

"Would you like some tea?" Georgie nervously asked, trying not to make eye contact with Macateer again.

Denis turned and faced Macateer, then quickly said, "Two teas, honey! Can we use your helicopter to fly down to your dad's house at Forest Lodge?"

Georgie frowned, wondering why they wanted to go down there again. "Surely you have cleared everything out of the house by now?" Georgie asked, questioning their reasons for requiring the helicopter.

"We have two dead agents down in the underground passage. We have to dispose of their bodies as soon as possible," Wadsworth said, as Macateer looked at her distrustfully.

"Who are the dead agents?" Georgie asked.

Macateer butted in. "Mind yer own business," he said abruptly. He stared at Denis Wadsworth, but at the same time, he was letting Georgie know that she was no longer trusted.

After drinking their tea, both gunrunners made for the helicopter and took off, heading for Forest Lodge.

Georgie Watson Harkin Burke watched with relief, glad to see the backs of them.

Back at the Orchy Hotel

The phone was ringing at the Orchy Hotel bar, and Carol McBride answered the call. "Good morning! This is the Orchy Hotel, and you are speaking to Carol. How may I help you?"

The voice at the other end of the line belonged to her friend Georgie Watson Harkin Burke. "Hi, Carol! Georgie speaking. Could you ask Frank Mulholland to call me as soon as possible? I have some very important information for him."

Carol was still jealous that Frank was having contact with her, and she asked, "Is there something going on between you and my fella, Georgie? If there is, then you and I will be falling out and I will be coming to see you, even if it means a four-mile walk to your house," Carol added, emphasizing her intent to have it out with her.

Georgie instantly tried to ease her mind. "It's purely business, Carol. And it could maybe save his life."

On hearing this, Carol told her that she would pass on her number to him. She hung up the phone and made for the dining room, some doubt churning around in her head.

Suddenly, a piece of paper was thrown onto the table in front of Agent Mulholland. He quickly looked up to see Carol glaring at him. "You're to phone her right away, Frankie boy. And, there better be now't going on with you and her," Carol said, determined to let him know where they stood.

Frank didn't have to ask whose number it was. Based on Carol's reaction, he already knew. "Thank you, honey," he said rather sheepishly, picking up the paper from the table and looking at the number.

Removing the bleeper from his inside pocket, he punched the required digits and listened to the ringing sound.

Georgie was hovering by the phone, and she quickly picked it up. To her relief, she realised that it was Mulholland. "I have some information for you, Frank. I may be able to help you," answered Georgie in an excited tone of voice.

"What can you tell me, sweetheart?" Frank said.

"My uncle Denis and that rat Macateer are on their way down to my dad's house at Forest Lodge in my helicopter. They said that there were a couple of dead bodies down at the lodge that they have to dispose of. Earlier I overheard Sharon Gallacher and Sean Macateer saying that one of the bodies was Russian pilot Dimitry Baranovsky. If that's the case, then they may be a pilot short for the evacuation of my planes tonight."

Frank listened intently, the gears grinding inside his head.

"Have you got some kind of idea in that lovely head of yours?" Frank asked, wondering what she was going to come up with.

"I was thinking that if I offer to fly one of the planes to Russia, then I would be in the position to escape. I could then transport the plane to a Scottish RAF Base such as Lossiemouth or Leuchers. This may be a way of saving at least one of my planes," Georgie said excitedly.

Frank asked Georgie who the other pilot was and warned her to be careful that she didn't fall foul of any of the people inside the mine.

"The other pilot is Russian, and her name is Alexei Vispedov," replied Georgie. "She's a very good pilot. She has flown MiG-21 fighter planes."

Frank already knew this, but it confirmed to him that Georgie was telling the truth and probably was sincere about transporting the plane to a Scottish RAF Base. Frank was a little worried that she may try to escape with the plane when his team was about to take the gold mine. Her life could be in danger.

He thought for a few seconds then blurted out, "If you're taking one of the planes, then make it as early as possible – say, around half past eight, when it will be dark. Frank said this to try to give her a hint to get out as quickly as possible, without telling her about the MI6 mission tonight.

"I'll try to be as discreet as I possibly can be. In fact, my Uncle Denis and Sean Macateer are away at this minute. Maybe now is a good time to check things out," Georgie said, glancing out the window. To her horror, she noticed Sharon Gallacher coming down the hill towards the farmhouse from the mine. "Frank, I'll have to go. Devil woman's about to visit me."

Frank had told her that Sharon Gallacher's real name was Alexei Smirnoff and she was a Russian agent.

This information surprised Georgie. She had known her only as Sharon Gallacher from their university days together.

Sharon Gallacher entered by the kitchen door, and Georgie quickly asked her if she would like a cup of coffee. Gallacher stared at Georgie through cold blue eyes. The look told her that she was disappointed with her for being so stupid as to bring an MI6 agent into the area.

Georgie apologised profusely and burst into some fake tears. She was hoping that Gallacher would ease off and accept her back into the fold. Chancing her luck, she asked Gallacher if she could go up to the mine with her.

"Absolutely no chance of that happening. Sean Macateer would have my head on the block," Gallacher said, looking at Georgie strangely, as if wondering why she had asked that of her.

Georgie Watson Harkin Burke was disappointed but not surprised at this answer from Gallacher. Georgie knew that she was as scared of Macateer as she was.

Sharon Gallacher looked sternly at Georgie and told her that the only reason that she was there was because Macateer asked her to keep an eye on her.

Georgie was disappointed at hearing this. She had hoped that she could win her friend over and maybe use her to get inside the mine. The tone changed in Gallacher's voice, and she asked Georgie whom she was phoning before she entered the house.

"I was calling my friend Carol over at the Orchy Hotel, that's all," replied Georgie, trying not to sound suspicious. Gallacher seemed to accept this explanation, which was of great relief to Georgie.

After finishing her coffee, Sharon Gallacher said she was heading back up to the mine and warned her friend not to try to follow her. "Your life could be in danger because Sean Macateer warned all the others and told them about your escapade with the MI6 agent," Gallacher said.

Georgie watched as Gallacher trudged through the snow on her way back up to the mine, wishing she could make the same journey.

Alexei Smirnoff! That's a new one on me, thought Georgie, who now realised that her friend had been using her all along.

Down at Forest Lodge

A fter the helicopter landed, IRA agents Wadsworth and Macateer
made their way through the forest to the underground passage.
Lifting the flap, they descended beneath the ground. A few
minutes later, they appeared, dragging two dead bodies towards the
helicopter. Unknown to them, they were being watched by MI6 agent
Brian McDonald, who had been positioned in the forest to keep an
eye on anyone entering the lodge. Agent McDonald quickly contacted
Big John Aitken and gave him a rundown of the situation. "Baith
bodies seem tae hiv been wrapped up inside a blanket an' are definitely
weighted doon at the neck an' ankles," said Brian whispering.

"Whit direction ar' they headin tae wae the whirlyburd?" Big John
asked urgently.

"Ah'll be able tae tell ye in a meenit, as soon as they lift aff the
ground," said Brian, watching the helicopter as a hawk would eye a
mouse. John Aitken was waiting patiently for an answer so he could
inform Frank Mulholland.

After a few minutes, the silence was broken as agent McDonald
spoke. "Ther' heading fur Loch Etive. And ma guess is ther' gonnae
dump the bodies intae the loch."

"OK, Brian. Keep yer eyes peeled, in case ther ar' oany mair visitors
doon there. Ower an' oot," said JBA. He urgently began pressing in
Frank Mulholland's number.

Back at the Orchy Hotel

Frank was wondering how Georgie Burke was getting on at the farmhouse, but he was afraid to give her a call in case it landed her in more trouble with the people down at the mine. He heard his bleeper and saw that it was Big John Aitken.

"Hi, big man. What can I do for you?" Frank asked.

"Jist tae let ye ken that twa agents wer' doon at Forest Lodge, an' they took twa bodies awa' wi them. They wer' heading ower tae Loch Etive, possibly tae dump the bodies at the bottom o' the loch," Big John said.

"OK, JBA, I'm pleased to hear that information because it has confirmed what Georgie Watson Burke told me earlier. It probably means that she is on our side now," Mulholland said.

Big John was sceptical and replied by warning Frank that she may be putting him into a false sense of security. "Ye dinnae really ken her," warned JBA.

"Dinnae worry, mate! Ah think she may be of value tae us. An' yer delivery will be doon ther' aroond midday," Frank said in his best Scottish accent, which made Big John laugh.

Frank's breakfast was cooling down. Suddenly, a hand appeared and lifted a sausage from his plate.

It was agent Tom Sommerville's hand. "If you're not going to eat it, then I will, mate."

Frank slapped the back of his hand, but was too late, as the sausage was entering his laughing buddy's mouth. Mulholland glanced at the time on the clock in the dining room. It showed 10 a.m. He filled Tom in on the information regarding Georgie Watson Burke stealing and flying the plane to a Scottish RAF base.

151

"Can we trust her to do what she said?" Tom asked with a deep sigh.

"I hope so, mate. Because she is going to try for it earlier, at my request," Frank said, with a little puff of his cheeks.

"Geez, Frank. You're putting your reputation in her hands, and she may let you down with a bump," Tom said, sounding worried for his friend.

"I had to ask her to try for it earlier, as our team would bring the plane down if she took it out later."

"I couldn't tell her of our mission tonight," Frank said, an exasperated look on his face.

Frank was worried that something may happen to her or the mission.

Suddenly, barmaid Lorna McBride appeared, clearing away the empty plates. "Would you like a pot of tea to take to the barroom?" she asked.

"That would be fine ... and no sugar, sweetheart," Tom said, giving her the eye. Lorna smiled when Tom told her that she looked like Carol.

She suggestively replied as she walked away with a grin, "Maybe Frank will get us mixed up."

Frank was unsure as to whether that was an invitation. "I better watch what I'm doing, after what happened with Georgie Watson Harkin Burke. I don't want to put my foot in it with Carol again," Frank said.

They made their way to the barroom. They were about to sit down when in walked Sergeant Murdoch.

"Lorna, please make that a pot of tea for three," called Frank.

"Guid stuff, Frankie boy. Ah'm gaspin' fur a cuppa tae help me get ower ma celebrations last nicht," Murdoch said.

"Celebrations!" Tom remarked.

"Aye, mate! Yesterday St Mirren beat Glasgow Celtic by three to one in the Scottish Cup, an' it wis a richt guid fiery match," Murdoch said, looking as though he was still celebrating.

"I didn't know you were a St Mirren fan," Tom said.

"Och! Aye! Me an' Tommy Anderson hiv been goin' tae Love Street fur years noo," Murdoch said, smiling like a Cheshire cat. "Dae you twa lads support oany team?"

The agents looked at each other, saying that they supported their local team, Arsenal, down in London.

"Unfortunately, our job doesn't allow us to go to the games much now, which was just as well because we lost five to four to Aston Villa yesterday," Agent Sommerville said.

Frank changed the subject and reminded Murdoch to be at the Inveroran Inn with the helicopter at 6 p.m. on the dot. "Don't forget to bring Tommy Anderson with you," Frank said jokingly. He knew that Tommy was the pilot of the helicopter.

To a loud cheer, Lorna the barmaid arrived with the tea and biscuits. The plate had almost emptied before it reached the table. The lads were pulling her leg, so to speak, as she made her way over to the Robertson family, who were sitting over at the window.

"Give them all a drink and put it on my bill for room number seven!" shouted Mulholland. The Robertsons acknowledges his generosity with a wave of their hands.

"Crivvens! You ar' gonnae hae some bill by the time ye get awa' frae here," Murdoch said, laughing.

"Ach! Dinnae worry aboot it, mate. 'Cause we ar' chargin' it tae the Tyndrum polis," said Frank in his best Scottish lingo, grinning at the sergeant.

On hearing this, Murdoch nearly choked on his biscuit. "Aye, that'll be richt. Yer oan a loser ther'." Murdoch gulped his tea to clear his throat.

Frank decided to check out the helicopter and make sure everything was OK for tonight. The MI6 agents made for the exit to give the helicopter the once over.

They were happy that everything was OK and that nobody was paying special attention to them.

They noticed an army truck coming towards the hotel and quickly waved it down.

"Is this the way to Inveroran?" the driver asked.

Frank introduced himself and told them to go over the bridge and turn right and follow the road. "You can't miss it."

"What! Over that bridge," said the driver, pointing. "Is it not a bit on the narrow side?"

"Don't worry, mate. You'll get through. But don't damage it, because it's been here since seventeen fifty-one," said Agent Sommerville, showing off his knowledge of the area again.

Frank looked at his smiling buddy and shook his head. "Sommerville! You're a bit of a blowhard. But at least the delivery to the team is early."

Frank took out his bleeper and listened. "Thanks, mate. Over and out," Mulholland said. Tom was looking curiously at Frank. "That was Agent Kane informing me that two trucks have arrived at the gold mine this morning."

As the agents made for the warmth of the hotel, they met Sergeant Murdoch, who was leaving to make his way back to Tyndrum Police Station. As Frank began reminding him about 6 p.m. at Inveroran, Murdoch butted in.

"Ah ken, Frankie boy. Ma mind's no gaun' doolally yet." He made for his Land Rover, waving back to the agents and shouting that he would let Constable Anderson know. Tom grasped the door handle and jerked the door open, allowing both agents entry to the hotel just as barmaids Carol and Emma were leaving.

"Where are you two ladies off to?" Frank asked.

They replied in unison, "Fort William, here we come!"

On hearing this, Agent Sommerville burst into laughter and looked at his fellow agent.

Carol explained that they were supposed to meet their friend Georgie Burke at one o'clock down at Tyndrum, but she had informed them that she had other arrangements. "So we have decided to pay a visit to Fort William instead," Carol said, pointing at the bus coming towards them. They gave the guys a quick kiss and then stepped onto the bus. The agents were left gobsmacked as the bus pulled away, the girls waving cheerily back at them.

On hearing Carol's words, the agents were also concerned. "I wonder if that means that Georgie Watson Burke was going to try to escape in one of the planes during daylight hours," Frank said.

Agent Sommerville quickly grabbed the door handle again and pulled the door open, allowing both men entry. "Surely not, mate. It would be more difficult to enter the mine, as we well know, when we got too close for comfort just the other day," Tom said.

"Yes, I suppose you're right. Vladimir Bazarov will probably be keeping a close eye on her," Frank said.

A ringing sound was heard, and barmaid Lorna was scurrying behind the bar to lift the receiver before it rang off. "Yes, he is walking across the room at this very minute," Lorna said, handing Frank Mulholland the phone. Frank took the phone from her and listened intently, with Agent Sommerville wondering who was at the other end of the line.

After a few minutes, Frank said, "Be very careful, honey. These guys are mean characters, and they wouldn't hesitate to kill you. Thanks for the information. Give me a call at the hotel sometime tomorrow if all goes well."

Frank eased himself over to the fireside table, and both agents warmed their hands in front of the fire. Tom asked Frank what that was all about. Frank began by telling him that it was Georgie, saying that she told him two trucks had arrived at the mine that morning. "She also told me that she was dyeing her hair black to try to change her disguise in the hope that they will confuse her with the other pilot, Alexie Vispedov. Georgie will be wearing some of Sharon Gallacher's clothes, and it may give her time to get to one of the planes inside the mine," Frank said.

Tom looked at Frank with confusion. "How would she get the plane out when she would require the roof to be raised before lifting off?" Tom asked.

Frank looked at his buddy sternly, as if he didn't want to tell him something, and Tom picked up on this.

"What are you worried about, mate?" Tom asked.

Frank looked at him again and nervously blurted out his next words. "I couldn't let her try in daylight. I've told her what was happening tonight – that we are going to blow the main door of the mine at around ten. She may be able to enter the mine before or during the confusion and fly the plane out of the front entrance, if the roofs aren't raised."

"Jings! Crivvens!" Tom said, alarmed. "Mate, you're putting the whole mission in jeopardy by telling her that information – and our lives are at risk too."

"I feel that I can trust her. At least I hope so," Frank said, nodding his head and trying to convince his buddy that everything would be OK.

"You better not let the team down at Inveroran know about this or they will crack up," Tom said. This problem caused Agent Sommerville to have some doubt about the operation later tonight.

The clock is ticking

Frank looked at the time on the clock behind the bar and saw that it was 11:40 a.m. "This is going to be a bit of a drag today, mate," Mulholland said with a frown.

"Yes. Especially with Carol and Emma on their way to Fort William," answered Tom, smiling.

"What did Sergeant Murdoch mean when he said he would tell Constable Anderson?" Tom asked.

"I've asked him to ask Tommy Anderson if could come down here and take us on a flight at one o'clock," Frank said quietly, making sure that he couldn't be overheard.

Agent Sommerville noticed Diane Macintosh coming along the hallway and gave Frank a nudge. "There's that Russki bitch coming towards us, so watch what you're saying," Tom said. Both agents glanced at her as she made her way to the dining room.

"I'm surprised that she's not down at the Cononish mine by now, with the rest of their mob," said a worried Mulholland.

"We'd better watch our backs, mate, in case Alyona Aslanov has been left here to take us out of the equation," Tom said with alarm.

"Aye! Ye micht be richt, mate. So we will hiv tae watch her like a hawk," Frank said in his best Scottish lingo to ease the tension he was feeling.

Frank noticed barmaid Lorna behind the bar and called out for two beers. Just then, Ian Chapman entered the bar. "Make it two beers and a cider for Chappie," Frank called out.

Lorna acknowledged with a wave of her hand that she had gotten the message.

Chappie sat down, blowing on his hands and then holding them in front of the fire. "By Christ, it's bloomin' freezin' oot at the watter's edge the day," he said, rubbing his hands together and looking at both agents for sympathy.

"What are you doing down at the water on a day like this, anyway?" Tom asked.

"Ah've set one or twa lines tae see if ah kin catch oany' salmon or trout that micht be heading up tae the loch," Chappie said, just as Lorna placed the drinks on the table.

"Ah micht no hiv oanything tae sell tae ye. The snaw is keepin' the rabbits doon in ther' burrows, and things ar' no lookin' sae guid wi' the fishin' either," Chappie said, shrugging his shoulders. Chappie was clearly expecting some kind of response from her, but she simply shrugged her shoulders and made for the bar.

Chappie's hand shot forward, and he lifted the poker from the fireside bucket. He began moving the burning logs around, making room to add another log to the fire. "That's a wee bit better," Chappie said placing a new log into position.

"Enjoy your drink and heat yourself at the fire," Frank said, feeling a little sorry for him. The three men were chatting when Frank noticed that Tommy Anderson was coming into the hotel. He quickly moved over to meet him.

"Hi, Tommy! Good to see that you're a little early. Would you like a tea, or a coffee, or something stronger to drink, mate?"

Tommy reminded Frank that he didn't drink when he was working. "Could we leave immediately, as ah hae tae get back tae Tyndrum as soon as possible efter we return tae the hotel?" Tommy asked.

Frank looked over at Agent Sommerville and pointed to the exit. He called over to Chappie that he would see him later. The wee man smiled and held up his glass to the agent.

Unknown to the threesome, as they left the hotel, they were being watched by Russian agent Alyona Aslanov, alias Diane MacIntosh. But unknown to her, Chappie had noticed that she was paying special attention to the actions of the agents.

Checking out the lead mine

On arriving at the helicopter, Frank made another quick inspection to make sure that Alyona Aslanov had not been tampering with it while they were sitting comfortably at the fireside.

"OK, Tommy. Everything seems to be OK, mate," Frank said. Tommy shook his head and laughed.

"You wouldn't be laughing if it blew up when you started the engine," Agent Sommerville said, eyeing Tommy.

"Well, it hasnae' happened yit," Tommy said.

"We are living in dangerous times at the moment, my friend," Sommerville said with a serious look. Frank informed Tommy that he would like to establish a landing place somewhere out of sight, where they would be able to cover any escape route from the lead mine at Tyndrum, in the possibility of some of the Russkis escaping through an underground passage inside the mountain.

Tommy offered the smile of a confident man and said, "Ah think ah hiv the very place tae land."

He zoomed away in the direction of Tyndrum.

A few minutes later, the helicopter settled down in a small clearing among the tall fir trees which were whipping around in the draught created by the rotors.

Frank was a little concerned at their destination and asked Tommy if he would be able to find this spot in the dark of the night.

"Nae problem, Frankie boy. Ah've got my readings tae work aff o' an' ah'll tak' a note o' them the noo," said Tommy. As the rotors slowly stopped, the guys jumped clear and made their way down through the trees. Suddenly, the entrance to the lead mine came into view.

"How will this spot dae ye, Frank?" Tommy Anderson asked, grinning at both agents.

Frank stared down at the entrance to the lead mine below. "Wow! What a viewpoint, mate. From here, you'll be able to take out anybody that leaves the mine," Frank said.

"I'll be supplying you with night goggles so that you can see in the dark," Mulholland said.

Tommy nodded and replied, "Ah've a'wis wanted tae try them nicht goggles oot."

As they admired the view down towards the village of Tyndrum far below, Agent Sommerville said, "It is hard to believe that the village was built on a battlefield."

"C'mon! Let's get back to the whirlybird," Frank said, smiling as they made their way back through the forest. On climbing back into the helicopter, Frank quietly said, "Bridge of Orchy ..."

He smiled at the other two guys, who were nodding their heads and shouting, "Here we come!"

Back at Georgie's farmhouse

Georgie Watson Burke was about to begin dyeing her hair when she saw her helicopter approaching the house. She watched as her uncle Denis Wadsworth and Sean Macateer stepped out onto the snowy ground. She was mightily relieved when they split up, with Macateer making his way towards the gold mine and her uncle coming to the house. Georgie filled the kettle with water in anticipation of her uncle arriving at the kitchen door.

As Denis entered, Georgie said, "Hi, Uncle Denis. Would you like a coffee?" she asked, trying to appease for her earlier misdemeanor. She was half expecting a bit of a rollicking from him.

Denis merely informed her that there might be a change of plans for tonight. "But word would have to come from Macateer himself, as he needed to discuss everything with the team up at the mine," said Denis.

Georgie was trying to find out any information that she could from him, but to no avail.

Denis had obviously been well warned by Macateer, and it would be more than his life was worth to tell his niece anything.

"When I finish my coffee, dear, I'm going up to the mine to assist in the evacuation," said Denis.

When the phone began to ring, Georgie lifted it and listened. She handed the phone over to her uncle. "It's for you. It's that rat Macateer," Georgie whispered.

Denis listened and then put the phone down. "I have to go up to the mine, honey. That rat Macateer wants me up there immediately," said Denis with a grin.

Georgie's face was sad at the fact that she couldn't get up to her beloved aeroplanes.

"C'mon, honey! Turn that frown upside down," said Denis.

His comment brought a smile to her face as well, and her uncle Denis left by the back door to head on up to the gold mine.

Georgie was watching him trudging through the snow when, to her dismay, she saw Macateer and Gallacher making their way down the hill towards the farmhouse. They stopped and spoke to Denis Wadsworth. Georgie was hoping that they were coming to speak to him, but to her horror, they parted, and her worst fears were realised when they walked towards the farm. Georgie was beginning to panic as they approached the house. She wondered what was about to happen, especially after the beating they gave her yesterday. The back door swung open abruptly, and in walked Sean Macateer, with Sharon Gallacher tagging along.

"What do you two want from me?" asked Georgie, feeling intimidated.

Macateer's right arm swung forward, and his hand released the keys of the helicopter towards Georgie. With an instinctive move, she caught them in mid-air, slightly stinging her hand. Before she could prepare herself for anything that might happen to her, Macateer had grabbed Georgie and pinned her against the wall, with her ex-friend Gallacher looking on with terror in her eyes. Macateer's face was now pressed firmly against Georgie's face. He whispered in her ear that he would finish her off if she let him down again. A very nervous Georgie was desperately trying to apologise as she gazed into a pair of wild, staring eyes.

"It was a mistake, and it won't happen again," Georgie said, squirming. Macateer had wrapped his hand over her throat, and Georgie's head was pushed firmly against the wall. Her toes were barely reaching the floor. Macateer pressed his lips firmly onto Georgie's lips, kissing her forcibly while she struggled for breath. Macateer was enjoying his power over her, but at the same time, he was letting Sharon Gallacher, alias Alexei Smirnoff, know that she would be next if she crossed him.

Georgie's feet were now dangling clear of the floor and her bulging eyes were beginning to roll in her head when Sharon Gallacher called out, "You'll kill her, you stupid bastard."

This brought Macateer to his senses, and he released his hold on Georgie's throat. Standing back, he watched her slither to the kitchen floor, where she lay coughing and spluttering.

The terror in her eyes returned when Macateer grabbed her blonde hair. Looking straight into her watery blue eyes, he said fiercely, "You, madam, are flying one of those planes to Moscow tonight. If it doesn't get there, then what you have just had is only a sample of what will happen to you when I get to you."

Through terror-stricken eyes, all Georgie could focus on was his gold tooth flashing before her.

Macateer pushed her head firmly against the wall, and then he stood up and made for the door.

Sharon Gallacher watched him walk away and stepped forward to help her friend up from the floor.

Pushing her away, and with tears running down her face, Georgie shouted, "Leave me alone, you bitch! I want nothing to do with you from now on."

Sharon tried desperately to explain that she had no other option but to go along with him. "I'm too scared to cross him because he is a very violent person!" she screamed, tears filling her eyes. "The Russians are paying the IRA a lot of money and weapons for the supply of these planes." Gallacher looked her friend in the eye. "It would go a long way to funding the IRA's fight against the British government."

Sharon Gallacher was not aware that Georgie knew that she was a Russian agent and that her name was Alexei Smirnoff. Georgie decided to let her think that she was softening towards her by allowing her to help her up from the floor. Thanking her, she then asked, "When will I be taking the plane out of the gold mine?"

"I'm not sure," replied Sharon. "It will be after dark, and that is all I know." Sharon headed for the door.

Turning the cold water tap on, Georgie began wiping her face, trying desperately to refresh herself. She then watched as Sharon Gallacher left, trudging through the snow on her way up to the gold mine.

When she felt it was safe to do so, Georgie gave the Orchy Hotel a call and asked for Frank Mulholland, but barmaid Lorna McBride informed her that he was away on business.

"Would you please ask him to call me as soon as he returns to the hotel? Just tell him Georgie called," said Georgie, ending the call. All thoughts of dyeing her hair had now vanished. She worried that maybe Frank Mulholland may not get back to her in time for her flight out of Cononish Glen.

Back at the Orchy Hotel

Tommy's helicopter was making its way back to the hotel when Tom asked if he could fly over the Auch Viaduct, as he would like to take a photo of it for his album.

"Nae problem, mate. It's a crackin' view, especially when there is a train crossin' ower it," Tommy said, smiling as they closed in on the viaduct.

"Wow! That scene looks good with the mountains beyond covered with snow," said Agent Sommerville.

"That mountain is called Beinn Mhanach, and to your far left, gents, is Beinn Achaladair and Beinn A' Chreachan," Tommy said, putting on his tour operator voice.

"Geez! Ah dinnae ken ye could speak oany English," Frank said in his best Scottish lingo as they all laughed. "That doesn't look like the Beinn Achaladair we were on top of last Tuesday," Frank said.

"Yer lookin' at it frae the back o' the hill. Ah'll fly ower it, fur tae gie ye's a better look et it," Tommy said.

About ten minutes later, the helicopter was lowering behind the hotel, and the agents thanked the big man for the flight. Frank reminded him to be at the Orchy Hotel by 6 p.m. Tommy made for his Land Rover and the journey back to Tyndrum Police Station. When the agents entered the hotel, they were met with silence.

"Where is everyone? Tom asked, raising his eyebrows.

Suddenly, the voice of head barman Tam Cameron answered. "Ther' aw awa' tae the hills fur the ski'in' and climbin'."

"Geez! You're in early today, Tam," Frank said, glancing at the clock behind the bar, which showed half past one.

"Aye! It's the girls' day aff, an' ther' awa' tae Fort William fur the day. Ah've got tae cover fur them," Tam said, tipping his trilby.

Both agents were twiddling their thumbs and at a loss as to how to pass the time.

"Crivvens! Even Chappie's away," Tom said, staring at the empty fireside table.

"Aye! He's awa' doon tae the river tae try an' catch me a couple o' fish tae top up ma supply," said Tam. Frank was about to ask Tam when the girls would be back when he noticed a reflection on the glass panel of the door as Tam entered the bar. It was room maid Diane MacIntosh, alias Alyona Aslanov, and she was paying attention to the movements of both agents.

"Whit wer' ye gonnae ask me, Frank?" Tam said.

"Nothing, mate, nothing," said Frank, dipping his eyes.

The MI6 agents decided to check the equipment in the boot of the car for tonight's mission. "Everything seems to be OK, and we know the helicopter is fine," Frank said a little nervously.

Tom noticed this and asked Frank what the problem was.

"Oh, it's nothing, mate," Frank said. "I'm always a bit nervous when we have time to kill before a mission. I wish it were six o'clock and we were on our way to Inveroran."

"C'mon! Let's go for a walk down to the Auld Brig and stretch our legs for a while," Tom said, trying to ease his tension.

"Good idea, Tom. It'll take our mind off things," Frank said, and they headed for the Orchy Bridge.

While the agents were standing on the bridge, they noticed an army truck coming towards them from the direction of Inveroran.

"Well, at least the MI6 team have their equipment for tonight," Tom said, pointing his camera at the hotel and mountains beyond. As Tom focused on the hotel, to his dismay, as he zoomed in, the face of Diane MacIntosh was peering at him from one of the windows.

I'll give Big John B. Aitken a call, just to make sure everything was OK," Frank said.

"Frank! Everything will be OK, so stop worrying. But Christ, that Russki bitch is checking us out," Sommerville said anxiously.

Frank's head spun towards the hotel, and he took his bleeper from his inside pocket and called JBA. "Hello, big man. Is everything in the delivery to your requirements?" Frank asked.

"Nae problem, mate. We hiv everythin' ye asked for," said big JBA.

"Who is covering Forest Lodge at this moment in time?" Frank asked.

Aitken answered rather meekly, "Ah've sent Hardie doon tae keep an' eye oan things."

"C'mon, big man. You can't keep putting the boot into Hardie," Frank said, trying to make John Aitken feel differently towards him.

"Ach! Aw richt, Frank. Ah'll get somebody else tae go doon an' relieve him. Ah'll see ye the nicht at eighteen hundred hours."

This agro between Aitken and Hardie was adding to Frank's concern for tonight's mission, on top of the worry about Georgie Watson Harkin Burke and the solar aeroplanes.

Frank informed Agent Sommerville that he saw the Russian agent Alyona Aslanov listening in on their conversation with Tam the barman. "I thought she would have been called down to the mine by now," Mulholland said, smiling but showing concern that she was still around.

"When we go out later, we'll have to keep a lookout for her," Agent Sommerville said, pointing a finger to his eye.

Frank smiled and nodded his head in agreement. "That's strange! I haven't seen Chappie. Did Tam not say he was going down to the river to try to catch some fish?" Frank asked curiously. The agents looked over both sides of the bridge, but Chappie was nowhere to be seen.

"Ach, he'll be aw richt. C'mon! We'll heid back up tae the hotel," Tom said in his best Scottish accent. Both men began laughing.

On nearing the hotel, they noticed that Chappie's bike was still leaning against the wall where it had been since earlier in the day. Frank shook his head and indicated that Chappie's crossbow was hanging over the handlebars.

"What the hell is he doing? Anyone could lift that from his bike," Frank said, entering the hotel. They were about to question Tam on his whereabouts when they saw Chappie sitting on his usual seat at the fireside with a pint of cider in front of him. "Wid you twa lads like a beer tae keep me company fur a wee while?" asked Chappie. Both agents agreed that that would be a good idea. The agents sat down beside the fire, and Tom asked Chappie why he wasn't out fishing.

"Whit!" Chappie said. "It's too bloomin' cauld oot ther. I've just set a couple o' fixed lines doon at the watter's edge. Ah'll go back doon later oan an' see if oanythin' has ta'en the bait,"

A little later, in walked forestry worker Davy Blackwood and road worker Brian Greene, along with his gaffer, Harry Bain. Frank was curious as to why they had finished work so early in the day.

Harry stepped forward and spoke. "We ar' expectin' mair snaw the nicht, an' if we dae get it, then it'll mean a richt early start fur us the morra. An' we will hae tae clear the roads again," said Harry.

On hearing this, Frank Mulholland was concerned and wondered if maybe they should be moving in on the gold mine earlier than they had planned. Frank returned to the fireside table and whispered to Agent Sommerville that they should go to his room. On entering room number seven, Frank informed Tom that Harry Bain had just told him about the impending snowfall tonight. "We can't move in earlier, mate. We have to wait for the cover of darkness," Tom said, reminding Frank that darkness was their ally.

"Yes, I know that, mate. I'm just getting a little panicky about everything. It all stems from not knowing if I can trust Georgie Watson Harkin Burke with this bloody aeroplane," Frank said, looking anxiously at his partner. Mulholland checked his watch for the umpteenth time. "Geez, time is dragging. It's only four o'clock, and it's been a bloody long day up until now." He puffed out his cheeks in exasperation.

Agent Sommerville had never seen Frank so edgy, and he told him to calm down. "We'll have a long night ahead of us, and you'll probably find that time will fly once we get started," Tom said, trying to ease his buddy's mind.

Suddenly, Frank put his finger to his lips, informing Tom to be quiet as he tiptoed quietly towards the door. Grabbing the handle of the door, he swiftly pulled it open, only to be faced with startled barmaid Lorna McBride. Frank grabbed her arm firmly and pulled her into the room. "How long have you been standing outside this door?" Frank asked.

She nervously answered that she had only just arrived. On closing the door, Frank caught a glimpse of Alyona Aslanov, alias Diane MacIntosh, walking down the corridor and entering another room. Lorna informed Frank that she had a message for him from Georgie Burke. "I forgot to tell you earlier to phone Georgie. You were away when she called. I think it was probably around one o'clock or thereabouts," Lorna said apologetically.

Frank asked her not to mention this to anyone, as it could cause Georgie Burke problems down at Cononish.

"Do you not mean that it could cause you problems with my sister, Carol," Lorna said, smirking as she exited the room.

Frank informed Tom of the Russki Aslanov who was out in the hallway when he let Lorna into the room. This gave both agents a little concern. Frank lifted the room phone and immediately called Georgie Watson Harkin Burke.

Georgie answered the call but gave Frank some concern when she said, "I'm sorry, Carol, but I won't be able to come down to meet you tonight. I have some business to attend to after dark," Georgie said.

"Is there someone with you?" Frank asked.

"Yes – Carol," she replied. "I will be going out around nine o'clock, but I'll try to see you tomorrow at some point in time." Georgie ended the call.

"Georgie is flying one of the planes out after dark, at approximately nine o'clock," Frank said.

"Christ! That will be a bit dodgy. Big JBA might shoot her down the minute she appears out of the gold mine," Tom said, looking at Frank sternly.

The agents decided to kill some time by going for an early dinner, and they made their way to the dining hall. After enjoying an excellent meal, they made for the bar to await the arrival of Sergeant Murdoch and Constable Tommy Anderson. As they sat at the fireside table discussing their protocol for later, in walked the three white-faced amigos, blowing into their hands as they made their way to the bar.

"By Christ, that is a cauld wind oot ther!" exclaimed Brian Greene, rubbing his hands together.

"Wid you twa laddies like a beer alang wae us?" Davy Blackwood asked. Frank, trying to be discreet, nodded his head horizontally as if to say no thanks. He pointed at the door to let them know that they were leaving shortly.

Two minutes later, in walked Sergeant Murdoch. He signalled with a wave of his arm for the agents to follow him out of the door. They quickly made for the exit, waving goodbye to the three amigos, who were settling into their usual seats beside the fire.

On exiting the hotel, Mulholland gazed up at the sky. To his dismay, the dark clouds he had seen earlier were now above them. "Crivvens! That's a cold wind – and look at those bloody clouds above us. I hope it doesn't snow later," he said.

Frank made his way to the car and quickly opened the boot. "Here!" Mulholland said, handing out snowsuits, night goggles, crampons, bulletproof vests, automatic rifles, and handguns and ammunition to each man.

"Crivvens! Ar' we goin' intae battle wae this lot?" Sergeant Murdoch said, laughing at the agents.

"You may well be. And if you are, then believe me, you will need everything you can lay your hands on," said Frank.

The lads made their way to the helicopter as the cold icy wind bit into their faces. Frank climbed in and faced the other guys. "Pass the equipment to me and I'll put it all at the rear," Mulholland said. After loading up the whirlybird, Frank threw a quick glance over at the hotel to check if they were being spied upon.

To his relief, all seemed to be quiet as the helicopter lifted upward, with Tommy saying, "Inveroran, here we come!" The lads smiled at his comment as the whirlybird zoomed towards the Inveroran Inn.

Two minutes later, the helicopter settled down next to the inn. The noise of the rotors and the swirling snow attracted the attention of JBA, who came out to meet them.

"Just leave the equipment inside the helicopter, lads. We'll be first off tonight," Frank said as the men made for the inn.

"Christ! That's a cauld wind that's blawin," Big John said, wiping his watery eyes before quickly pulling the door open, allowing the team to enter.

The final briefing

As the agents entered the inn, a smiling Peter MacInnes pointed towards the conference room. Frank Mulholland acknowledged his signal and asked for a round of drinks to be brought into the room. Walking over to the drawing board, Frank asked the men to pay attention to what he was writing on the board. He began by introducing Sergeant Murdoch and Tommy Anderson to the rest of the team and informed them that Tommy would be flying them into position tonight. "Due to the equipment we will be taking with us, Tommy has asked me to make four drop-offs instead of the three that I originally asked for." Facing Brian McDonald, Frank asked if he was happy with the explosives that he had been supplied with.

"Aye, Frank, but ah think we micht get awa' wae just blawin' four o' the ventilation shafts," Agent McDonald said.

"Why do you think that, mate?" Mulholland said. "Would it not be better to make sure by blowing six shafts?"

Agent McDonald looked at Frank and smugly said, "Jist leave it tae me, Frank, 'cause ah ken whit ah'm daeing. Ah've got a box o' grenades that we picked up doon et Forest Lodge which belanged tae the Russkis. We kin drap them doon the shafts to help wae the strength o' the blast, an' Ah'm pretty sure the roof would fall in," McDonald said convincingly.

Frank had heard good reports on agent McDonald's ability with explosives and decided that he should know better by giving him the thumbs up signal.

Frank informed the lads of the procedure again and asked if everyone was clear on his part in the mission. The team all agreed that everything was clear and they were ready to go.

Frank informed the team of the order that they would be transported down to the Cononish Gold Mine. "First off will be Agents McDonald, Sommerville, and myself. We'll be dropped off will make out way along the hill, positioning explosives to the front entrance door and four ventilation shafts." Mulholland emphasized the word *four* and smiled at Agent McDonald.

"Second team off will be Agents Wilson and MacNeill, who will be dropped off and make their way to the front entrance of the mine, ready to enter when the entrance door is blown off.

"Third team off will be Agents Aitken and Hardie, who will be covering the escape hatches of the aeroplanes. If they do try to escape, JBA will bring them down with the rocket launchers.

"Not peashooters, as first intimated," Mulholland said, looking at JBA and laughing.

This comment lightened the atmosphere and brought laughter from the team at J. B. Aitken's expense, but he took it all in good-natured fun.

Frank quickly continued. Agent Hardie will give cover to Agent Aitken with gunfire if required. On hearing this, Aitken gave George Hardie a look that could have turned him to stone.

"Ye better cover ma back or ye'll be hearin' frae me efter," Big John Aitken said.

Frank Mulholland butted in, calming the situation between both men by reminding Big John, "If he doesn't cover you, then there won't be an *after* … mate. The fourth, and a super team they make," said Frank, wafting his hand in the direction of both police officers, "is Sergeant Murdoch and Constable Tommy Anderson."

A loud cheer rang out as the team acknowledged their presence. "These two guys will cover the other end of the mine down at Tyndrum, making sure that nobody escapes through the mine when Agent McDonald blows the roof in," Mulholland said. He reminded the men to wear bulletproof vests.

"Agent Sommerville would justify that point from the last mission, as it certainly saved his life," Frank said. Tom nodded in agreement with what Frank had just said by jokingly sticking his tongue out and clutching his chest.

"Gentlemen, make sure you wear snowsuits and have crampons on your boots to help with gripping in the snow. Remember to wear your night vision goggles because, believe me, it's pitch dark when you are up there on the mountain. You will have about a thirty-minute walk along the hill, through deep snow, to get into position for the attack. Make sure you have your bleeper with you so that I can communicate with you all – and don't forget your oxygen masks. Put silencers on all weapons in case we have to take any of them out before the explosion of the first airshaft. According to information I have received, there may be snow falling later. With a bit of luck, this may keep them inside." Mulholland looked around at the faces of his men.

Frank continued, emphasizing that everything would have to be done with military precision based on the timing of the first explosion. "I will inform everyone of the time that this will take place, depending on our explosive expert," Frank said. All eyes turned and focused on Agent McDonald.

Brian McDonald said, "Ten o'clock on the dot, lads, an' ah'll make sure that ah dinnae blaw ye's up alang wi' the ventilation shafts."

Frank continued with the procedure as the team all glared back at Agent McDonald. "We will make the first drop-off as soon as darkness falls. This should be around twenty hundred hours. It will take us approximately thirty minutes to reach the main entrance. At this point, we would attempt to wire the main door, which will have a timer set for one and a half hours. Hopefully this won't be discovered before we get the ventilation shafts wired up. Then at twenty-two hundred hours, the fireworks should begin gents. If everything goes to plan, all hell will break loose when agents Wilson and MacNeill, along with myself, enter the mine through the front entrance." Frank looked around the men for some response.

Suddenly, a gruff voice spoke out. It was JBA their team leader. "Ah've a wee question, sir. Whit happens if wan o' the planes leave before we hiv aw the explosives in place. Whit dae ah dae aboot bringin' it doon wae ma rocket launcher?"

Frank said, "Take it out, mate! Then we would have to respond to whatever happened inside the mine without the explosions of the air vents."

Agent McDonald butted in. "Ah hiv the very solution, Frank, an' it wis the Russkis who supplied the ammo. We hiv a box of grenades that we took frae them at Forest Lodge. If we drap them doon the air vent shafts, it wid bring the roof doon oan top o' them." He looked convinced that he had solved the problem. "It wull mean that ah wull hae tae run between the shafts, drappin' a grenade doon each wan as ah go," he added excitedly.

"Great stuff, mate! At least that would be a solution to the problem, and it would cause confusion inside the mine," Frank said, pumping his fist and smiling. He turned his attention to JBA.

"John, if one of the planes does exit the mine and it is being flown by Georgie Watson Burke, then I want you to let her go. I have a pact with her that would hopefully guarantee that one of the planes would be in British hands when this is all over," Frank said, swallowing hard.

"How wull we recognise this person caud Georgie Watson Burke in the heat o' the moment?" Big John asked.

"You'll recognise her because she is the one with blonde hair. The other pilot is Alexei Vispedov, and she is dark-headed," Frank said.

"But wull she not be wearin' oany heidgear such as a helmet?" JBA asked, confused.

Frank appreciated the predicament that Big John would have. "If you're not sure, mate, then just take the plane out." It would be better if none of them make it to Moscow rather than both," Mulholland said, making sure Big John understood what he had to do. JBA nodded, intimating to Frank that he understood his instructions.

Frank turned to face Tommy Anderson and Sergeant Murdoch. "These two guys are going to cover the lead mine entrance at Tyndrum, just in case any of their agents try to escape through the mine.

We think both mines are linked by an underground tunnel, and it may be a way out for them to escape," Frank said, acknowledging their worth to the team. Mulholland informed them that he would be in touch with them during the mission in case he needed them to assist down at the gold mine.

Frank checked his watch and asked the guys to synchronise watches, telling them that it was now nineteen hundred hours.

There is more than gold
in them thar hills!

Suddenly, there was a knock at the door, and Frank quickly covered the drawing board.

Peter MacInnes walked into the room with a tray full of beers. Placing the tray on the table, he nodded at Frank Mulholland. "Enjoy your beers, gents, because they are being charged to Frank," he said, laughing as he left the room.

Frank was still in the mode of leadership and asked the men if they were clear about tonight's mission.

The agents lifted their beers and all shouted together, "Cheers!"

The muffled sound of the cheering could be heard by Peter MacInnes, who smiled while rubbing his hands together.

Mulholland was pleased to hear this and asked them to prove that they were the best MI6 team by working and pulling together.

"Now, lads, I want you to go through the procedure for tonight."

The team began shouting in synchronization:

"Mulholland and MacDonald set explosives."

"Sommerville gives cover."

"Wilson and MacNeill cover the entrance."

"Aitken and Hardie take out the planes."

"Murdoch and Anderson cover the lead mine."

"The Iceman chills out."

"Once again!" Frank called out.

John B. Aitken began conducting the men through the routine, and this brought a smile to their faces as they repeated the procedure.

Mulholland wished everyone the best of luck tonight, and with a few brisk swipes of his right hand, he wiped the board clean.

Lifting his glass and holding it up to the men, Mulholland spoke. "Gentlemen, there is more than gold in them thar hills, and we are going to blast them out of that bloody mine."

Frank reminded the team that it would be a bit of a squeeze to get all the weapons and ammunition into the helicopter. So make sure that you only take what is required to do the job," Frank said, looking around at everyone. All the agents nodded in agreement with this comment.

Frank gave Georgie Watson Burke a call and walked over to the window to check out the situation of the darkness.

Georgie lifted the phone at the farmhouse and was surprised to hear his voice.

"Hello, Carol! I'm surprised to hear from you," Georgie said, letting Frank know that it was not safe to talk. Frank asked her if she had dyed her hair yet.

"No, Carol. I'm still a blonde," Georgie said with a chuckle.

Frank informed her to make sure that her blonde hair could be seen when she was flying the aeroplane tonight.

"OK, Carol, I'm going to wash my hair around ten o'clock tonight so that it will be dry before I go to bed," Georgie said, laughing aloud. "I'll see you tomorrow night over at the hotel." She ended the call.

Frank desperately tried to tell her to leave before 10 p.m. but was too late, as she had put the phone down. A quick flick of the curtain told Mulholland that it was almost dark enough to get the mission under way.

Frank informed the team that Georgie would make sure they were able to see her blonde hair. "It looks as though she is flying out at twenty-two hundred hours. This will give us time to get everyone in their positions," said a worried Mulholland, who had realised that Georgie would be leaving as the front door blasted out.

Back at Georgie's farmhouse

D enis Wadsworth was asking his niece what that was all about. Georgie informed him that she had told her friend Carol that she was going to dye her hair black for a change. That was why she couldn't go out with her tonight.

"But you're going to Moscow tonight, and you won't be back to meet her tomorrow night," Denis said, questioning her intentions.

"Yes, I know that, but I couldn't tell Carol that. Now I will just have to make up an excuse for tomorrow night," Georgie said, trying to sound convincing.

Denis turned away, muttering to himself, "Women, bloody women!" He took a sip from his coffee and then settled down into his chair.

Georgie Burke breathed a sigh of relief as she stared out the window at the impending darkness closing in.

Back at the Inveroran Inn

F rank began organising the team for the first liftoff, which would be in about twenty minutes' time.

"Would the leading team get their equipment together and load it into the helicopter, please?" Frank said. Instantly, agents Mullholland, Sommerville, and McDonald made their way to the door.

As they stepped out into the dark twilight zone around the inn, Tommy made for the helicopter. Agent McDonald made his way into the forest and broke the silence by calling out to the agents.

"Wid someone gie' me a hand wi' the box o' grenades. They ar' a wee bit oan the heavy side tae manage by maself," agent McDonald whispered. Frank immediately responded to his request and entered the forest to help him with the lifting of the box over to the helicopter.

"Jings! And we have to carry that box for about half an hour along the top of this bloomin' hill," Mulholland said, worried.

"Nae wae mate! We ar' dividin' the contents up between us an' we ar' puttin' them intae these three bags tae carry ower oor shoulders," Agent McDonald said, smiling. He quickly opened the box and began dividing the grenades between each of the agents.

Frank loaded the ammunition and explosives into the helicopter as Tom repositioned both their rifles and handguns to make space. Frank told the other agents to put on their snowsuits and caps in preparation for the return of the helicopter.

"We are talking about twenty minutes between each pickup. Try to be a bit discreet, gents. This is a Holiday Inn, and we have to consider and respect Peter and Jessie's business," Frank said. Mulholland looked at his watch for the umpteenth time. It showed 7.55 p.m.

The men were champing at the bit to get out onto the hill and attend to business. Frank was adamant that they don't go before 2000 hours. He stared up at the darkening cloudy sky, hoping that it wouldn't snow later. "OK, lads, it's time to put on our snowsuits and caps. We want to be as inconspicuous as possible when we step out into the snow," Mulholland said, as the team prepared for the arduous task ahead of them. Before stepping into the helicopter, Frank wished the men the best of luck. With a quick glance at his watch, Mulholland whispered, "Cononish Gold Mine, here we come!" The lads all smiled and gave out a stifled cheer.

On the way to the drop-off point, the nervous tension was felt; hardly a word was spoken. Suddenly, the helicopter slowed down and lowered gently onto the snow-covered hill. The MI6 agents grabbed their weapons and explosives and stepped out into the deep snow, which reached above their knees. Tommy's helicopter rose gently above the agents as the snow swirled around them from the draught of the rotors. Frank instructed the men to stay together and to put on their night goggles. "It would be easy to lose sight of each other in the dark as we head on up to the main entrance," Frank Mulholland said.

The going was pretty tough and tiring, but the agents were making good time as they trudged through the snow. Mulholland was paying attention to the dark, threatening clouds above. "There don't seem to be any guards positioned on the mountain," Frank whispered. In the distance, they could hear the sudden sound from the rotors of Tommy's helicopter.

"That must be the second drop-off arriving," Frank said, shining his torch onto his wristwatch.

"Yes! It'll be agents Wilson and MacNeill arriving to give us cover," Agent Sommerville said.

"That must mean that we are roughly halfway to our target, lads. We can take a breather for a couple of minutes," Frank said. With relief, they settled down into the snow.

Tom whispered that it is quite hard going trudging through this snow and carrying the weapons and explosives at the same time.

"It sure is, mate. Maybe we are getting soft in our old age," Frank said, quietly laughing.

"We canny sit here much longer or the lads will catch up wae us an' we'll never hear the end o' it frae them," agent McDonald said softly.

"Jesus," gasped Mulholland, "those dark clouds are getting angrier by the minute." He informed the lads that it was time to move on. With a deep sigh, they picked up the equipment and trudged onward.

Fifteen minutes later, they were almost in reach of their target.

Frank told Agent Sommerville to wait there and act as a lookout. Frank pointed out the positions of the hatches where the planes would emerge. "Tom, stay clear of them in case a plane leaves unexpectedly," Mulholland said. "We're going down to set the explosives at the main door. Keep your eyes peeled for any movement of their agents and tip us off."

Frank was feeling some tension as he stared once again at the angry clouds above. "C'mon, Brian, but be very careful as you go down this hill because it is quite steep and slippery," Mulholland said.

Both MI6 agents were digging their crampons into the snow as they slithered their way downhill towards the front entrance.

Agent McDonald began setting the explosives at the far side of the door, while Frank was at the near side. They were positioning the explosives around the large hinges, which, according to Agent McDonald, should blow the door off completely. The agents could hear some form of commotion coming from within the mine as agent McDonald trailed the cable over the top of the door towards Frank. "I thought we were using explosives with timers," Frank said, looking at the trailing cable.

"This is just a wee safeguard in case oany' o' the timers' disnae work. This means that we kin still blaw the door aff' manually by using the plunger. We'll cover the cable wae snaw so that it canny be seen if oany bugger comes aboot," Agent McDonald said. He trailed the cable over to some tree cover, while Frank Mulholland was frantically covering the cable as they moved along.

The silence was broken when Agent Sommerville appeared. "There's a pair of headlights coming through the glen towards the mine," Tom whispered. Frank responded quickly by frantically brushing the snow over the remaining cable.

"What if they see the cable when the door lifts up?" Frank said, looking with alarm at Agent McDonald.

The agents heard a noise, and they quickly dove for cover, slithering through the snow and into the trees. With some relief, they soon realised that it was Agents Wilson and MacNeill coming towards them.

"Over here lads," Frank said softly, "but be quiet about it. There is quite a bit of noise coming from within the mine, and there is a vehicle coming along the glen. We are going up to wire the ventilation shafts. Take cover here and wait for the first two shafts to blow. When they do blow, the front door should blow almost instantly. If the front door doesn't blow, then hit the plunger to blast the door off."

With a quick tap on agent McDonald's shoulder, both men disappeared into the night and were scrambling on up the hill, leaving the other agents to attend to the entrance.

As Mulholland and McDonald made their way along the hill, they heard a slight crunching of snow in the near distance. "I hope that noise is JBA and Hardie, because if it's not, then we will have to take whoever it is out and maybe blow our cover," Frank said in a whisper.

Suddenly, the gruff voice of Big John Aitken was heard. "Christ, Ah could hae taen the twa o' ye's oot a minute ago wae the noise ye's ar' makin'," JBA whispered.

Frank informed JBA that the escape covers were only about forty yards farther on and the rest of the team were in position to enter through the main entrance when it blew. "Now, John, remember to look out for Georgie's blonde hair and to let her go with the plane," Frank said. "But make sure that you take out the other plane, as we can't afford to let it reach Moscow."

Agents Mulholland and McDonald made their way onto the appropriate ventilation shafts and positioned the explosives in a way to get maximum advantage from the explosions.

"We'll drap in a few o' these wee fellahs doon inside just tae help it alang," McDonald said, smiling. He dropped seven hand grenades into each ventilation shaft before setting the timers to go off ten seconds apart.

"Will that do the business?" Frank asked.

"Frankie boy, there is enough explosives in ther tae blaw up the entrance tae your wallet. An' believe me, that takes some doin'," Agent McDonald said, quietly giggling.

"C'mon, ya bugger, and let's get back down to the entrance before I slip this grenade with the pin taken out into your bag," Mulholland said, quietly laughing.

Back at the entrance
to the gold mine

The MI6 team watched closely from their hiding place as the headlights that they had seen earlier approached the mine. "Ah hope that they've set the cable well doon in the snaw, mate," agent MacNeill said, whispering to Agent Sommerville.

"Dinnae worry, Jim. It is weel hidden," Tom said, trying to convince his fellow agent that everything was OK.

All eyes were on the driver of the truck as he blasted the horn for someone to allow him entry to the mine. Suddenly, the door swung open and IRA agent Sean Macateer appeared, extending his hand up to stop the truck from entering.

Macateer turned and signalled for another truck to exit the mine. A minute later a fully laden vehicle drove forward and manouvered around the truck waiting at the entrance. Frank Mulholland was observing the scene, and he checked his watch to see that it was 21:45 hours. To his dismay, he could see Georgie Watson Harkin Burke and Sharon Gallacher approaching the mine.

"Geez! That's all we need. She only has fifteen minutes to get one of the planes out of there before the door and air vents are blasted," Mulholland said to Agent McDonald.

"C'mon, mate. As soon as this truck enters the mine and they close the door, we'll slide down this hill," Mulholland said. They saw the fully laden truck setting off down the glen, distancing itself from the gold mine. Another truck exited the mine and parked beside the truck, waiting to enter. The light from the exiting truck's headlights were shining too close to the hidden cable for comfort, and the MI6 team was showing a nervous concern.

The driver called on Sharon Gallacher to come over, and he jumped down into the snow as Sharon approached. While they were chatting, Sharon Gallacher noticed footprints in the snow leading over to the trees where the MI6 team was positioned. Sharon Gallacher was suspicious of the footprints in the snow and decided to investigate by following them into the darkness. Slowly but surely, she was closing in on the MI6 team, who were beginning to panic as they realised that she may discover the plot before the mine blew.

Agent MacNeill's hand reached down and withdrew a knife from the sheath hanging from the belt around his waist in preparation for Sharon Gallacher discovering them.

"Jings! This is looking dodgy. Try to finish her off as quietly as possible, mate," Agent Sommerville whispered.

The tension was building as Gallacher slowly edged nearer. Agent MacNeill was anxiously holding his breath, his fingers twitching on the handle of the dagger. She was now only ten yards from the MI6 team. Suddenly, Sean Macateer called out for the truck to enter the mine. At this point, Sharon Gallacher, alias Alexie Smirnoff, began to return to the entrance of the mine.

"Phew, that was close," agent MacNeill said, replacing his knife.

"At least she didn't see the cable under the snow," Sommerville said, swallowing hard.

Sharon Gallacher had now entered the mine, leaving the truck driver alone to finish smoking his cigarette. A few quick puffs later, the driver nonchalantly flicked his cigarette down onto the snow before jumping back into his cabin and preparing to leave.

Frank Mulholland arrived at the hiding location of the other agents, who were pleased to see him. He informed the men that Agent McDonald was going to drop grenades down the air vents if the timers didn't work.

"Crivvens, Frank! You cut that neat. When we saw the first truck leaving, we thought about taking that lot out instead of waiting for the explosives to go off," Agent Wilson said, looking at Agent MacNeill for confirmation of what he had said.

Frank informed them that he was glad that they didn't. "We have to hope that Georgie Watson Burke takes one of the planes out before we go in."

Agent Wilson noticed the mine door opening again and gave Frank a dig in the ribs. To their dismay, a smaller van appeared, with Sharon Gallacher behind the wheel and Sean Macateer in the passenger seat.

"Crivvens! Where are they going?" Agent Sommerville asked.

The van manouvered around the truck, causing its headlights to shine into the trees where the agents were positioned. With synchronised motion, the team dove for cover and the van made its way down the glen, following the truck, which had left a few minutes earlier.

"Jings, that was a close thing. Is ther' oanybody left inside the mine?" Agent MacNeill jokingly asked.

Agent Sommerville quickly confirmed that there was still another truck said that six men had come out of it when it entered the mine. "Don't forget about our Russki friends, the chemical experts, and the giant Vladimir Bazarov and pilot Alexei Vispedov," Tom said, convincing the men that this would be no walk in the park.

Frank gave Sergeant Murdoch and Tommy Anderson a call down at the other end of the mine to make sure they were prepared for action.

"Hello, Frankie boy. Whit hiv ye tae tell me?" Murdoch said.

"The first two vents will blow at twenty-two hundred hours, so be prepared for some action, guys, and the best of luck. Over and out," Mulholland whispered. Murdoch looked at his watch and quietly told Tommy Anderson, "Five minutes, mate. Get yerself set fur some action."

Frank gave Agent Kane a call. "John, just let the truck and van leave; we have bigger fish to fry up here at the mine. There's another truck sitting at the entrance of the mine, and it's leaving as we speak, with two men that we know of on board. After the mine blows, take out anyone who tries to leave, mate."

"OK, Frank. Over and out," said the Iceman, preparing for some action.

Georgie takes flight

One of the hatches abruptly began to open. Big John Aitken and George Hardie dove into the snow. Their eyes were straining, trying to focus on who the pilot was. Slowly but surely, the plane appeared from within the mine, the blonde-haired figure of Georgie Watson Harkin Burke at the controls.

"Christ! This gets up ma humph, lettin' her fly awa' wae that plane. But we'll hiv tae dae whit Frank asked," JBA said, glancing around at Hardie, who was facing in the opposite direction and watching their backs.

Georgie's plane hovered above the escape hatch, and in the blink of an eye, it was gone.

"Bloody Nora! Did ye see the speed o' that thing as it took aff?" Aitken said.

"Christ! Ah'll hae tae be quick oan the draw when that ither yin appears," Aitken said, glancing at Hardie to make sure he was covering them. "It's almost twenty-two hundred hours, so, be prepared fur an explosion at oanytime," JBA whispered. He had no sooner mentioned this than an almighty explosion occurred farther back on the hill.

"Jesus, sufferony! Whit did Brian McDonald put doon those vents? It nearly scared the shit oot o' me," said Big John B. Aitken. Almost simultaneously, the other three vents were blowing and the ground was violently shaking as the night sky lit up.

George Hardie began firing at a couple of silhouetted figures who were coming towards them in the darkness and brought them down. Both figures slumped to the snow-covered ground.

"I've took them oot, big man. Ah'm glad we hiv these night goggles or a micht no ha'e seen them," said Hardie.

Aitken was congratulating him on a job well done when suddenly the other plane appeared from inside the mountain. J. B. Aitken took aim with his rocket launcher. His finger was anxiously hovering over the trigger. *My timing has got tae be richt wae this shot,* thought Big John. The plane was just about to accelerate into the night sky when Big John's itching finger sent the missile on its way.

"Take that, ya bass," called JBA as the missile reached its target, catching the plane around its engines and sending it spiralling upwards and over towards the tall peak of Ben Lui.

With an almighty explosion, the plane crashed high up on the face of the mountain. A sickening crunching noise was echoing down the glen, along with the rumbling sound of an avalanche, as the cascading snow tumbled downwards. The crash, which could be heard for miles, ended the life of pilot Alexei Vispedov. Aitken and Hardie immediately rushed over to the escape hatch before it closed to gain a vantage point for whatever was happening inside the mine.

The Iceman prepares

Agent John Kane was on high alert as he listened to the noise coming from the direction of the gold mine. He was watching the headlights of the escaping truck coming in his direction. Both agents were about to face their worst nightmare, as the Iceman had prepared for some action by planting an explosive trip wire across the snow-covered road. It had annoyed Agent Kane that he had to sit back and allow the first truck and van to leave unchallenged just a few minutes earlier.

An explosion high up on the mountain called Ben Lui sent the Iceman into action, and he dove for cover, awaiting the explosion from his trip wire. The fleeing IRA men had heard the explosions from the mine and were desperately trying to distance themselves from the area.

Back at the gold mine

A s the main door blew off, Agents Mulholland, Wilson, MacNeill, and McDonald were firing at anyone who moved inside the mine, where absolute chaos was taking place. Bullets were flying around, and all hell was breaking loose. Frank Mulholland slipped inside the mine and moved in on Russian Stanislav Balsunov. He fired two bullets, sending the Russki slamming into the wall of the chemical room and slithering to what looked like his certain death. Frank fired at the Russians who were positioned behind a large metal box. This allowed Agents Wilson and MacNeill to enter the mine and take up position on the opposite side. Some Russkis were running down the tunnel, trying to find some protection from the influx of bullets that the agents were spraying around.

Agent MacNeill could see the giant of a man called Vladimir Bazarov, and he let rip with a round of bullets. This caused the big Russian to dive for cover behind a large metal container. Bazarov crawled to the far side of the container to gain a better view of his assailant and was homing in on agent MacNeill with an automatic rifle. Suddenly, a bullet zipped into his forehead from above the escape hatch, and a smiling George Hardie gave agent MacNeill the thumbs up. On seeing this, one of the Russians quickly pressed the button to close the hatch, just as Big John Aitken took one of their agents out with a spray of bullets from his machine gun.

The MI6 agents were closing in on the panicking men, who were scrambling around trying to escape the blistering assault that was taking place.

Agents Sommerville, Aitken, and Hardie entered the mine and were firing at two IRA men who were taking refuge behind a machine against the wall, just beyond the chemical room. Agent Sommerville screamed at the men, reminding them to be aware of the chemical tank or they would all be blown up. All three agents crawled along the floor to achieve a vantage point farther along the mine. A burst of firing came from the opposite side of the tunnel, and both IRA men scrambled for cover, trying to gain protection from the assault as a bullet ripped into the leg of one of them. It was Frank Mulholland firing. As the MI6 agents closed in from both sides, they knew they had a problem.

Farther down into the mine, shots could be heard from the weapons of MI6 agents Wilson and McDonald. With this thought in mind, the IRA men held up their hands in surrender.

"Drop your weapons and get down on the floor!" agent MacNeill shouted. He watched as the IRA men hit the deck. Agent MacNeill immediately kicked their weapons aside and told both men to lie still. More shots could be heard from the direction of Agents Wilson and McDonald.

The Iceman is cool

The fleeing truck had just struck the tripwire, and the explosion had thrown it over onto its side, with both occupants desperately trying to escape the burning vehicle. In such a short time, Agent Kane had closed in on the men, who were dazed and because of the darkness had still not seen their pursuer. The Iceman who was wearing night vision goggles had seen both men escaping from the burning truck, and he took aim with his automatic rifle. With a quick squeeze of his finger on the trigger, bullets were now heading towards both of the fleeing agents. Screams could be heard in the night air as the men fell into the soft snow.

Agent Kane was rushing through the deep snow to attain a better view of the fallen men when abruptly a shot rang out. The Iceman felt a burning sensation high up on his left arm. *Christ! Ah've been hit,* thought agent Kane as his body sprawled through the snow.

The situation had changed because he now knew that the fleeing assassin was still alive and obviously had night vision goggles. Agent Kane was now in a most precarious position as he crawled towards his target. The silhouetted figure of one of the assassins could be seen just beyond the burning truck, and the Iceman sent a bullet towards the fleeing agent. A loud scream was heard as the man tumbled down the steep roadside embankment and slithered towards the fast-flowing River Cononish. The Iceman was clutching his injured arm as he made his way back to his hiding place. Agent Kane was relieved that he did not have close combat with any of the fleeing agents. He still had nightmares about when he stabbed the Russian soldier with the icicle near Murmansk. As he trudged through the snow, his thoughts went back to that event at the Norwegian-Russian border. Even to this day, three years later, he could still see the look in the dying soldier's eyes. A bullet zipped past him, and MI6 agent Kane dove into the snow.

Christ, one of them is still alive, thought the Iceman, feeling a blood-rushing pain on his injured arm. Agent John Kane was under a great deal of pressure because he now realised that he was dealing with an escaping assassin who was fighting for his life. The Iceman was crawling slowly through the deep snow, hoping to glimpse the injured assassin. Suddenly, a slight movement off to his right sent the agent springing into action. His hand quickly grasped a grenade from his pouch. With a quick removal of the pin and a bowling action which would be the envy of any cricketer, the grenade was on its way towards the escaping man. Seconds later a blast was heard, along with the screams of the dying agent, eerily filling the night air. Agent Kane breathed a sigh of relief and was about to make his way back to his hiding place when a ghostly figure threw himself forward and engaged in a fight with him. As both men tumbled downhill through the snow, the Iceman quickly stuffed a handful of snow into the assassin's face, temporarily blinding him. This action gave Agent Kane the upper hand, and he reached for his knife. With a quick stabbing motion, the screaming assassin tumbled downhill and into the Cononish River to his ultimate death.

There must hiv been fower o' them in that truck, thought the Iceman. "It is just as weell that Brian McDonald gave me that grenade," he muttered as he trudged through the snow and back to the relative safety of his snow house.

Back at the gold mine

Agents Wilson and McDonald were on the tails of two Russian spies, and they were closing in fast. The Russkis met a wall of boulders where the roof of the mine had caved in. A smile broke out on Agent Wilson's face when he realised that Agent McDonald's explosives had blocked off their escape route through the mine. "Super job you've done here, mate. But we have still tae tak' these twa oot," said Agent Wilson, congratulating Brian on a job well done.

The agents were crawling along the floor trying to catch a glimpse of the two Russkis who were hiding among the debris lying around. They glimpsed a pair of legs of a dead agent protruding from the boulders which had obviously crashed down on top of him. Agent Wilson whispered that he had seen something move behind a large boulder off to the right. Agent McDonald dipped his hand into his ammunition bag and pulled out a grenade. Showing it to Agent Wilson, he quickly removed the pin – then, with a quick lob, the grenade was on its way. The clinking sound of the grenade bouncing around the rubble sent the two Russkis scrambling for cover from the impending blast. This allowed the MI6 agents to take them out in a hail of bullets. Both MI6 agents dove for cover just as the grenade exploded, sending vibrations around the debris. When they checked that the Russkis had been taken out, they soon realised that one of them was the Russian female called Veronika Bogrov.

"Geez, mate! Ah hate it when it's a woman that I hiv taken oot," Brian Wilson said, almost feeling sorry for her.

Everything had gone quiet inside the mine now that the agents seemed to have completed their task. They made their way back towards the entrance of the mine, their eyes scanning the area as they joined their fellow agents, who were questioning the two IRA men. A sudden shot rang out, and a body slumped to the floor over in the corner beside the chemical room.

"Aye, it's jist as weel that ah'm keepin' ma mind oan the job or ye's wid aw be deid the noo," George Hardie growled at the men. Big John Aitken extended his hand towards Agent Hardie and congratulated him on his professionalism in finishing the job, thus ending the life of Stanislav Bulsanov.

Frank Mulholland's eyes dipped because he thought that he had killed the Russian earlier. He slipped into the chemical room. A quick inspection confirmed that there was nobody hiding inside. Mulholland relayed this message to his team.

The two Brians were smiling as they joined the rest of the team. They informed Frank Mulholland that the mine was closed off.

Over at the Tyndrum lead mine

Sergeant Murdoch and Constable Anderson were waiting patiently. They could hear a lot of noise in the distance, from the direction of the gold mine. "Jings, there is quite a lot happening doon ther'. We better be oan oor toes," Murdoch whispered to his mate. Suddenly, a truck came out of the mine in great haste. Considering it was about to attempt the drive down the mountain on a road with lots of hairpin bends, it was obvious that the driver was in a great panic. Unknown to the driver, he was about to meet his worst nightmare as Murdoch and Anderson threw themselves down into the snow.

"Here we go, mate. Lets gi'e them hell!" Murdoch shouted, and a hail of bullets ripped into the driver's cabin. The truck skidded out of control and slid over to the edge of the steep hill. Bodies were jumping clear from the vehicle as it edged closer to the cliff and the plunge downwards to its ultimate destruction. The four escaping men were clinging desperately to the side of the hill as the truck slithered over the edge, with the driver slumped over the wheel. Moments later and far below, the truck exploded and burst into flames. The fleeing agents had now realised that they were pinned down, and they tried to get themselves into a position to be able to return fire by spreading out along the edge of the cliff. Murdoch and Tommy were in the prime position and began to pick the men off with relative ease as two of the fleeing agents fell to their deaths. The other two men desperately tried to escape the hail of bullets coming from above. But they soon found that they were fighting a losing battle.

"Only twa tae get buddy an' we hiv done oor job," Murdoch said. A bullet from below whistled past his ear. "Christ! That wis close. Whaur did it come frae?" he anxiously asked.

"Wan o' them must hiv sneaked ower ther' just behin' that big rock, an' he must ha'e night goggles tae be able tae see us," Tommy said. "Ah'll make a move, an' you kin spot him if he tries tae get me." He slid across the ground, and seconds later two shots rang out.

Murdoch shouted, "Only wan tae go noo mate!" as a body slithered over the cliff edge, plunging to the ground far below. "If we split up, then we kin tak' the last yin oot easily enough, but keep yer heid doon, as ah dinnae' want tae lose ma best mate tae a bullet."

The agent far below was terrified. He knew that he was in a vulnerable position. He desperately tried to crawl along the road using the side of the hill as cover.

Unknown to him, Murdoch was crawling through the snow and achieving the ultimate position to take the terrified agent out. Tommy Anderson opened up with a burst of firing, and the man scrambled along the roadside with bullets zipping around him. This allowed Murdoch time to pick out his target. With perfect aim, a bullet ripped into the agent's shoulder, sending him spinning across the road to the cliff edge. The agent let out an agonising scream of pain, but before the man could adjust himself, another bullet came crashing into his body, sending him tumbling over the edge of the cliff to his ultimate death.

"That's them aw, mate!" Murdoch shouting to his buddy. "But we better keep an eye oan the mine jist in case ther' ar' oany mair comin' oot."

Taking up their positions, the men settled down into the snow, but it seemed as though their action was complete.

Back at the gold mine

rank Mulholland was staring down the Cononish Glen, and he could see flames in the darkness. Grabbing his bleeper, he called agent Kane. "Hello, John! I can see something burning along the glen, and I was wondering if it was the truck that left just before we entered the mine," Frank said.

"Yeah! It sure is, an' ah took the four occupants oot," said Kane.

"Good man, John. Could you make your way up to the mine and meet up with the rest of the team?"

Frank gave Sergeant Murdoch a call to find out the situation at their end of the mine. "Nae problem, Frankie boy. Ther' wis only wan truck wae five men inside it, an' we took them aw oot," Murdoch said, chuffing at their achievement. "Frank, these night goggles are bloomin' brilliant."

"How would you guys like some more action?" Mulholland said. "Come down to the gold mine immediately."

Ten minutes later, the beating sound of rotors could be heard as Sergeant Murdoch and Tommy Anderson appeared above the entrance to the mine. Agents Mulholland and Sommerville rushed over to meet them as they settled into the soft snow.

"Whit dae ye need us for, Frankie boy?" Murdoch asked.

Frank explained to them that four IRA agents had left in a truck full of weapons, with a van transporting Agents Sharon Gallacher and Sean Macateer behind it. "They left about thirty minutes ago, and we have to stop them from escaping," said a very animated Frank Mulholland. Frank had no sooner spoken than the sound of a helicopter's rotors was heard reverberating in the night air.

The Phoenix takes flight

"Geez! Someone is taking Georgie's helicopter. We'll have to stop the *Phoenix* from escaping," Frank said. With some urgency, all four men scrambled into Tommy's helicopter. They were immediately up in the air and racing after the flying whirlybird, which was heading down the Cononish Glen.

"Ther' it is. Ah kin see its navigation lichts in the dark!" shouted Tommy Anderson, pointing down the glen.

"Ah wonder whaur they ar' heading tae!" Murdoch shouted as the helicopter closed in on its target. The pilot in the fleeing helicopter soon realised that someone was on his tail and tried to take evasive action, which gave the MI6 agents time to see who was inside the fleeing whirlybird.

Frank Mulholland peered through his night vision goggles. "It looks like Denis Wadsworth, the IRA gunrunner!"

"Will ah try to tak' him oot, Frank?" Murdoch shouted, trying to be heard above the noise of the rotors.

"Now is as good a time as any, Sergeant. Get yourself down on the floor and I'll hold your ankles so that you don't fall out when Tommy manouvers the chopper," Agent Sommerville said. Murdoch quickly dove to the floor, with Tom grabbing the sergeant's ankles as the helicopter swung to the right and upwards.

Murdoch let rip with a volley of bullets that smashed into the gunrunner's cabin, catching him on the arm. This caused him to veer violently. A spray of bullets zipped into the MI6 team's plexiglass windscreen, shattering it and sending fragments into the faces of the team. One of the bullets just missed Agent Sommerville and embedded itself in the seat that he had been sitting in.

"Crivvens, that was close! I'm glad that I'm not sitting in my seat, lads," Tom shouted. As both helicopters buzzed around trying to take each other out, a cold icy wind blew into the cabin as Frank let rip with a hail of bullets, causing the gunrunner to take evasive action. The helicopters swung away in opposite directions, ready to face each other in an all-out attack.

"Oh! Christ. This is lookin' a bit dodgy, mate. It looks as though we ar' gonnae have a face-off, the noo!" Murdoch shouted as they flew towards each other.

"Ah'm gonnae swing ower tae the richt, Sergeant, so that you and Frank kin get a potshot at the bugger before he homes in oan us!" Tommy cried.

All hell abruptly broke loose, and they traded bullets. Georgie Burke's helicopter, the *Phoenix*, began spiralling towards the ground. With a sickening crunching sound, it crashed into the River Cononish and burst into a ball of flames.

"Phew! That was looking dodgy for a while, but at least we're OK. I wonder who was firing back at us from the helicopter," Tom said.

"Yes, I wonder who!" Frank shouted. "Because Wadsworth was too busy flying it to be able to return any gunfire."

Tommy Anderson spoke out and anxiously informed the agents that they had a problem. "Wan' o' the bullets has done some damage, an' it looks as though we ar' oot o' commission noo. Ma instruments ar' tellin' me that we ar' losin' fuel rapidly."

"There's smoke belching out the back!" Sommerville shouted anxiously.

"Oh no – that means the truck and the van will get away now," Mulholland said despondently.

"Can you make it tae Crianlarich headquarters?" Murdoch shouted.

"Ah'll try ma best, mate," replied Tommy as they limped along with smoke trailing behind.

Frank asked Murdoch what he had in mind when they got to the police headquarters. "Ah'll get the keys tae wan o' the Land Rovers, an' we wull be able tae track them buggers doon, as long as we ken which wae they hiv gone," Murdoch said, trying to boost the agent's hopes.

A loud crunching noise could be heard coming from the stuttering, stalling rotors.

"Aw jings, Ah dinnae like the sound o' that!" shouted Tommy Anderson.

The guys were on the edge of their seats at every abnormal sound that they heard coming from the engine and the rotors. Suddenly, a stuttering sound was heard from the engine, and the men all stared at Tommy.

"Christ! Whit wis that?" gasped Murdoch, grasping his buddy's arm.

Tommy was desperately trying to keep the whirlybird under control as they approached Crianlarich. "Ah'll hae tae keep awa' frae the hooses in case we come doon!" Tommy shouted with a grimace. The other three guys were right on the edge of their seats, willing the big man to get to their destination.

"There's the headquarters ahead of us!" Mulholland shouted anxiously.

"We ar' runnin' oan empty," Tommy exclaimed as the whirlybird began its approach.

Another crunching sound rang out, and all eyes were staring at Tommy for some kind of response.

"Hing oan, lads, because this is gonnae be a bumpy landin'!" shouted Tommy, who was desperately hanging on to the controls. His teeth were clenched in a grimace, and his pale face looked like grim death. On the final approach, the helicopter was shuddering as it closed in on the car park. With a bump, the whirlybird bounced along the tarmac and finally came to rest, to the relief of everyone.

"Well done, Tommy!" shouted the guys excitedly, slapping his back.

"Jings, mate. You've come tae rest oan Inspector Hugh Smith's parking place," Murdoch said, laughing heartily.

Tommy slumped back onto his seat and puffed out his cheeks with relief as he stared at the building through the shattered windscreen.

Frank informed the team that headquarters had called him earlier with news of a Russian submarine.

"Sir Jeffrey Merriday told me that a Russian submarine was tracked into the Firth of Forth. It was last seen near the Bass Rock. Also, we have a nuclear sub down at Rosyth Dockyard that was in for repair, and this could be where they are heading," Mulholland said.

"Surely not, Frank. The guns will be for the IRA, mate. They must have a boat somewhere awaiting them over in the Firth of Forth," Tom said.

Tommy spoke, suggesting that they would be taking the Callander to Dunblane road if they were heading for Rosyth. He said they should take that road as well. Frank Mulholland reminded Murdoch to make sure he picked a Land Rover that had lots of fuel in the tank, as they may have to divert to another location somewhere along the way.

"Nae problem. Ah'm no as daft as ah look," Murdoch said, smiling as he made for the entrance door. Tommy jumped clear of the helicopter and watched as Sergeant Murdoch entered the building. Murdoch quickly reappeared, dangling a bunch of keys. He gave them the call to jump in and quickly threw the keys over to Tommy.

"This wan wull dae us fine 'cause ah filled it wae fuel earlier," Murdoch exclaimed as the lads piled inside.

The chase is on

"They havnae' got that much o' a start oan us, because it wid hae taen them a while tae get oot o' the Cononish Glen wae aw that snaw that wis lyin' aboot," Murdoch shouted. All eyes were on the road ahead as Tommy put the boot to the floor. Murdoch called out for him to watch what he was doing and to keep the speed down.

"Slow doon in plenty time tae tak' the bends oan this road 'cause, as ye weell ken, ther' ar plenty o' accident spots, mate!" shouted Murdoch, wiping his eyes, which were straining to see in the dark.

About twenty minutes later, Agent Sommerville called out, "There! The taillights of a vehicle about half a mile ahead of us – and we are closing in quite quickly."

"Aye, Ah kin see it!" shouted Tommy. His foot went back to the floor, and he accelerated.

"Christ, man! Ar' ye trying tae kill us aw?" shouted Murdoch as the two MI6 agents spurred Tommy on to go quicker. The team were closing in quickly and soon realised that it was the truck they saw leaving from the gold mine.

"Yes, that's the lorry, and not only that, but there is also a van driving in front. It looks as though it will be the IRA team!" exclaimed Agent Sommerville, getting a little excited at the prospect of catching them.

As they came around a long bend in the road, there was no sign of the vehicles. "Crivvens, where are they? Where have they gone?" asked Frank, his eyes wide in astonishment.

"They must hiv turned doon intae the Killin road, said Murdoch. "If that's the case, then we hiv got them. The brig ower the River Dochart is narrow, an' they wull hiv tae slow richt doon tae cross ower it."

"Quickly! Turn aroond and go doon the Killin road," shouted Murdoch excitedly.

"Whit ar' they goin' this wae fur? It is a lang wae alang this road tae get tae Rosyth!" hollered Tommy Anderson, dipping his eyebrows.

"Maybe they have realised that we are trailing them, and are hoping that we would take the other road," said Mulholland, peering ahead into the darkness. As they were nearing the village of Killin, they saw the truck just up ahead.

"Crivvens! They ar' goin' far too fast tae turn ontae the brig!" Murdoch shouted.

No sooner had the sergeant mentioned this than his prediction came true and the lorry slithered and crashed into the bridge. Tommy closed in on the fleeing agents and then slammed on the brakes, allowing the team to jump clear of the Land Rover and take cover behind the riverside wall. Frank was leading the way as the team crawled along using the drystone dyke as cover. The IRA team were frantically trying to get the stalled engine up and running again. Gunfire was coming from the area around the far side of the bridge. Sean Macateer was spraying bullets in the direction of the MI6 agents.

Sergeant Murdoch made a beeline for the wall across the road. Evading bullets from the gun of Macateer, he achieved a better angle to return firing. "Take that, ya bass!" shouted Murdoch, firing at the Irishman who was hiding behind a wall. Sharon Gallacher, alias Alexei Smirnoff, was sitting in the awaiting van with the engine revving. The four IRA agents were still frantically trying to start and free the truck from the corner of the bridge when Mulholland and Sommerville let rip with a hail of bullets which brought down two of them. Agonising screams filled the night air. The driver eventually managed to clear the vehicle, only to feel the pain of a bullet from Sergeant Murdoch ripping through his body.

Gunrunner Sean Macateer was now in a panic. He now knew that his agents had been taken out and the cache of weapons had been lost to the MI6 team. Macateer let rip with a hail of bullets as he made his way over to the revving van, with Sharon Gallacher screaming at him to hurry.

As Macateer reached the van, Gallacher was literally pulling away as he struggled on board. A hail of bullets from the MI6 agents made their way towards the escaping couple, but to no avail.

"Christ, were going to have to move this truck before we can continue the chase," said Frank.

The men ran towards the stranded vehicle with guns at the ready. Suddenly, a bullet whizzed just over Murdoch's shoulder, and the guys realised that one of the IRA agents was still alive. The MI6 team dove for cover. Frank was thinking that the speeding van was distancing itself from the situation. He signalled to the team to try to manouver themselves into a position where the man was surrounded. Considering the River Dochart was on the left and the inn was on the right, they felt their options were limited.

Tom pointed out that he was going to jump over the wall to try to approach from the river's edge. As he threw his body over the wall, a bullet ricocheted against the wall, narrowly missing him. Now the IRA man had a problem because the agents were coming at him from three directions. He panicked and decided to make his escape by running across the bridge to the far side of the river. As he approached the central arch of the bridge, a hail of bullets brought him down and his bullet-riddled body tumbled over the side and into the fast-flowing River Dochart, to his certain death.

Almost immediately, Sergeant Murdoch climbed into the truck. With a crunching of gears, he reversed the vehicle, allowing them to cross the bridge.

The team climbed into the Land Rover and crossed the bridge quickly, but to their dismay, the local police had been informed of the disturbance and had blocked the road with their vehicles. Frank jumped out and informed them that they were MI6 agents. "We are in pursuit of IRA gunrunners! Could you please clear the road immediately?" Mulholland anxiously shouted, his arms flailing about.

The local police began checking out his details but decided to let him go when they heard Sergeant Murdoch calling out from the Land Rover. This caused unnecessary delay in their pursuit of the gunrunners.

"Geez! We are in for a long night now," Frank said, looking at his watch, which showed 1.30 a.m.

"Put the boot down, mate!" exclaimed Mulholland. They sped off in pursuit of the van, which had a fifteen-minute start on them.

"Christ! Is there any way they can turn off this road? Frank asked, looking at Tommy, who was peering into the darkness ahead.

"No way, Jose!" said Tommy. "They ar' oan this road fur a wee while. We ar' passin' Loch Tay, and we ar' headin' doon tae Kenmore, an' then, et that point, they hae options."

"If they are going to Rosyth, then do you know which road they will take?" Frank asked.

"Oh aye, ah ken whit road they'll tak', mate. Dinnae worry, Frankie boy," Tommy said, smiling at the agitated Frank Mulholland.

"Well, which road will they take?" Frank sternly asked.

"They'll tak' the Aberfeldy road and then head doon the A9 tae Stirling, where they will make their wae alang tae Rosyth," said Murdoch.

"How long will it take for us to get there?" Frank anxiously asked.

"Aboot an' hour frae Aberfeldy," Murdoch said, sighing.

This rather annoyed Agent Mulholland. He had hoped that they would apprehend them long before this, as he had further business to attend to back at the Cononish Gold Mine.

About an hour later, the MI6 team caught sight of the fleeing agents and the chase was on. Sharon Gallacher could see the police Land Rover in her rear-view mirror, and Sean Macateer took aim with his rifle.

Tommy swerved to avoid the Irish man's gunfire. Frank Mulholland leaned out the window and returned the firing. This caused the van to swerve dramatically, taking it off its intended route.

"We're on the wrong road now!" Gallacher shouted. She looked at Macateer with a worried frown on her face.

"Where are we heading now?" Macateer asked, frantically trying to see in the darkness.

Suddenly, before their eyes was the outline of the Forth Railway Bridge, shrouded in the mist which was hovering above the water of the Firth of Forth. The IRA twosome realised that they were in a no-win situation when they saw the road sign for North Queensferry.

"Agents Mulholland and Sommerville were firing at the van's wheels. This caused the vehicle to spin and crash against a wall before turning over. Sharon Gallacher, alias Alexei Smirnoff, was lying unconscious and trapped inside the damaged vehicle. Sean Macateer had struggled free and let rip with a hail of bullets towards the MI6 agents before jumping over the wall onto the railway track.

Sergeant Murdoch returned some firing, and Macateer dove to the ground, responding with some more lead coming towards the MI6 team.

Frank signalled to Agent Sommerville that he was going to jump over the wall and pursue the Irishman along the railway track. Macateer was running through the mist and towards the bridge to gain some cover. Agent Sommerville acknowledged Frank's intentions and opened up with a spray of gunfire which caused Macateer to dive for cover. At this point, Mulholland had jumped the wall and was moving along in pursuit of the Irishman. Agent Sommerville fired again and then jumped over the wall to assist his fellow agent, while Mulholland made for the bridge and some cover.

Macateer was in an anxious state. He now realised that he had two agents on his tail. He fired his weapon, but to his dismay, it had run out of bullets. Mulholland and Sommerville moved in for the kill and were about to take the Irishman out when Macateer took a handgun from its holster and fired back at the agents. Dodging the bullets, Agent Sommerville returned the firing, which allowed Frank Mulholland to cross the railway line just before the overnight mail express train from Aberdeen came hurtling by.

Tom was peering underneath the train and could see Agent Mulholland closing in on the Irishman.

Macateer's gun was now empty, and Mulholland raced towards him. In sheer frustration, he threw his weapon at Frank, but Mulholland's reflexes were razor sharp and he fended off the flying obstacle with his forearm. Macateer screamed at the MI6 agent, but he knew the end for him was near. Frank hit Macateer in the midriff with the butt of his rifle, sending him sprawling towards the train which was thundering past. As the Irishman landed close to the passing train, a spray of steam blasted into his face, causing him to scream aloud, temporarily blinding him in his left eye. Mulholland saw his opportunity and leaped on top of the gunrunner.

As the men traded blows, their bodies moved seriously close to the speeding train. Agent Sommerville was on his knees trying to get off a shot, but the train seemed to be never ending as it thundered past, with Mulholland and Macateer trading further blows and bruising their knuckles in the process.

Agent Sommerville was desperately looking to see when the last carriage would pass so he could assist his buddy. Macateer and Mulholland were having a real set-too when Frank stumbled on one of the sleepers of the railway. This gave Macateer the chance to pick up an iron bar and strike Mulholland's arm. This put Frank in grave danger, as his arm was now in a state of malfunction.

Tension was showing on Mulholland's face, his eyes bulging and straining to see his attacker through the thickening mist. Macateer's ghostly figure moved through the damp soggy mist and in for the kill. The MI6 agent was under pressure as he dodged another blow from the Irishman, who had now realised that he had the upper hand.

As Macateer moved forward to finish Mulholland off, two shots rang out, and the Irishman, screaming in pain, staggered back against the side railing of the bridge. Frank Mulholland seized his opportunity and grabbed Macateer around his legs, forcing the terror-stricken gunrunner over the side railing of the Forth Bridge. The strain was showing on Mulholland's face at the effort required to lift his struggling attacker over the railing. Macateer was now hanging upside down, with only the grip of Mulholland's single arm saving him from his impending fate.

Macateer's eyes were bulging, and the thin blue lines on his temple were pulsating at his predicament. His teeth were clenched tightly and showing complete terror on his scalded, pale face as he now realised his fate. The badly injured Mulholland was struggling to hold on to the terrorist and was relieved to let go of his flaying legs. Sean Macateer was now falling into the cold water of the Firth of Forth far below, to his certain death.

Frank Mulholland's hair was dripping wet from the damp mist that had settled on it, and his face was contorted with the pain that he was feeling on his badly bruised arm.

With a swish of his hand, Agent Sommerville wiped the wetness from Frank's forehead and asked, "Why did you not shoot the Irishman?"

"Quite simply, mate, I ran out of bullets before I got to him," said a relieved Mulholland. "It's just as well you put a couple of bullets into him because I didn't fancy getting an iron bar over my head," said Frank, wiping the damp mist from his eyes.

Agent Sommerville informed Frank that he had only fired one shot.

A gruff voice suddenly said, "Aye, it wis me that fired the other yin, Frankie boy. An' it'll cost ye a pint o' Guinness in the Orchy Hotel the morra," said the smiling Sergeant Murdoch.

To their dismay, when the team eventually returned to the Land Rover, they found that Sharon Gallacher had gone. "Christ! Where is she, man?" Frank asked anxiously, looking at Tommy Anderson.

"She's still alive. Ah've tied her up an' stuck her in the back o' the Land Rover," said Tommy, smiling at the worried faces.

"That's good enough for the Russian bitch," Frank said.

Sergeant Murdoch looked at the agents in confusion. "Russian, did ye's say? Wae a name like Gallacher?"

"Aye! Her richt name is Alexei Smirnoff," Agent Sommerville said in his best Scottish accent.

Tommy Anderson jokingly replied, "Ah could dae wae a wee Smirnoff the noo." This brought laughter from the team as they boarded the vehicle.

The drive back to Orchy seemed to be never ending. Frank Mulholland looked at his watch for the umpteenth time. "Geez, it's going to be about five o'clock before we reach Orchy, and I've still to inform the authorities about the bodies at the mine and over in the Firth of Forth," said Mulholland. He yawned and closed his eyes.

"Ah'll dae that fur ye, Frankie boy, when ah inform Inspector Hugh Smith at Crianlarich aboot everythin' that has happened," said Sergeant Murdoch.

At this point Mulholland was falling asleep, muttering, "Bridge of Orchy, here we come!"

Tommy Anderson mumbled, "Aye, its aw richt fur you lot tae go tae sleep. Ah'm the wan that's got tae drive us back."

"Keep yer eyes oan the road then an' gi'e us a shout when we're nearly there," said Murdoch.

By the time they had reached Bridge of Orchy, Tommy's eyes were literally rolling in his head due to tiredness. "Richt, you lot! We're here noo, so ye's kin waken up," said the big man, shouting to stir the men from their sleep.

Frank rubbed his eyes and then ran his fingers through his blonde hair. With a shivery shrug of his shoulders, he sprung into action by asking Tommy to open the back of the Land Rover.

"Jings! We should have put her in a cell at Crianlarich," Murdoch said, staring at the tired faces.

"I'll take that Russian bitch Smirnoff to my room in the hotel," Mulholland said, yawning. "The army will be coming to get her in a couple of hours' time."

Sergeant Murdoch reluctantly released the Russki into Frank Mulholland's charge. The two policemen said their goodbyes and drove off in the direction of Tyndrum. Frank made for his car and opened the boot, refilling his Smith & Wesson handgun with bullets. The agents grabbed the Russki by her arms and frogmarched her towards the hotel and room number seven, where Frank sat her down on his bed. This awakened Carol, who looked at the tied-up woman.

"Hey, Frankie boy, are you into the bondage stuff now?" Carol asked.

Frank told her that she was under arrest for espionage. "She will have to be held in this room until the army come in the morning to take her away," said Mulholland.

"Oh no she won't, Frankie boy. I want you all to myself," Carol said sternly, grabbing his arm. This caused Frank some pain on his badly bruised arm from the fight with Macateer up on the Forth Bridge. He winced. Carol apologised for hurting him and told Frank that he could put her down in the beer cellar until they came to pick her up.

"C'mon – follow me. I'll show you where to put her," said Carol, opening the door and leading the way to the cellar. After tying their prisoner up to a post, Carol and Frank locked the cellar door. Carol hung the key on a hook behind the bar as Frank looked up at the time on the clock.

"Crivvens, it's five thirty in the morning. It'll be daylight in another hour," said Frank.

Carol knew by now not to ask Frank where he had been. She slipped her arm around his waist and helped the injured agent to his room. When they entered the room, she observed that his arm was badly bruised.

"Oh my goodness, how did that happen?" she asked.

"It's a long story, so just leave it at that," Frank said, rubbing his limb. "At least it's not broken." He smiled, trying to make light of the situation.

She gave him a cuddle and whispered into his ear. "Would you like a cup of tea to warm you up."

"Yes, honey, I would love a cuppa, but I would prefer your sexy body to warm me up," Frank said, laughing as he walked through to the shower room.

"I have to go to the kitchen at six o'clock to prepare the breakfasts for the guests in the hotel," Carol shouted, trying to be heard over the noise of the running water.

Frank appeared to be feeling the result of the bruise more than he was letting on. He cagily massaged his arm. Suddenly, Carol appeared in the shower room and was horrified when she saw the condition of his arm. "I'll have to go, darling. Your tea is on the bedside table. I'll come back and see you shortly," she said, feeling sorry for her lover. With a quick glance in the mirror, she grasped her black hair and twisted it into a ponytail before exiting the room.

Frank made his way to the bed and flopped down on it. While sipping his tea, his mind ran through his actions for the day ahead. *Geez, that's the daylight coming in now, and I'm feeling shattered,* he thought, laying his head down on the pillow. The adrenalin from the action during the night was keeping him awake, and he tossed and turned, trying to find a comfortable position for his injured arm. A couple of hours later, the door of room number seven opened, and in stepped Carol, who was now facing a rather drowsy agent.

"Geez, honey, I must have dropped off," Frank said, glancing at the time. It was now eight.

"Frank, I'm really sorry, but I don't know how it happened," Carol said, showing a lot of stress and bursting into tears.

Frank jumped up from the bed and asked her what was wrong.

"She's gone, Frank. I don't know how, but she's gone," Carol said through tear-filled eyes.

Frank knew instantly who was gone, and he asked, "When was the last time you checked her out?"

Carol told him that she had looked in on her at half past seven and she was still tied up to the post.

"She can't have gotten very far, then. While I get dressed, will you give Agent Sommerville a call?"

Mulholland dressed quickly and put on his bulletproof vest again. He then made for Agent Sommerville's room to discuss their plan of actions to salvage the situation. While they were discussing their options, Frank looked out the window. To his surprise, he could see Diane MacIntosh, alias Alyona Aslanov, and Sharon Gallacher, alias Alexei Smirnoff, making their way towards the old bridge over the River Orchy.

"There they go!" Frank shouted, quickly throwing Tom his handgun as he made for the door. The agents exited the hotel from the back door and chased after the two Russians with gun in hand. The two Russkis were now aware that they were being followed, and they took up position at the bridge, prepared to thwart the MI6 agent's advancement.

As Frank and Tom approached the bridge, both Russkis let rip with a volley of bullets. The agents quickly dove for cover as lead zipped around them, a bit too close for comfort. Frank crawled through the snow to try to take up a position which would allow him to see both assailants. In the distance, the beating sound of a helicopter's rotors could be heard.

"They must be making for that helicopter!" shouted Frank. Tom nodded in agreement, and he fired a volley of bullets at the Russkis, which allowed Frank to close in on them. Suddenly, Sharon Gallacher made a move and Frank took his chance to open fire, sending Gallacher squirming through the snow and screaming in pain as the bullet ripped into her shoulder. She was writhing in agony as the snow changed to a bright red around her. Alyona Aslanov let rip with a hail of bullets towards both agents. Frank Mulholland returned the firing and closed in on the two Russkis. In a split second, a bullet zipped past his head and ricocheted against the Auld Bridge.

This caused Frank to slip on the icy surface and crash down on his bruised arm. Frank let out a yell, and his face contorted with the pain. He was in agony, and this gave Aslanov some hope that she would prevail.

Lifting her head, she tried to seize the momentum of the situation confronting her as she took aim at the sprawling Agent Mulholland. Agent Sommerville had quickly assessed the problem his partner was facing, and he fired his Smith & Wesson in the direction of the Russki, causing her some distraction.

Silence unexpectedly filled the air, and Diane MacIntosh, alias Alyona Aslanov, was slumped on the ground in a heap. The MI6 agents were staring at each other, wondering why all this silence.

Slowly they slithered through the snow, making their way towards their assailants.

To their obvious relief, they found that both Russians were dead. Frank turned Aslanov over, and to his dismay, he found that she had an arrow through her neck.

He made his way over to Sharon Gallacher, alias Alexei Smirnoff, and found that she was in a similar situation, with an arrow piercing her heart. Frank summoned Tom to come over immediately. He glanced back towards the hotel, where some of the guests were peering from the windows.

"Jings, who did this?" Tom asked, looking at the arrows that had penetrated both Russian's bodies. Frank looked at his buddy despairingly. Then they exchanged a knowing look.

"Surely not, mate. It couldn't be, Chappie?" Sommerville asked.

"Well, do you know anyone else who owns a crossbow?" Mulholland asked, staring back towards the hotel.

"We'll have to close off this bridge until the army uplifts the dead bodies," said Frank.

The agents crossed over the bridge and made their way back to the hotel as the muffled sound of a helicopter's rotors could be heard fading into the distance. The beating sound of the helicopter's rotors gave the MI6 agents some concern.

"I wonder who was flying that blooming helicopter, mate," Agent Sommerville said.

When the agents arrived at the front of the hotel, they were surprised to see that Ian Chapman's bike was not in its usual place, leaning against the wall of the hotel.

"Crivvens, I expected to see Chappie's bike. Maybe it wasn't him who fired the arrows at the Russians," Tom said, shrugging his shoulders and looking pensively at Frank.

"I'll be checking that bugger out later on anyway," Frank said, smiling at his buddy as they entered the hotel.

Frank took out his bleeper and called headquarters to report the outcome of last night's actions. Sir Jeffrey Merriday congratulated him on their efforts and told him that the army would be arriving at the hotel within the hour to pick up the Russian bodies before the situation caused too much of a commotion.

"Good stuff, sir! It won't be good for the hotel's business if they are lying around too long," said Frank.

"Oh, remember we have six dead bodies down at the Cononish Gold Mine, four down in the glen, and four at the village of Killin that have to be picked up."

Merriday quickly replied that they had already picked up the bodies at Killin. Inspector Hugh Smith called MI6 very early this morning," he said, emphasizing the words *very early*.

Frank informed him that they had been awake all night, and he laughed aloud at Merriday's expense.

"Yes, I know, Frank. Tell the lads well done for last night. Over and out, my friend," Merriday said, ending the call.

Mulholland called J. B. Aitken down at the gold mine to inform him of what was happening and told him that he would be down shortly.

When the phone rang behind the bar, Carol answered it, saying a moment later, "It's for you, Frank." She was giving Frank a serious look while waving her finger at him, prewarning him.

Frank listened and then asked Carol to put the television on the BBC News, which began broadcasting the following segment:

Good morning. This is an urgent report from the RAF base at Leuchars, near St Andrews in Fife. This morning, staff at the base arrived to find an unusual surprise awaiting them, in the form of an aeroplane. This aeroplane had some uncharacteristic features. The base is carrying out further inspection of this strange aircraft. There is an investigation into how it arrived at the base.

According to security, no sound was heard. The Ministry of Defence has people en-route to Leuchars to investigate, and we hope to have further information in our later bulletin.

Frank thanked Georgie Watson Burke for not letting him down. Georgie asked Frank if she could see him at some point in time, in the not-too-distant future.

"Of course you can, sweetheart," Frank whispered, trying not to let anyone hear their conversation. "How about Wednesday? Agent Sommerville is going on a short training course, and I'm sure that I can make myself available once I have wrapped everything up around here."

"Meet me in the George Hotel in Inveraray at midday for lunch. I would like to ask you questions about if or when I can return to my home at Cononish," Georgie said.

"I'll find out as much information as I possibly can," Frank quietly said.

"I asked my Uncle Denis to distance himself from everything that was going on last night because he is a truly nice guy and shouldn't be involved with that lot," Georgie said.

Frank decided that silence was the key regarding Denis Wadsworth and her helicopter, the *Phoenix*.

Georgie asked him if Carol McBride was standing close by and keeping an eye on him. "You seem to be scared to say more than you have to," Georgie said, sensing that he was not alone.

"Yes, just like the proverbial hawk, watching over me," Frank whispered.

Georgie told Frank that she was looking forward to Wednesday. She asked him not to let her down.

"OK, Georgie! Thanks for calling me, and goodbye," said Frank, ending the call.

Carol immediately asked Frank why she was phoning him. She was still suspicious of her friend talking to Frank. Frank kissed Carol's lips and told her that he would have to kill her if he told her secret information. He walked away laughing aloud, going to speak to Agent Sommerville. The men turned and made for the exit and the car park, with Carol shaking her fist at Frank.

Tom asked where they were going, and Frank replied with a smile, "Cononish Gold Mine, here we come!"

Down at the gold mine

After a precarious drive along the single-track road, the agents eventually arrived at the mine. Big John Aitken was directing the army truck into the mine like a police officer directing road traffic.

"You would make a good policeman, mate. I'll see if Sergeant Murdoch requires any traffic cops," called Frank, laughing at his team leader. Big JBA cursed at Frank under his breath and held two fingers up.

"I don't need to go to lip reading classes to understand what the big man was calling me," said Frank, looking at Agent Sommerville with a huge grin.

The agents glanced up at the sight of a British Bristol Type 192 helicopter hovering above the crash site on Ben Lui. Frank whispered, "Geez, I don't think there'll be much left of the solar plane – or Alexei Vispedov, for that matter – judging by the explosion we saw, mate."

Frank and Tom spoke to their team of agents and congratulated them on their performance on taking the mine last night. Frank informed them that he had word from headquarters that chemical experts were on their way to check out the safety of the mine.

Noticing that agent Kane had his arm in a sling, they approached him. "Well done on stopping the truck last night, but what happened to your arm?" Mulholland asked.

"Ach, Frank. It's oany a wee scratch. Wan o' them hud a lucky shot afore ah took them oot."

Frank gave him a pat on the back on a job well done. As they made their way back towards the rest of the team, Tom whispered to Frank that the Iceman was a tough cookie.

Agents MacNeill, Wilson, Hardie, and McDonald were all jokingly standing to attention and saluting their fellow MI6 agents. Frank and

Tom told them that they were simply the best. Both agents took a walk through the mine to assess the damage.

Frank called back to agent McDonald, "Good job on bringing the roof down, mate." Brian McDonald smiled and clapped his hands in gratitude for the comment.

Frank Mulholland stooped forward and picked up something from the floor.

"What's that you picked up, mate?" Tom asked.

Frank held out his hand to reveal a small piece of gold. "Do you think there's enough gold in this nugget to make a ring for Carol?" asked Frank.

As they made their way back along to the entrance, the army team were, as Frank called it, tidying up. They had lifted the body bags onto the truck and were placing them out of sight. At this point, Big John B. Aitken stepped forward and grasped the hands of his fellow agents.

"Well done," said Mulholland, easing his hand clear of the agent's powerful grip.

"Aye, we mak' a guid team, mate," said Big John, smiling.

"Yes, John! As I told the rest of the lads, we're simply the best," said Frank.

Big John repeated, "Simply the best ... Noo that wid be a guid title fur a song, mate."

"Did MI6 pick up the two agents we held captive from last night?" asked Mulholland.

"Aye! They sent doon agents Davy Kerr and Sammy Balmer frae their posting et Kinlochleven. They are transporting them tae Faslane fur interrogation. They are definitely in safe haunds noo because Davy and Sammy are a pair o' tough, reliable characters."

Frank looked seriously at JBA and said. If Merriday sanctioned it, maybe they could be brought into our team for a mission sometime in the future."

"Ye could dae a lot worse than Davy and Sammy. You've got ma vote fur them," said Big John Aitken.

Frank informed the men that they would have to cover the mine for a couple of days.

"This is a gold mine, and if you find any gold while you are here, I don't want to know about it," said Frank, grinning. Frank told JBA to make up a rota to cover the mine for the next two days, in case there were any unwanted visitors.

As the agents were making their way out of the mine, Frank called back to the men that there was a ceilidh in the Orchy Hotel tomorrow night. "I expect to see you over there for a celebration and a few beers," said Frank, tilting his hand up to his mouth. The team let out a cheer before making their way down into the mine with eyes focused on the floor, looking for gold.

Frank and Tom made for their car and the drive back to Orchy. As the agents were travelling along the Cononish Glen's long and winding road, they looked down at the truck that Agent Kane had blown up. It was lying over on its side in a burnt-out condition. Farther along the glen, they were looking into the river at the sight of the smashed-up helicopter. "Christ! We better check out Georgie Burke's helicopter that we shot down with Denis Wadsworth and another occupant on board," said Frank. He slammed on the brakes, causing the car to skid slightly on the hard-packed snowy surface.

Frank jumped out and made his way down to the helicopter, which was in a crumpled state and overhanging the river's edge. As he approached the whirlybird, he could see only one person inside. *It looks like the burned body of a female,* thought Mulholland. Frank's eyes quickly scanned the area as he made his way back to the car. *Christ! Don't tell me Denis Wadsworth escaped that explosion last night.*

Tom asked him who was in the helicopter with Denis Wadsworth.

"I don't know, mate. The body was burned, but it was a female, and she was the only person inside the helicopter," said Frank, dipping his eyes.

"What! Do you mean that Denis Wadsworth escaped again?" said Tom, shaking his head. "Does that bugger Wadsworth have nine lives?"

Frank called Sir Jeffrey Merriday on his bleeper, informing him of the helicopter down in the Cononish River and of the burned dead body. "Sir, there could be another body floating downriver. We know there were two people on board when it went down," said Mulholland.

"OK, Frank. I'll arrange for a search party to check out the area," said Merriday.

The agents were closing in on the Orchy Hotel. "I don't know about you, mate, but as soon as we get into the hotel, I'm going to my bed to have a good sleep," said Frank.

"Yep! I couldn't agree more with you," said Tom, already with that thought in mind.

On entering the hotel, Frank informed Carol that he was putting a Do Not Disturb notice on his room door. He was giving her the hint to stay away and allow him to sleep. He smiled back at her as he made his way to room number seven while waving the card in the air.

About six hours later, Frank Mulholland was awakened by the sound of his pager bleeping. It was Sir Jeffrey Merriday at headquarters, informing him that the body of Irish gunrunner Denis Wadsworth had not been found. "I'm sorry, Frank, but we have searched along the stretch of the river where he would have been expected to be found, but to no avail, my friend," said Merriday.

This news worried Mulholland, as he knew the capabilities of Wadsworth in regards to rebuilding the gunrunning structure again.

"Oh, geez! Surely he couldn't have survived that crash, especially with the helicopter bursting into flames, sir," said Mulholland.

Merriday told him that the search would continue until they were sure of the situation.

"OK, sir. I'll keep in touch with you on this one. He is a dangerous character we don't want to be let loose. Over and out," said Frank.

Frank looked at his watch and knocked on the room wall to awaken his buddy. The impatient Mulholland made for room number eight, but as Frank entered Tom's room, he was taken aback when he found barmaid Emma MacNamara's eyes peering at him from behind the bedcovers.

"Crivvens, Frank! Can I not get a little privacy in my own room?" Tom asked.

Frank was embarrassed because that was the second time he had walked in on them. He quickly left the room, smiling and apologising as he called out instructions for Tom to join him in the dining room.

Carol and Janice Irvine appeared from the kitchen and began serving meals to the guests.

"Hi, Frank! Have you seen Emma on your travels?" Carol asked, showing a little stress at her workload.

"She's in Tom's room, and they are certainly not just holding hands," said Frank, winking. "I'll go tell her you are looking for her."

"Good, Frank, because we need two people in the kitchen at all times and we no longer have Diane MacIntosh," said Carol, rushing back to the kitchen.

About two minutes later, an embarrassed Emma made her way to the kitchen with Agent Sommerville, heading for the dining room to join his buddy. Both agents were enjoying their meal when Sergeant Murdoch and Constable Anderson arrived at the hotel. Frank asked them what had brought them down to the hotel at this early time of the evening.

"We ar' doon early because The Crusaders ar' back oan the nicht again, et eight o'clock, on a special request," said Murdoch.

"Good stuff, lads! You can get the beers in while we finish our meal and we'll join you shortly," said Mulholland, smiling back at the two officers.

The agents made for the bar, and a welcome beer was awaiting each of them. "Brilliant! That beer is looking good," said Frank Mulholland. That's when he spotted Ian Chapman making for the bar.

"Mr Chapman, can I have a word with you in private?" Frank asked in a professional tone of voice, which caused Chappie a little concern. Frank and Chappie made for the quiet of the dining room, and Frank asked him where he was at around nine that morning.

"Whit dae ye want tae ken that fur?" Chappie asked.

Frank asked him if he was anywhere close to the hotel.

"Ah wis doon et the Inveroran Inn and Forest Lodge area aroond that time," said Chappie, looking a bit nervous.

"So if I were to go out and check your bike, would I find your crossbow around the handlebars?" asked Mulholland.

"Aw, naw, Frankie boy. Ah took yer advice an' left it et hame, in case oany bugger stole it aff ma bike," said Chappie.

"Yesterday, my friend, you had four arrows in your bag. So how many have you got now?"

"Ah've oany got twa in ma bag. Ah lost twa o' them when ah wis oot shootin' game," said the worried-looking rogue.

"What! A super marksman like you missed twice today?" said Frank, laughing.

"Ach! Ah wis a wee bit hungower this morning," said Chappie through tight lips.

"You are sure that you weren't near the hotel this morning, mate? Because someone helped us out this morning, and I would like to thank that person," said Frank, changing his approach.

A few beads of sweat appeared on Chappie's forehead, and he wiped them off with his sleeve.

Chappie was in deep thought, and he stammered, "N-naw! It wisnae me doon et the hotel this mornin'."

"OK, wee man! Thanks for your help. I'll inform the Swiss Tourist Board that William Tell's reputation is still safe," said Frank, smiling.

With some relief, Chappie quickly made for his usual seat at the fireside.

Frank looked over at Agent Sommerville, who seemed to be wondering what the outcome of his discussion was. Frank waved his hand, signalling for Tom to come over.

"Well, what did he say?" Tom asked.

"He denied that it was him down at the brig, but I'd bet my wages on it that it was him who took out the two Russkis," said Mulholland through tight lips.

"Well, he did us a favour this morning, mate. So let's just leave it for now and enjoy the music which is about to start," said Tom.

Frank stared at Tom and said, "We have a license to kill, mate. But I don't think Inspectors Hugh Smith and M. D. Johnstone will treat their deaths as government business when they see the bolts embedded in their bodies."

Three hours later, Frank and Carol were dancing as the band played the last song of the evening. Frank asked Carol what the future held for them.

"Are you proposing to me?" Carol asked gingerly. "I don't think it would work out for us, Frank. You would be away far too often, and I would always worry whether you would return at all."

Frank asked her where they'd go from here, now that he would probably have to move back down to London.

"Let's just enjoy the rest of our time together and see what happens," said carol, smiling at Frank to ease his mind.

The band had finished playing, and the dance ended with Frank now feeling a little awkward about the situation with Carol. She broke away from him and began clearing the glasses from the tables. Frank noticed that Carol was talking to Emma and Janice. He felt that they might be discussing him and his sort of proposal to her. This made him feel even more embarrassed and awkward.

The guests were beginning to disperse and make their way back to their rooms. Brian Greene approached and asked, "Wid ya like tae join me an' Davy Blackwood in the morning aroond ten o'clock, oan a climb up ontae Beinn Achaladair?

"Yes, mate! I would look forward to that, although my arm is pretty sore at this minute in time," Mulholland said, looking at Agent Sommerville, who was giving the invitation the thumbs up.

"OK, mate. We'll go for a walk up the mountain," Tom said, convincing Frank that it would be nice to have a day of leisure.

Frank reminded Tom that he was going to meet Captain Walter Duffy down at Coulport Submarine Base on Wednesday morning for his mini sub training.

"Yes, and I'm looking forward to that," Tom said.

Sergeant Murdoch and Tommy Anderson shook hands with the agents and then made their way to the awaiting taxicab. "Are you coming down to the ceilidh tomorrow night, gents? The night will be on me," called Mulholland as the two police officers made for the cab.

"Of course we ar', especially when a Londoner is payin' the bill!" shouted Murdoch as the taxi pulled away.

"Well, I don't know about you, mate, but I'm shattered. I'm going to my room for a good night's sleep," said Frank.

Frank's head had barely touched the pillow when there was a knock at the door and in walked Carol with a cup of coffee in her hand.

"Would sir like a nightcap to help him sleep?" asked Carol seductively. She placed the cup down on the bedside table and laid a couple of pills next to it.

Frank grabbed her and pulled her down onto the bed, kissing her passionately. "I don't need pills, honey. I need *you* to take my mind off the pain," he said.

She removed her clothes and slipped under the sheets to join the agent in a night of pleasure.

"I didn't think you would come to my room tonight," said Frank, gazing into her eyes.

"I decided to stay with you tonight because with your sore arm, you wouldn't be able to reach your coffee," Carol said, laughing as she visualised him trying to reach his coffee cup.

Frank kissed her passionately, and his hand slipped over her sexy body. This brought Carol to a high state of excitement, and they made passionate love.

Beinn Achaladair, here we come!

The following morning, Frank awoke to the sound of Carol exiting the room, and he quickly reset the alarm for eight o'clock. In what seemed like no time at all, he was wakening to the sound of the alarm. *Oh, geez! My arm is sore,* he thought to himself as he massaged his sore limb and made for the shower room.

Suddenly, there was a knock on the door, and in walked Carol. She called on Frank to come out of the shower. Frank appeared and was surprised to be faced with two women in his room. The embarrassed agent quickly wrapped a towel around himself. Carol informed him that the woman's name was Sheila Black. She was a nurse and was one of the guests in the hotel. "She would like to check out your bruised arm, honey," Carol said, introducing the woman to him.

"It's just as well that I had my medical box in the car because you need to be strapped up, my friend," Nurse Black said, a concerned look on her face.

Fifteen minutes later, Frank was feeling a lot better with his arm wrapped up in bandages.

"Will I be OK to go hillwalking today?" he asked.

"Yes, just just as long as you are not planning on doing any actual climbing. Get it checked at a hospital," the exiting nurse called back as she made her way back to her family.

Carol left with the nurse, who was shaking her head in disbelief. Frank rapped two knocks on the wall to let Agent Sommerville know that he was almost ready to go for some breakfast.

A few minutes later, both agents made for the dining room, and Frank smiled at Nurse Black to acknowledge his gratitude for attending to him. The dining room was quite busy, and the agents scanned the area to find a table.

"Geez, I'm looking forward to this full Scottish Breakfast," said Frank shortly after they'd ordered.

"Yes, especially the square sausage, which tastes fabulous," replied Agent Sommerville, rubbing both hands together in anticipation.

Carol and Emma soon appeared and placed their food on the table.

"Just take it easy when you are up on the hills today, honey," Carol sarcastically said, rubbing Frank's sore arm.

"Don't worry … I'll save my energy for you, darling," Frank said, laughing.

Both girls made for the kitchen, giggling at Frank's comment.

Tom changed the subject and asked Frank who he thought would have been flying the helicopter yesterday morning when they took out the two Russki girls at the bridge.

"I have my thoughts on that one, mate. But I hope that I'm wrong," said Frank, looking at his buddy.

"Yes, I think you have the same idea as me. Could it be Georgie Watson Harkin Burke?" Tom asked.

"Well, the girls were her friends, and she was possibly trying to rescue them from the situation. I wonder how and where she got the helicopter."

"Tuck into your breakfast, mate," Frank said, changing the subject quickly to defuse the situation.

A little later, the agents lifted their coffees and made for the barroom to await their climbing partners for the day ahead.

"I'm looking forward to our visit to Beinn Achaladair today," said Sommerville.

"Yes, it'll be nice to be up there and not worry about Russian spies having a pop at us," said Mulholland with a laugh. Just then, Davy Blackwood and Brian Greene entered the hotel.

"Aye, and whit hiv you twa tae laugh aboot?" Brian asked, settling down beside the agents.

"Nothing, mate, but we are looking forward to our hill climb in the company of two semi-professionals today," Frank said, grinning at his own comment.

"Well, the sooner ye get yer gear oan, the sooner we'll get awa', Frankie boy," said Davy, gesturing with his hands at both agents to get a move on. The agents took the hint and made for their rooms to put on their hillwalking jackets and boots.

"I don't think we will need the bulletproof vests and snowsuits today," Frank said, laughing.

The agents were dressed for the hills when they arrived in the barroom, and Carol and Emma began whistling at them. This caused all the others to laugh as they quickly made for the exit.

"We'll heid up tae the Bealach between these twa mountains, Beinn an Dothaidh and Beinn Dorain. Then we'll cut across the hills tae Achaladair," said Davy, pointing at their route from the hotel.

"Before we set off, have ye brought yer crampons wae ye, lads?" Brian asked.

As they crossed the road and made for the hills, the agents confirmed that they had them in their bags.

About three hours later, the lads were posing at the cairn on the summit of Beinn Achaladair "Geez! What a tremendous view of the Rannoch Moor and the Glencoe Mountains that you get from up here," said Agent Sommerville, pointing out the various locations.

Brian Greene opened his bag and produced from within a half bottle of Chivas Regal.

"Cheers, lads! This is tae celebrate yer first 'Munro'. An' aw the best tae ye's twa. Ah hope that this is the first hill o' many," said Brian, smiling as he passed the bottle around.

"Jings! That is a braw whisky, mate," said Mulholland as he passed the bottle to his buddy.

"Here's tae the Hill of Hard Water," said Agent Sommerville, rubbing his throat as the liquor went down.

Earlier in the week, Brian Greene had informed both agents that the English interpretation of Beinn Achaladair was the Hill of Hard Water. This was a vital clue in their investigation.

Meanwhile, Frank Mulholland was gazing down at the farmhouse far below. "Davy, have you brought your binoculars with you?" Frank asked.

"Sure have, mate," replied Davy. His hand reached into his rucksack, and he passed them over to Mulholland.

Frank had gone quiet and was showing concern on his face as he watched a car drive away from the farmhouse far below. "Are you coming to the hotel tonight for the ceilidh, at my expense?" asked Frank eventually.

"Ye better believe it, mate. Ah widnae miss it fur the world. Especially if an Englishman is payin' fur the bevvy," said Davy, laughing heartily.

Brian picked up some snow and threw a snowball at the agents. Before long, they all joined in on the snowball fight.

Two hours later, the guys were approaching the Orchy Hotel. Davy and Brian informed the agents that they would be heading home and they would see them tonight for the ceilidh.

The agents made for the hotel, and Tom pulled the door open. On the way into the hotel, Frank pointed at Chappie's bike leaning against the wall, his crossbow hanging over the handlebars.

"His crossbow is there, but there are no arrows," said Agent Sommerville.

On entering the bar, Frank ordered a couple of beers. "And a pint of cider for Chappie!" shouted Frank, trying to attract Chappie's attention. The wee man gave him the thumbs up sign and a big smile as both agents joined him at the fireside table. Chappie's jacket was lying across one of the chairs, and Frank could see a pouch with crossbow bolts protruding from his inside pocket.

"Do you always keep your arrows on your person?" Frank asked.

Chappie held his glass up. "Always, Frankie boy. They are never out of my sight frae the meenit ah get them at Dalgetty's shop in Tyndrum," said Chappie. He tipped his glass. "Cheers, Frankie boy."

The ceilidh night

T he hotel was absolutely packed with guests, and the band were in place as some of the MI6 agents joined the locals for the night of music and dancing to the ceilidh band called Schiehallion. Feet were tapping, and hands were clapping to the beat.

"This band is good," said Frank. Just then, Carol came over and dragged him up for a dance. All the lads were cheering him on as they hit the dance floor.

"Hey, Frankie boy is daeing aw richt oan the dance flair," said Brian Greene, clapping his hands as the couple danced past.

A few hours, a few drinks, and many dances later, the lads had thoroughly enjoyed themselves. Emma and Tom were up on the floor for a Canadian Barn Dance. They were proving to be pretty good as they danced past, urging the guys to get up on the floor. The bandleader asked everyone to take a partner for "The Gay Gordons".

With a loud cheer from the team, Sergeant Murdoch and Emma MacNamara, along with Brian Greene and Moira Malone, made for the dance floor. Frank grabbed hold of Nurse Sheila Black and joined them on the floor in anticipation of the music starting. Everyone was jumping around trying to find a partner. The bandleader described the dance they were about to do. The music began, and the hall started to rock as they all danced around enjoying themselves while hoochin' at the tops of their voices. "That band is bloody good," was regularly heard from the guests throughout the night.

"Ah've never seen sae many people sae happy. Ah'll hiv tae book this band Schiehallion again," said head barman Tam Cameron to Carol.

"Yes, Tam. They're a good ceilidh band, and the dancing brings everyone together," Carol said, smiling at her boss.

The bandleader asked everyone to get up for the last dance of the night. Carol made her way over to Frank Mulholland, and Emma clung on to Tom Sommerville.

"Ladies and gentlemen, would you all join hands and make a circle for the last dance, which is 'Auld Lang Syne'?" the bandleader requested.

Everyone stood in anticipation of the dance beginning. A cheer rang out as the band began playing.

"Here we go noo!" shouted Sergeant Murdoch.

The hall began rocking to the beat. Everyone was singing and dancing during the last dance of the evening.

"Jings, it's great tae see everywan enjoyin' themselves," Tam said excitedly. He dove into the middle of the circle and began dancing a highland fling with his trilby held high in his right hand. The crowd danced around him, cheering and clapping their hands and with smiles on their faces. Frank grabbed Tam's trilby and placed it on his head. He began impersonating Tam's actions impeccably, to a loud cheer from everyone.

"Brilliant night, Tam," was regularly heard as the band finished playing.

Frank removed the trilby and bowed to Tam. Then, with a flick of his wrist, the trilby was flying towards Tam, who caught it in mid-flight. Placing it on his head, Tam quickly tipped his trilby back, earning a cheer from everyone. With both hands, Tam twirled the ends of his moustache, receiving an even louder cheer.

It's a pity that JBA and Agent Kane couldn't make the ceilidh tonight, but we have to monitor the situation down at the gold mine," said Frank. "I'm really surprised that Aitken didn't make George Hardie cover the mine tonight."

"Although I can understand that the Iceman was injured and wouldn't have been able to dance anyway," Agent Sommerville said, trying to justify agent Kane's absence. "It's a good sign that maybe JBA has softened toward Hardie and they have sorted out their differences, mate."

"Aye, maybe," replied Frank Mulholland, looking at Tom unconvincingly.

Ten minutes after the last dance had finished, some of the agents were boarding a taxi for the short trip down to the Inveroran Inn. "Ah'm lookin' fur a guid night's sleep," said Brian McDonald as he tumbled into the awaiting cab, his fellow agents laughing heartily at his predicament. Agents Mulholland and Sommerville waved at the men as the cab disappeared over the old bridge.

Frank reminded Tom that he had an appointment with Captain Walter Duffy down at Coulport Submarine Base at ten o'clock tomorrow morning.

"Are you driving me down to the base?" Tom asked hopefully.

"Of course I will, and you will be there at ten o'clock on the dot," Frank said, emphasizing the time by pointing to his watch.

Frank's intentions were to drop Agent Sommerville off at Coulport and then make his way over to Inveraray to meet up with Georgie Watson Harkin Burke for a day of pleasure. Then he would return in time to collect his fellow agent at the submarine base.

The agents made their way back into the hotel and joined the local guys, who were still sitting around the fire in the barroom. Tommy Anderson was taking centre stage while telling some of his jokes. The sound of laughter could be heard as Tommy's joke reached the punch line.

Frank gave Chappie a hug because secretly he knew that the man had fired the arrows from the crossbow that killed the two female Russian agents and ultimately saved the lives of both MI6 agents.

"Christ almighty! Look et them twa huggin' wan an' 'ither!" shouted Murdoch, pointing at Frank and Chappie.

"We're just good friends," Frank said with a laugh.

Carol approached. "Taxi for Murdoch, Anderson, Blackwood, and Greene!" she called.

"I don't think Brian Greene will be going in the taxi because, last seen, he was heading down to room number twelve with Moira Malone," said Agent Sommerville, nodding in the direction of the room. The other three guys made for the taxi, with Chappie cadging a lift from them. Most of the guests were off to their rooms, and the guys in the band were packing their instruments into the awaiting van. Tam Cameron was tipping his trilby and thanking them for the entertainment during the evening.

A tall, slim dark-haired man eased his way from the bar towards the exit. Unknown to the MI6 agents, IRA Commander Thomas Gallacher's piercing dark eyes had been scrutinizing their every move. Revenge was in his thoughts as he slipped out into the darkness.

Frank whispered to Tom that it may be a good idea to make for their rooms and get a good night's sleep.

"Yes, mate, that's a good idea," Tom said, impersonating silent movie star Stan Laurel. He then made his way to room number eight while impersonating silent movie star Charlie Chaplin.

Carol called out to Frank Mulholland. "What can I do for you, honey?" Frank asked suggestively. "Would sir like a coffee brought to his room?" Carol asked, a sensual tone in her voice.

Frank smiled because he knew that Carol was coming to spend the night with him again. He nodded at her request and then quickly made for his room.

All the girls were clearing the glasses from the tables and bringing the place into some kind of order. "This wull ease oor workload fur the morning," Tam Cameron said as he washed up the glasses.

Ten minutes later, the door of room number seven eased open. In walked Carol with a mug of coffee in her hand. She placed it on the bedside table. Frank grabbed her and pulled her down onto the bed beside him, kissing her passionately as she fell into his arms.

"Oh, Frank!" Carol moaned, breathing heavily as he brought her to a high state of excitement. Minutes later, both of them collapsed in a heap. Frank's hand reached out for his mug of coffee as Carol snuggled into his body.

As Frank sipped his coffee, his thoughts turned to his meeting with Georgie Watson Harkin Burke and to the whereabouts of her uncle Denis Wadsworth, whom he had seen earlier, leaving Achaladair farmhouse, through binoculars from the top of Beinn Achaladair. *He seems to be the proverbial cat with nine lives*, thought Mulholland, snuggling closer to Carol.

Printed in the United States
By Bookmasters